THE
GOOD
GARDENER

a novel

SUSAN EHLERS
O'CONNOR

THE GOOD GARDENER

ISBN 978-1-66784-277-6 (Print)

ISBN 978-1-66784-278-3 (eBook)

To Patrick, my good gardener

When designing a garden, it is wise to turn to the philosophy
of the Good Gardener: Cultivate seeds that will germinate
the kind of majesty in which you yourself can grow.

The Art of Gardening by Emily Mayfield

CHAPTER 1

Along the Texas coast, weather and water eat away the land, and
natural coastal vegetation and large boulders known as rip-rap armor up
the shore against erosion. Living on the coast for years, I began to appreciate change, learned how to live with it, redirect it really, so for me the
whole business of erosion felt personal. The best years of my youth had
succumbed to another kind of erosion, eaten away by memories that I
wouldn't let go of—pin pricks of remorse, occasionally nightmares that left
me groggy and sad for days. And yet I learned a thing or two that would
eventually nudge me in the right direction. Still, as youthful indecision will
prevail, I chose to run away until, like ceaseless waves that roll in and out,
they wore me down so slowly I barely noticed my threadbare resilience.

After I had moved away and had my own family, the flashbacks
began. I was dropping off the twins at the entrance to the school gym one
night when a memory apparition appeared, roused from its dormancy by
the bright lights illuminating the lot. The boys hopped out as I sat quietly trying to shake off the abrupt sense of darkness despite the light. The

championship basketball game was in our gym that year—we were playing against a major rival, the Lakeside Lions, and my support was required inside. Undefeated, we should have been in good spirits even though their dad was out of town on business. I was prepared to cheer them on for the both of us, but I couldn't ignore my untimely angst even as I watched my towering senior athletes maneuver around the opposition. I began tumbling into that gloomy night, and it was half time before I realized my boys had scored.

May, 1966, a small town in south Louisiana. A crowd was steadily growing as cars drove up and kids poured out behind the gym too dark to see much of anything. They say darkness travels at the speed of light, but it couldn't have felt more like slow motion. Soon red-tipped cigarettes, lit and inhaled, glowed off and on like blinking lights while the odd flash light swept across the bloodied face of the Negro boy lying motionless on the ground. When I looked down at him, I couldn't breathe—was he dead? I looked around the crowd of students to see if I could recognize anyone else. I knew this boy. Hours earlier I had watched him walk across the stage to receive scholarships and honors. Months earlier he had offered friendship and out of kindness spared me the humiliation of a mistake I made. I couldn't move. Until the patrol car's screeching siren dispersed the onlookers who began scattering like ants. My friend lay there alone in the dark bleeding, and I, too, ran.

After that night, I thought running away was the easiest way to deal with anything unpleasant. I'd tell myself that denial might be cowardly but it was nevertheless convenient, and vacating trouble was after all practical. So, with diploma in hand, no obligations and with the bogus arrogance of a self-assured college graduate, I convinced myself that my leaving was propitious, perhaps better still an adventure and a duly earned reward. It could even have a literary bent akin to the ancient seafaring Greeks who sailed away in search of discovery—Odysseus looking for Ithaca. I was too naïve to know that the truth always catches up with you.

In 1974 living with an illusion continued to feel easier than being honest with myself. Soon after graduation I boarded my vessel, a used Oldsmobile Cutlass, and launched down the highway in a westerly direction. A change of scenery, I thought, would calm the recalcitrant battle raging inside. The reality was I had to get out of Carlton fast, away from the birthplace of repressive memories that seemed to define me. Carlton tried its best to cling to its old Southern ways, and soon I found it difficult to live under its influence. The town was a reminder of all I hadn't done for the people I cared about and the things I had done for the ones who betrayed me. In the end, the smell of gasoline and burning wood—a fiery cross stuck on our front lawn late one night, and two weeks later the death of an innocent young woman, murdered against the backdrop of the Civil Rights Movement and the Viet Nam War haunted me. So I ran.

Mimi Schwarz herself hired me the day I left Carlton. There I was, a college graduate with a degree in history, yet I would be working behind a cash register, mindlessly selling knick knacks in a gift shop off the beach on the south shore of Galveston Island. When I saw the sign in her store window, I walked in and went up to the counter where a man was unpacking boxes. I asked about the job and he told me to come back in an hour when the owner would return from lunch. Did I want to wait at the café next door?

I ordered a sandwich and a coke from Addie's Cafe and decided to sit in a booth and relax for the next hour. Only that morning I had arrived on the island and begun to explore the streets just off the beach, hoping to look for nearby apartments. I'd never rented one and had no idea what to do, but after an unsuccessful search up and down inland streets, I turned my attention to several gift shops close to the water. Searching for a help wanted sign in one of them, I spotted Mimi's on the corner. Even from the outside it seemed a tourist's delight selling gifts, beach wear and post cards. Souvenirs and jewelry made from little shells occupied one window, but filling the one opposite was an incongruous assortment of old pink and blue and yellow glassware gleaming in the light. I couldn't stop looking

3

at it. All that glass reminded me of home, the very place I'd been trying to leave behind. Suddenly thirteen again, holding my mother's pink glass cake plate up to the kitchen light, I asked her where she bought it, and she said she hadn't—no store she knew of sold it. Her own mother had pulled it from a box of laundry soap like a prize, but one day without any explanation, the only contents of a box of laundry soap went back to being just soap. When I asked her why, she put her newspaper down, thought a moment, and said she really didn't know, but wasn't it a shame to stop surprising people with such lovely gifts in ordinary old boxes of soap powder. Then she picked up her coffee, took a long sip and went back to reading the paper. It was her way—uncomplicated acceptance of the inevitable. And yet there were times when her little cup of hope would spill over into the lives of others. In 1966, in a town where the lines of race were beginning to blur, it saved Reginald Washington's life.

I looked at my watch and realized only twenty minutes had passed. With nothing to do but wait in the cafe, thoughts continued to flood my senses, and with too much time on my hands, the difficult ones ushered in the grief I was avoiding.

My mother became very sick my third year of college and when she finally succumbed to the illness, I tried to live in the house again by myself. Once I called out to her to come and look at the wild violets that had sprung up under the oak in her garden. The minute I uttered her name I was so taken aback I began sliding into a sinkhole of anxiety, unable to deal with the fact that she was gone and I would live without her. My father left long before that, the year I turned five, so I didn't really know him. I have two vague memories of him. One, seeing him at the breakfast table, a stranger with brown hair telling me to drink my milk, and two, my mother talking on the phone to a man named Everett. He called a few times after he left, once all the way from New Zealand. Mama said he'd been there during the war on a mine sweep and longed to return. My father had finally done it, and for all we knew he had sailed away and made a new life for himself there, maybe even a new family. That was the last she heard from him, and so the two of us resigned ourselves to living alone until I was twenty.

I couldn't sell the house fast enough. At the time I convinced myself that leaving a scene of shame and guilt was just as good as dealing with it. I wanted to put it all behind me, and to my relief it sold quickly, a simple bungalow my mother bought when my daddy left. It was a small wood frame structure with an ample tree lined back yard that she and her yard man Reggie later turned into a garden. The day it officially became hers, she hired someone to paint it sunshine yellow, as if a happy color could alleviate the pain of being abandoned. She never talked about my father, but over the years the white trim peeled near the back screen door, and she left it, she said, as a sort of marker. Although she would never say exactly what it marked, I had enough understanding even as a child to avoid broaching it or him again.

After all the paper signing, I looked at the house for the last time—the garden that had once been a show place, the screened in garden house, the rusty old swing, like bookmarks in the storied years we spent there. I walked toward the little house—the shed, as Reggie used to call it, tugged at the rickety old screen door, and went inside. Empty now. All of the contents had been given or thrown away, and yet if I closed my eyes, I could still see Reggie sitting at the table showing me his plans for the beautiful garden he was going to create for my mother. So many memories came back to me as if the walls themselves whispered their secrets—one warm October night when teenagers experienced bliss in the pitch black darkness of that shed. A blood soaked shirt stuffed between the cushions of a chair. The Bertrands' house next door had new occupants now, but it too had served as silent witness to all that had happened. Almost a year had passed when President Nixon made a television appearance announcing the end of the Vietnam War, and the year before that—or was it two, we lost Philip Bertrand in that conflict. But discord persisted. A young woman lost her life and a shell-shocked family fled the scene.

I was more than a hundred miles down the road before I began to feel that I was finished with Carlton, or maybe it had taken all it could wrangle from me before tossing me out. The town was slowly on the precipice of change, like it or not. For years Tinsley's, the only department store in Carlton, was known for its water fountains in the back of the store marked White and Colored. The absence of Negroes in most public places and a class system circumscribed by wealth rather than education helped to define the town itself. But the Civil Rights movement changed everything, and in the midst of the community's struggle against uncomfortable reforms, Mama, beloved teacher at the local high school, found herself without a husband one day with no recourse. Added to this burden was a duty to raise a daughter who didn't particularly stand out in any way and welcomed the anonymity. Through the years, the people on our street, especially the Bertrands, came to love her generosity and warm presence in the neighborhood despite her lack of a spouse, but no matter how many meals she delivered to the sick or cakes she baked for the school cake walk or seniors who had prospered under her tutelage, she was a divorced woman and that alone placed her outside the norm. So the two of us lived on the periphery of society. It would be a long time before I would accept with finality that I could never reconcile my place in it, however near or far that change may be.

I loaded what few possessions I had into my blue and white Cutlass. The plan was simply to head west. On impulse I turned south and drove across the Louisiana border toward Galveston, suddenly longing for the image of freedom in sea and sky. When I reached the dock, I drove onto the ferry. Seagulls begging for bits of bread tossed by passengers flew close to the boat, screeching as they cheered me on to a promising adventure. Energized the minute we landed on the island, I disembarked and drove around to get a feel for the place. I knew I would stay, at least until I could gather my thoughts and make adjustments to the plan suddenly bubbling to the surface.

A woman behind the counter was talking to a young girl of ten or eleven when I entered the shop again.

"Excuse me," I whispered. Louder this time. "Excuse me. My name is Lizzie Rowan and I'm looking for work." They both looked up at me wide-eyed. Embarrassed, I turned down the volume as I pointed to the front window. "Sorry. I saw your sign?" It sounded like a question amidst my lack of decorum—I was too old for social ineptness, but Mimi didn't seem to hold it against me. In one swift move, she reached under the counter and handed me a job application.

"You can sit at that table and fill it out if you like," she said and pointed to an old table that I later learned was one of the antiques she was trying to convince herself to sell. That explained all the old glass in the window. When I finished, I handed it to her and she gave it a cursory glance before asking me when I could start.

"Oh," I said, startled at the hasty but not unwelcomed request. "I just drove in and don't have a place to live yet," I replied. The girl by her side stepped up.

"Hey, Mom, what about Gran's? Isn't she trying to rent that room on the first floor?" With the self-assurance of one much older, she said, "Hi, I'm Janie Schwarz. This is my mom Mimi—you know, the owner. You'd love my Gran's house and it's only a few blocks from the shop." I glanced at Mimi. Clearly ambushed, she wasn't ready to share that information yet.

"Honey," she hesitated, "I'm not sure that room downstairs is ready yet." Janie, ignoring the covert warning in her mother's response, wrote the name and number on a slip of paper and handed it to me anyway.

"Look, just go to this address and see my grandmother, Mary Stiles. When you walk out this door, turn left and walk three blocks straight ahead. It's the pinkish-orange two story house on the left. Gran says it reminds her of canned salmon." I flinched at the mention of salmon and Janie giggled, but Mimi just smiled thinly and said nothing. She watched the whole transaction between her daughter and the stranger standing before her in stunned silence. Before she could object, it was done, for Mimi knew her reticence was an implicit agreement, and she accepted it. I thanked both of them after we determined that I could begin the next day, and, combating the January island chill, I turned up the heat and drove three blocks to the home of Mary Stiles.

The house wasn't difficult to locate. Even though most of the dwellings in the area were wood or stucco painted in shades of sand and sky, Mrs. Stiles' house was indeed the color of canned salmon. I knocked on the door of the first floor for several minutes before I heard a woman's voice.

"Nobody down there, pet. Up here." I looked around me but couldn't place the accent with a face. "Up here, love. Can you come up." I moved over to look at the second floor where I saw a woman on the porch and walked toward the stairs. A simple "Grand" was all she said. The sun blinded my view of who had spoken, but when I walked up the steps into the shade, a woman in loose clothing draped over her small bones, her graying hair secured loosely in a top knot with errant wisps framing her face, stood at the top. Long thin fingers wrapped around the porch railing to steady herself. The petite woman before me was not the Mrs. Stiles I imagined, the mother of the tall blonde owner of the gift shop.

"Hello, I'm looking for Mrs. Mary Stiles. I was told she lives here?"

"What are you selling, pet?" she said, wasting no time on polite conversation.

"No, no…. I'm not selling….," I assured her. "My name is Lizzie Rowan. Mrs. Stiles' granddaughter Janie Schwarz told me she had a room for rent. I'll be working at the gift shop starting tomorrow, and they said she had a room available," I repeated myself nervously. "I think this is the address Janie gave me," I said, looking at the slip of paper again, afraid I had made a mistake.

"Ah, sure, you'd be the one. The girl called me and said she thought you might be coming round. Well, come in then, and I'll put the kettle on." Relieved, I continued up the stairs and through the door. We sat in her living room as Mrs. Stiles refilled my cup until the teapot was emptied twice, and I was sure a gallon of tea was sloshing around in my stomach. But she was full of stories about Ireland and the war, her family and living on her island home, and I was a willing listener, captive maybe, but I was pleasantly surprised at the connection already forming between us. We didn't talk about living arrangements right away. She simply wanted me to listen and insisted that I call her Mary. It was late when I finished moving in downstairs, but I already knew I'd be sharing many more cups of tea with Mary Morgan Stiles.

I went to work the next day waiting on customers, what few there were. Happy to have a job, I nevertheless wondered why Mimi wanted help in tourist-sparse January, but the next week she showed me how to take care of the books, order supplies, and do odd jobs around the shop. After that I saw her only once a week. I opened, I closed. In those days I still had the old Cutlass, but the room I rented was a straight three block distance, so I rode my bicycle, weather permitting. Along almost any side street that ran perpendicular to the beachfront drive, colorful houses, two and three stories tall and built close together off the ground to protect against yearly hurricanes, lined the streets. Mrs. Stiles' house was one of those pastels, and my room was on the first floor under the wooden stairs that led to the second floor. A bedroom with a bath was all I needed and space underneath the staircase to store my bike, and for six years I called this room three blocks from the beach, home. The living quarters exceeded what I expected. Mary starched and ironed the bed sheets, an undeserved luxury I had never known or thought I needed. My room was papered with stripes and flowers while framed water colors of palm trees and orange and red sunsets on the beach and a photograph of pelicans perched on pilings near the shore further embellished each wall.

My landlady was sixty-eight years old and rarely left her house, but several times a week she would stand on her porch and invite me in for tea. This kind of inducement usually meant a meal, but sometimes it was tea or coffee and a taste of whatever sweet delicacy or soda bread she had baked, which in the roughness of her khaki trousers and collared shirts made her an anomaly. Mrs. Stiles was a widow, her husband Carl having died a number of years earlier, before his time she said, but she stayed on despite the intermittent agitation of her son's arm twisting. His main tactic implied a kind of shame he might force on her, offering to move her to Little Rock where he had settled with his family. She never said directly, but from time to time he mentioned his desire for babysitting, in the guise of a need for her to have greater access to her grandchildren. Surely his mother must miss her grandchildren, reason enough for her to move closer to him. But Mary's daughter Mimi lived nearby, and she had seen Galveston through good and bad times, including a storm surge that had flooded the first floor, which included my room. She knew in her heart that she would end her days in this home teeming with memories of Carl. They had shared intimate knowledge of the war years in England and Ireland, and that bond had brought the two of them to his home in Galveston. While I was running away from my memories, hers were solid gold.

Mary Stile's home upstairs was an amalgamation of the trappings of her life and her husband's, mingled together with loving remembrance, unmistakable in the way they dominated each room. Crocheted doilies protecting wooden tables and antimacassars resting on the backs of chairs lay juxtaposed with sea shells and watercolor seascapes from her husband's brush. They adorned walls and shelves of books, reminding visitors and Mary Stiles as well of where and how she lived. Against one wall stood an old upright piano with sheet music resting above the keys, as if waiting to be released on her command. Every detail convinced me it was a happy place where lines between past and present were vague. She and Carl had made it a home in which harmony would abide, even long after Carl was gone. Each morning I unlocked my bike from under the stairs of this house of mirth and pedaled my way to Mimi's. On busy weekends, especially in the summer, I went mad trying to manage the cash register, but it worked the trick because it kept me from thinking about Mama and home and the regrettable events of 1967. Until Judy Anderson walked in.

Mimi had attached a string of bells to the door so that every time it opened, the soft jangling could be heard from anywhere in the shop, even the back room where she had stored the old furniture. I grew accustomed to its tinkling music. It meant another customer, surely a good sign, so I stopped what I was doing—dusting the antiques again, and stepped behind the counter. Judy didn't recognize me at first, not the way I spotted her. I would have known her anywhere. She still wore that dark brown page boy, out of fashion now, her eyes sad and turned down a little in the corners. When she walked toward me, unexpected panic accompanied the look of recognition. Judy turned away as if she wanted to run, but we both knew she was trapped.

"Judy?" I stared at her until she looked up at me. "What brings you to town?" She managed an ambivalent smile and I spoke again to fill the awkward silence. "It's Lizzie. You do remember me, right?" I was sure she did, but my apprehension over her sudden appearance led to inane prattle.

"Lizzie. This is a surprise." Her smile twitched as she seemed to remember our last encounter, and she shot over to a shelf where she spied old comic books, clearly an effort to avoid the disquiet of seeing me again. Regaining momentum but not enough to look at me, she added, "I'm here with my husband. Business trip, a medical convention—he's in sales. I'm on my own for a couple of hours. Thought I'd have a look around, do a little shopping," she babbled nervously. She finally looked at me. "You remember Jimmy Bertrand?" She waited for me to say something, as if I didn't know the Bertrands had been our neighbors for fifteen years. "The three of us used to hang out at Jimmy's...." I waited for her to get to the point. "Oh, of course, how silly. As if you wouldn't remember your neighbor—time flies, huh? Well, anyway, I married him."

I listened but it was old news. They eloped the week after we graduated from high school, their final caper, but by then our friendship had collapsed under the weight of Judy's cruel betrayal and we never spoke again. "No kidding," I said looking down, hoping she would leave soon. I suddenly felt sick and began rifling through papers under the counter. Judy grabbed a handful of vintage comics so she could make a quick exit. I rang them up for her.

"These for Jimmy?" I asked, harvesting the good memories of my old neighbor and friend.

"Yeah. He loves comic books. Still reads them all the time. They just cost more now. He has every single one since….since….you and I…." She ceased limping through contrived twaddle, remembering no doubt how our exhausted friendship had eventually bowed to its bitter end. "Hey, whatever happened to that yard boy your mother hired? What was his name? Ronald?"

"Reggie. Reginald Washington. I don't know where he is, but I'm sure he's doing well. He was a clever boy, capable of overcoming the worst…." I paused to let that sink in, but despite her marriage to Jimmy, I had my doubts that Judy would ever understand the pain of others or the generous salve of kindness. "Will this be it?" Her eyes met mine a moment too long, as if remembering something unpleasant, before she returned to the task at hand.

"Yeah. Jimmy'll be thrilled to get these."

"That'll be twenty even." Judy dug in her purse and handed me the bill. I thanked her and gave her the receipt and the bag of old comics. She began walking toward the door when she abruptly turned her head around, forcing a smile.

"Thanks, Lizzie. I'll tell Jimmy I saw you."

"By the way, whatever happened to Jimmy's brother?" I couldn't help myself. I should have let her go, but inviting the dark side into our conversation felt strangely comforting.

"Randy?" She was quiet for a moment, as if planning what to say next. "Oh, you know. He did what everybody else does after college. Got a job. Got married. Had a kid. The usual." Had I expected her to tell the truth? She had turned mollifying the facts into an art, breathing new life into them. Indeed, lying mitigated Judy's dependence on any truth she couldn't accept. She needed to reconstruct what really happened to all of us, especially Randy, for more than this chance meeting, I suspected. We both had lived through and survived the real version, the sordid details that had shame-lessly swept through Carlton.

"Is that so?" I retorted without challenging her bizarre invention.

"Well, gotta run. Meeting Jimmy soon, just around the corner," she said as she fumbled to open the door. The bell jangled abruptly. Judy was gone and I let out a sigh of exhaustion.

Despite our best endeavors, plants may be susceptible to damage or disease. Identify the cause and develop a plan for both prevention and control of the problem. Begin with symptoms related to soil and pests.

The Art of Gardening by Emily Mayfield

CHAPTER 2

1966 | The Andersons had recently relocated from Morgan City to the large white ranch style house around the corner. Since their only daughter Judy and I were both entering ninth grade, we gravitated to each other, and I wondered if she could possibly be the catalyst for change I so desperately needed. As there was a severe shortage of neighborhood girls my age, I had grown up with boys on both sides and was frankly outgrowing frogs and tree houses, war games and their concomitant battle tactics. My neighbors accepted me in these playtime antics, but I soon became hungry for girl things, and Judy filled the need, plain looking Judy who so wanted to look like Audrey Hepburn. She fantasized about her idol—sleek, dark haired, dark eyed—a fashion icon in her adoring eyes. One afternoon we were sitting in the garden when Judy pulled out an old movie magazine with Miss Hepburn on the cover in a film called *Charade* with leading man Carey Grant.

"Who's that?" I asked.

"You're joking, right?"

My mother had never encouraged going to the picture show. She said reading would improve my mind, but it was really because she didn't have the money for pictures. I didn't know the names of actresses then, not like Judy, but I felt certain that I about to be educated and Judy was going to make sure I looked silly for being so out of touch with the world. If she couldn't be glamorous, she would at least act like the expert who knew all about the people who were.

"She's just the most popular star in Hollywood, next to Doris Day, but Doris doesn't count." She rolled her eyes. "You're hopeless. You're never going to grow up to be a woman if you keep acting like you don't know anything."

"Why doesn't Doris Day count?"

"What?"

"Doris Day. What's wrong with her?"

"She's blonde and she smiles too much. That's why. And talk about someone who acts like she doesn't know anything—that's Doris."

"How do you know if you don't go see her pictures?" I asked.

"I just know. I read about her in my movie magazines. I have to keep up with the latest, don't I? You know, if you looked at them once in a while, you could learn a thing or two about....things a girl should know," she reasoned, tugging at her shirt and flipping her hair.

I left it at that. If I had any money, I'd buy books. I certainly wouldn't spend it on movie magazines so I could learn how to be a girl. And I wasn't about to argue with my only friend. Besides, I had no idea what being blonde had to do with anything, or smiling either. I had brown hair pulled back in a ponytail, but, as my mother loved to point out, my blue eyes were my best feature and sparkled, so she said, when I was excited. She was fond of saying things only a mother would say, but I put up with it to placate her need to boast about her only child. At any rate, Judy had made me feel less-than more than once, but I let it slide. The truth was, I needed a friend my age, a girl friend, and I was willing to subject myself to her mild abuse mainly because at the time I thought it was harmless.

15

"I tell you what," I said, changing the subject. "Let's go next door to Jimmy's house and see if he wants to go to the pool. And if he doesn't, we can just sit around and look at his comic book collection."

"Where are we going? Who's Jimmy?" she asked. I explained that Jimmy Bertrand and his family had lived next door to us since we were both six years old. I left out the details—those memories weren't for her ears, and I saw Jimmy with great affection because of the history we shared. Despite the fact that I was the only girl in the neighborhood, he agreed to play outside with me until we reached fifth grade. A small ditch ran between our houses and filled with water when it rained. One Saturday morning in late spring, when Jimmy found the ditch swarming with tiny frogs, he banged on our back door for me to come out and see, and I was happy to oblige. A bamboo hedge grew at the far end of our yard, to which Jimmy took his pocket knife. I always wondered how he knew those little frogs would jump on those split bamboo canoes and drift down the flooded ditch, but he knew and they did. We drew the other neighborhood kids to our yard, too, all boys, of course. A circus on the swing set, a jungle river expedition surveyed from our tree house boat, cowboys and Indians with stick guns and bows and arrows, and finally, when it got unbearably hot, endless games of Clue in front of his porch fan. As we grew older, Jimmy was still willing to be in the same space that I occupied, usually his screened-in sleeping porch, but it meant reading comic books together in silence with an occasional snicker from him. My classic comics evoked no laughter, but I was happy to be in his company. We didn't find it necessary to talk, and although we never acknowledged it, our silence made us mindful of the restorative quiet time that we both needed.

Judy vehemently opposed my pool idea. "No!" she snapped. I looked up at her, surprised. "I mean, it's too hot. We can go to Jimmy's if you want. But swimming's out," she said emphatically.

"Why? That's the whole point of going. To cool off."

"I just don't want to, that's why. Isn't that good enough?"

"It's not that time of the month, is it?"

"Maybe it is and maybe it isn't. What do you know about things like that anyway? You're such a—" She stopped.

"A what? I am fourteen you know. And I'll soon be fifteen."

"Never mind. Let's go. We can look at his comic books."

By the time we had stepped out the door and walked across the Bertrand's front lawn, our shirts were damp with perspiration. I led Judy around to the back door of the house that opened to the screened-in extension that had become Jimmy's room. He was just getting up and met us at the door in his pajamas. Judy giggled.

"Hey." He motioned for us to come in and then flopped down on his bed and, from the pile scattered across his unmade bed, picked up a comic without opening it. Judy boldly sat next to him and picked up an Archie. I settled on the rug in front of Jimmy, wrapping my arms around my knees.

"This is Judy. She's new but she'll be in our grade when school starts." Jimmy just nodded in her direction and picked up a stack of comics. "We were bored, so we thought we'd see if you wanted to do something," I said.

"Like what?" he yawned and stretched his arms out, then glanced at Judy and covered his mouth.

"Well, I wanted to go to the recreation center for a swim, but Judy doesn't want to." At that moment she shot a glance of terror at me, her body stiffening with a panic I hadn't seen before. I stared at her until Jimmy finally broke the uneasy silence.

"Wanna walk to the park?"

"It's pretty hot," I said.

"So?"

Judy threw the comic on his bed and stood up. "Okay. Let's go." She turned back to Jimmy and said, "You goin' like that?" He looked at her and whipped his pajama top over his head.

"Nope. Meet you outside." Judy stood there gawking until I pushed her out the door.

"He's so cute. Does he have a girlfriend?" she said as we walked out of earshot toward the sidewalk.

"Him? I dunno. Never thought about it before. Probably not. He's just Jimmy. Same as when we moved here almost ten years ago only taller."

"Oh. Maybe I can change that." Judy's whole face lit up. She was suddenly energized, and I realized she had just set her eyes on him as her new boyfriend.

Jimmy caught up with us. With his high tops on, he could sprint easily to the sidewalk in four steps. The swings were empty, unusual for a Saturday morning, but the sweltering temperatures kept people indoors in front of their window unit air conditioners and fans. Judy ran to the middle one and pushed off hard with her feet, accelerating into the air almost before I could sit down. Jimmy just leaned against a pole and watched.

"Lizzie," she yelled. "Let's see who can swing the highest. Jimmy, you be the judge." I shoved off, leaned back, and lifted my pony tail off my neck. As if crazed with the ever increasing altitude of her swing, Judy glanced my way and began squealing.

"I'm the winner! I'm the winner!" As quickly as she had reached the pinnacle, she released her grip on the chain and catapulted herself onto the dirt below. I followed her, sailing through the air and landing with a thud nearly on top of her. It was then that I saw it. There in the dirt with Judy on all fours, her long sleeved loose cotton shirt had crept up her back, revealing a broad strip of bare skin above and below her waist. Dazed for only a moment, she stood up and straightened her clothes, but I had seen it. Where pink flesh should have been, there were huge splotches of discolored purple and yellow skin, bruises days old and healing.

"My Lord, Judy. Did you get in some kind of accident?"

"What?" she said, still disoriented.

"Those bruises. Where'd you get them?"

"I don't know what you're talking about." She looked around for Jimmy, who was walking toward us, and I figured it was best not to say any more about it. I'd put my foot in my mouth once already. Five minutes of sitting in the stifling summer heat on the swings, we all agreed, was long enough to stay at the park, and I suggested we go to my house and get a

Popsicle. We could move the big fan to the back porch, cool off, and think of something else to do for the rest of the afternoon.

The oscillating breeze of the fan sent cool sticky sweetness streaming down my chin. I was in heavenly relief, but Judy in her long sleeved shirt and pants looked miserable. Suddenly I could feel my mother standing in the doorway.

"Hi, Mrs. Rowan." Judy always put on her best manners for my mother, an innocuous pantomime intended as respect, so I tolerated it.

"Well, hello, Judy, Jimmy. I see you all found a way to stay cool. Temperature's supposed to reach 98 today. Maybe you all could go down to the pool later."

"Actually, we were hoping to go to the picture show," Judy quickly interjected. "Audrey Hepburn's playing in *My Fair Lady*. It's a musical." I looked at Judy, surprised at the news she hadn't shared with me. Was this yet another one of Judy's performances?

"Oh, yes," Mama said. "I'd forgotten about it, but you're right, Judy. The Paramount's second run of *My Fair Lady*. I'm teaching Shaw's play in the fall. Might be good for the three of you to see it. Why don't you telephone your parents, Judy, and see if you can go? I can drop you off." I suspected the idea of seeing Audrey Hepburn in anything would have thrilled her, but when Mama suggested calling her parents, Judy's face dropped. Conversely she appeared aloof at the suggestion, expressionless, as if she had changed her mind and her fervor for going to the pictures had just expired.

"Actually, I think it's getting late. I better go, but thank you anyway. I just remembered I've still got some chores to do this afternoon." I knew it was an act, but I was clueless as to her motive. I soon learned that Judy was good at hiding her feelings when it suited her, a trait I presumed to be the beginning of a life of prevarication.

"All right. Maybe another time," Mama answered, and that was the end of our Saturday afternoon. Jimmy, who never said much, went home, and I accompanied Judy down the driveway from our back porch, determined to have the last word.

"Hey, I thought you loved Audrey Hepburn. And this is the first time in months my mother has actually encouraged me to go to the pictures." I was practically hissing through my teeth. "Are you crazy?"

"I have to go home." Judy quickly turned around to go and I ran to keep up with her. When we reached the end of the sidewalk, she stopped.

"My father's really mad at me. My mother let me come over today when Daddy had to see a client back at the office for a few hours. I need to get home before he does."

"What'd you do? Why is he so mad at you?" I sensed Judy might be telling the truth this time.

"I told Mother I was too tired to do the dishes and he thought I was sassing her. He got so mad—I mean really, really mad." Judy was staring at her feet.

"Oh. Is that all?"

"Is that *all*? He took off his belt." She shot a quick glance at me sideways, then looked down at the pavement, scraping her shoe on a crack in the sidewalk in a rare moment of honesty.

It didn't register at first how removing an item of clothing could do anybody any harm. I hadn't seen my own father for ten years, so I had no idea what fathers did when they were angry. I watched as Judy rolled up one sleeve. No sound came out as I stood there with my mouth wide open. The length of her arm was mottled with large purple and yellow bruises, and then I knew. When her father removed his belt, it was to beat Judy black and blue. I remembered the bruises on her back and whispered, "Does all of you look like that?"

"I dunno. I guess. I don't want to talk about it anymore. I need to go now." And then her sad, pleading eyes met mine in a moment of weakness that I might never see again. "Don't tell anybody, not even your mother. And especially not Jimmy."

"I promise." I crossed my heart as I stood there and watched her hurry around the corner before her father could find out she had left the house that day. I had no doubt about my loyalty to her. Her secret would be safe with me. I walked back to the house with the gnawing uneasiness that surfaces when childhood begins to crack and chunks of innocence fall off.

Enrich your soil with compost or manure before planting and water daily so that your flowers will thrive and provide you with the truly privileged space you have created.

The Art of Gardening by Emily Mayfield

CHAPTER 3

1974 | I had just pulled the car up the drive and was getting out when the weightless notes of Mary's piano keys flittered down like sparrows to the ground floor. She had a habit of leaving her front windows open, not only for fresh air but for the simple joy of seeing her lace curtains swaying gently in the island breeze. Her favorite songs entertained even the passersby on the street below, possibly unfamiliar with long-ago tunes. They were wartime songs, and Mary's role as lead singer in Dickie Wilson's band had entrusted her with a treasure-trove of music so sentimental that each one often brought tears to her eyes. I envisioned Mary coming to America. She would leave behind evenings of stardom where she embraced the spotlight, murmuring one minute and belting out the crescendo of each romantic ballad. Swarms of anxious servicemen clung to the promise of life and love while the orchestra escorted her—and them, through each silky refrain. It wasn't exactly the Moody Blues I heard that day coming out of her piano, but I had grown to love this nostalgic old music. She was singing that song again. Mary never got tired of it, and although she didn't need an excuse for playing it, she said it freed her mind from her worries. The words were clear and palpable as I climbed the stairs, and I imagined Mary singing to the memory of the man for whom she had traded such a life of glamour.

"Good night, sweetheart, sleep will banish sorrow. Good night, sweetheart, when we meet tomorrow...."

And then she stopped and sat very still. Mary hadn't heard me come in, so I cleared my throat and when she saw me, her faraway look became a smile.

"I think that's my favorite of all your songs, Mary."

"Cuppa tea?" She got up to fill the kettle without a word about her music. It was a private matter between herself and her memories of him, and she would not be sharing it that day. I followed her to the kitchen.

"I saw an old friend from Carlton today at the shop," I began, changing the subject and leaning casually against the counter. I rarely spoke of those days to anyone, not only afraid of unwieldy and delicate questions but also of dark memories that might surface, but Judy's unexpected arrival had vexed me all afternoon, almost to the verge of brooding. If I explained it to Mary, she would listen with little interruption and I would be grateful for her generous dose of wisdom.

"Ah, did you now? Tell me all about it. Come and sit here while the kettle boils." She motioned me toward our usual spot, a small gate leg table in the corner of her kitchen, turquoise paint worn off at the edges, and I began to unwrap the morning's events while she arranged tea paraphernalia on a tray.

"Her name was Judy Anderson but she ended up marrying a friend of mine, next door neighbor actually, so I suppose that would make her Judy Bertrand now." I paused. It was the first time I had said her new name, on permanent loan from a man now sadly nonexistent to me. I then explained why they were in Galveston, on business according to her story, her husband a sales consultant for a medical supply company and Judy stopping at several tourist shops on the beachfront. When I added that she ended up buying old comic books for Jimmy, I began to lay open my role in the Bertrand family saga. Surprised at how strangely erratic my chatter had become, I paused and looked at Mary, who was still listening, but kept going as if I were explaining it to myself for the first time. "The thing is, the thing is, there was bad blood—everything between us seemed to go wrong. I can't really blame her completely—I could have stopped her but I didn't, and on top of everything else that happened, she accused Reggie of a crime he didn't commit. Not long after that, I was certain she was partly responsible for his arrest for murder, which, again, he didn't do. My mother and I served as his alibi, and that was, as they say, the coup de grace—Judy abandoned me, expelled me from her new circle of friends. I felt betrayed but actually also relieved she was gone. When I saw her today, after all this time, the old feelings came right back, like they had been there *all this time* right under the surface."

"Reggie?" was all she said. It hadn't occurred to me that I had never mentioned him before.

"Oh. Reggie." Reggie would be another long story—there was so much to tell, and I wasn't sure where to start or how much to disclose. Mary Stiles was not someone you could lie to. She could see right through an embellishment of the truth which I learned right away. No matter what it was, she was clever enough to see through subterfuge, even flimsy excuses, so I began telling her the facts about Reginald Washington's journey to my mother's garden. Despite several painful and embarrassing omissions, I found that retelling my story would permit me to face the facts with enough distance between the actual events and the reliving of them to see them more clearly. While explaining this to Mary was one thing, making reparations with Reggie, unfinished and intertwined in secrecy, was another. Betrayal without forgiveness becomes mummified in the hot dry desert of denial. The truth, the whole truth about Reggie, wasn't going anywhere no matter what I did to it.

Halfway through my story she said, "So this Reggie—you say he was a close friend? How close?" I glanced up quickly to refute the boldness of her allegation, but her face revealed no presumptions about us at all. When

I didn't answer her, she said, "Never you mind, don't stop there. Go on. So this friend, Judy, betrayed you and your friend Reggie, and….." I picked up the conversation while Mary heated the teapot with boiling water. She emptied it after a minute and scooped in three spoonfuls of loose black tea.

"I guess the real issue is this mixed-up anger I still have toward this girl. I thought—I hoped I'd never have to see her again. I hoped." I stopped there and waited for her to speak, but she didn't say anything right away, just got up to pour the tea and think. The slow ceremonial gesture of preparing tea—warming the pot, spooning in the fragrant leaves, covering the pot with a cozy, and waiting for it to brew, gave her time to sort the facts from the emotions that she had discerned in my voice before she answered. She took her time with each step of the ritual, but I knew she was planning what to say to me. A minute of silence can sometimes feel like an eternity, but she sat down, teapot in hand, and began to pour the hot, dark brown liquid into our cups before speaking.

"I've always thought that people who hurt others have themselves been hurt. Tell me what caused your friend's pain and you'll have your answer. I think you'll see that she only meant to unload her pain on someone else who could carry it for her. The poor girl, bless her. Perhaps the burden was too heavy. I wish I had an easier answer for you, love. We humans are so deeply complicated."

"You're right about that. Thanks, Mary."

"Not at all, love."

It wasn't the answer I wanted to hear even though I knew she was right, yet my defenses took over and I snapped back. "But I've known about her troubles almost from the day we became friends. I just didn't want her to get off the hook that easy. Don't we all have personal tragedies that we have to deal with? I mean, look at you, Mary. You went through a war in England, away from Ireland, not even close to your own family. You saw terrible tragedy." Mary didn't say anything, only lifted her eye brows. I continued ranting. "Why should she behave badly because of a problem she never resolved? It wasn't my fault. Her father drank too much and beat her black and blue. Arms, legs, back—all hidden from view. Her clothes covered up what he did to her. And....and her mother knew what he did and let it go on for years. I mean, how could Judy's own parents hurt her like that?" Then I added, "Jimmy was fool enough to make her his girlfriend. I guess he wanted to make sure somebody loved her, and he had his own problems to deal with, too." I stopped for a minute. No matter what had happened between us, the precious years of history between Jimmy and me could not be erased. I had let the cat out of the bag but Mary was quiet. Then I remembered my anger toward Judy again. "So she had a terrible father. I didn't have one at all." I'd allowed the old irritation to chafe and Mary could hear it and see it in my face. At least we were diverted from dismantling my shrouded history with Reggie.

"Well," she started, "it seems like it wasn't all her fault either, love. I'm sorry for your friend, and her family, too." Mary shook her head and sighed. "She never had a chance. No child should have to grow up feeling she doesn't deserve the safety a parent should provide. What many of us never realize is that the greatest gift in this short little life of ours is to love and be loved, especially by the ones who are supposed to protect us." I didn't want to talk about it anymore, especially the love bit, not when Mary was taking her side. Love was painfully complicated. I hoped I hadn't given her the impression that I was jealous of Judy and Jimmy. I wasn't. Not exactly, anyway. It's just that he was my first real friend before Judy came along.

I told Mary it was getting late and I thanked her for the tea and talk and quickly hurried downstairs to my room. My attempt to shut out the past again was not going to happen overnight, so I curled up in bed to lose myself in a book until I fell asleep. I'd think about Judy and Jimmy and Reggie later.

A voice I didn't recognize outside my window woke me up early the next morning. I had overslept. I threw on some pedal pushers and a cotton shirt, ran a brush through my hair and slipped on some canvas shoes. I'd grab coffee and a roll at the café next to Mimi's. I was taking my bike out the driveway when I saw Mary and a man under the hood of her old Ford that resided in the garage in the back and was seldom used.

"Mornin', Mary," I yelled as I climbed on my bike and waved.

"Oh, good morning, Lizzie. Come and meet my mechanic." I was hoping she would leave it with our brief greetings since I was in a hurry, but I stopped where the two of them stood. "You'll be wanting to meet this nice gentleman, pet. He's the owner of your shop. Jack, this is my lovely tenant Lizzie Rowan. Lizzie, this is Jack Schwarz, my son-in-law."

"Oh," I said startled. I never considered Mimi having a husband, only a daughter. "Very nice to meet you, Mr. Schwarz. I'm on my way to work now," I said giving myself room to leave quickly.

"Jack, just Jack. Good to meet you, Lizzie," and he reached out and offered his hand. "My wife tells me how glad she is to have you in the shop, and our daughter Janie talks about you all the time." He turned to Mary with "I'd better get this thing running if you're going to make that doctor appointment."

"Mary, are you sick? I could have given you a lift." I got off my bike and moved closer to her.

"No, love. I'm fighting fit. Go on before you're late. Come round later for tea."

I nodded and rode off, down three blocks to Mimi's. No customers were at the door as I unlocked it, but I didn't want to be late again, especially after hearing how happy Mimi was with me. Galveston was supposed to be my fresh start sans trouble, and I was making an effort to keep it that way.

The shop was uncommonly busy that day. A busload of retirees from Houston landed right in front of the Crab Hut for lunch, which was convenient because they all walked across the street to Mimi's to shop for souvenirs. A cheerful bunch of mainly women, they laughed and strolled around the shop for almost an hour, and then suddenly all twenty of them lined up at the same time to pay for their purchases. Although the process was slow, I had nothing else to do and I saw them with new eyes—they were all sweet, kind Marys who were enjoying their sunny day in Galveston. The rest of the afternoon crept by with few customers, and after uncontrollable yawning, I closed the shop for ten minutes to buy a coffee next door to see me through the afternoon.

After locking my bike to the post outside my room, I ran up the stairs and knocked on Mary's door to check on her. The windows were closed and no one answered. Remembering her doctor appointment that morning, my uneasiness mounted. I began to worry. Was Mary all right? How could I find out? Mary still had not seen to the phone installation in my room, so I rode back to the shop, opened up, and used the shop phone to call Mimi.

"Hi, Mimi. This is Lizzie. Yes, everything is okay at the shop. I was wondering if you knew anything about Mary. She's not at home. Everything's shut tight."

"Well, she does go out from time to time," she laughed. "Don't worry. The doctor put her on a new prescription and she's sitting with me right here. She'll be home later this afternoon. I'll tell her you asked about her."

I felt foolish but it had been a long time since I had shared any part of myself with a confidant, restoring my faith in humanity, and I wasn't ready to give that up, letting people in and losing them again. When I left Mimi's, I bought a sandwich from the café and rode home. Mary arrived shortly afterward carrying a tray of marigolds. Arms full, she called out my name, but I had already heard her car in the drive and had seen her standing outside my window. I quickly opened the door and took the tray from her.

"I hear you missed me, pet. Well, here I am. Engine in my car and the one in my chest both working just fine. Come have a cuppa tea with me, but first help me get these in the ground out back. I have just the spot." Relieved to see her again, I followed Mary around the side of the house where she handed me a trowel. This would be an easy planting. The black soil was moist and rich where she had prepared a bed for her bright yellow flowers the day before. I refused the garden gloves she offered, thrusting my bare hands into the dirt instead. It felt good, sacred even, to be at one with such a powerful life force, and I closed my eyes and let the cool earth slide between my fingers. I was transported into Reggie's garden again, offering myself up to the earth in an act of submission, maybe even defiance. Everything seemed possible in Reggie's green world, the miracle of growth and second chances, and I was proof. Mama was right. Reggie's verdant heart made him a garden alchemist, and with my hands in the soil I felt the mystery of him close beside me.

The gardener cultivates carefully and respectfully, often wearing garden gloves, in full recognition of the sharp thorns that nature has provided to ensure the plant's protection.

The Art of Gardening by Emily Mayfield

CHAPTER 4

1966 | On the first Friday of September, the student council sponsored a welcome back dance following the game, aimed primarily at acculturating the ninth graders to high school life. Whether Carlton High's football team won or not, a victory dance followed the game and all the students gravitated toward the gym. Never suspecting Judy's plan to keep Jimmy isolated in a dark corner of the dance floor the entire evening, I agreed to tag along. For a long and painful thirty-five minutes, I stood on the side listening to 45s crooning one love song after another, so conspicuously alone, that I imposed on myself a maximum of suffering through two more songs. If no one had asked me to dance by then, I planned to slip out and walk home. Judy and Jimmy would never know I was gone. Once, Danny Simpson from my algebra class slowed down to check me out, but then he veered away and joined the rip-roaring cacophony of boys hanging out on the bleachers, not one of them with any intention of asking the wallflowers planted in the dim light of the sidelines to dance. The gym speakers were blaring "I wanna hold your hand" as I headed for the door. The teachers absorbed in conversation under the exit sign didn't seem to take any notice of my departure.

Stepping out into the soft light of the breezeway and into the pitch black darkness of the parking lot was like entering another world. Two teachers stood outside the door contributing to the stale air of cigarette smoke as I crossed the threshold and onto the sidewalk where I would journey to our little yellow house ten minutes away. An occasional car passed by, but for the most part, teenagers in Carlton were safely garrisoned inside the gym. I walked at a quick pace and was almost home when a pair of headlights flashed quickly, then turned left at the corner. It was only a few steps to the front door where inside I would continue my uneventful boring evening.

Like a Norman Rockwell, my mother sat posed in a familiar way, rocking chair facing the hearth, book in hand, reading glasses perched on the slope of her nose, smoke spiraling from the ash tray. She glanced up slightly as the door swung open.

"Didn't hear a car. You're home early. How was the dance?"

"Okay," I answered, disappearing down the hall.

"Pan of brownies on the side." I knew she hadn't taken her eyes off her book. Without looking up, she issued the welcomed pronouncement as if reading a line from the page she was on, successfully diverting me. My mother knew instinctively how to deliver comfort, even when there didn't seem to be a reason to do it. No discussion required, I headed for the kitchen.

I slept late the next morning. When fully awake, I stared at the ceiling like a movie screen where the vision of Judy and Jimmy and the miserable dance played again. Mama opened the door as the squeak of the bottom hinge gave her away. I quickly turned my head and closed my eyes.

"Lizzie, Judy's here. You awake? It's almost noon, hon." I kept my eyes closed and pretended to be asleep. It might have worked, too, but Judy pushed past Mama and plopped down on the bed so hard we both bounced a little. Judy fell against me and grabbed my shoulder.

"Hey. Get up. I know you're awake. Saw your eyes move."

"Well, I'm awake now." I rolled over and bolstered myself up, making a right angle with my arm. "What're you doing up so early? And why are you in such a good mood?"

"Why are you in such a bad mood? Never mind. I don't want to know. It'll ruin my day. Jimmy and I had so much fun last night. What happened to you? When all the lights came on at the end of the dance, we went around searching for our shoes, but I didn't see you. Did you leave early or something?"

"No," I lied. "I looked for you everywhere. You must have left before I did."

"Oh, sorry, Lizzie. Don't be mad. I guess I was paying so much attention to Jimmy. Isn't he just the greatest?" I didn't want to talk about Jimmy or the lies we both had just told.

"So why are you up so early? Were we supposed to do something today?"

"Well, I was hoping," she spoke in that sweet sing-song tone that precedes a request. "I was hoping you'd go over to Jimmy's with me. Please, Lizzie. I really want to see him again."

I turned over, mashed my pillow into a ball, and sank my head into it. "You don't need me for that. Besides, I'm gonna sleep all day."

"Oh, Lizzie, come on. I have to see him again. My father's in a rare mood and I'm finished with my chores. This could be such a good day. Don't spoil it for me. Please. I don't want to go by myself." I sighed and resigned myself for whatever reason, though I couldn't think of it at that moment, to humor her.

"Oh, all right," I said, sweeping the covers back in one swift motion.

"We don't have to stay long and I promise we'll come back and do whatever you want."

Next thing I knew we were walking across our neighbor's driveway to see Jimmy. His father's car wasn't there and no one came to the back screen door. When we went around to the front and knocked, Jimmy's mother appeared.

"Hi, Mrs. Bertrand. Is Jimmy home?" I asked.

"Well, good morning, Miss Lizzie, or is it already afternoon? Jimmy's not here, hon. He and Randy went fishing with Mr. Bertrand. Won't be back until, oh, I guess it'll be late tonight when they get in, most likely dirty, hungry, and smelling like fish," she laughed.

"Oh, okay. Well, thanks, Mrs. Bertrand." I stepped away from the door to go but Judy continued.

"Where'd they go fishing?" I looked at Judy, uncertain about her bold move.

"Oh, sorry, Mrs. Bertrand. This is my friend Judy."

"Nice to meet you, Judy. Hon, they went all the way to Pine Lake near their grandpa's house in Watts. I don't imagine they'll be back before nine or ten o'clock tonight.

"Okay. Well, would you tell him Judy came by to see him, please?" Thick as molasses she was.

"I certainly will, dear."

I was practically pulling Judy off the steps by this time. "Thanks, Mrs. Bertrand. See you later."

"Bye, girls. Try to stay cool today. Oh, and Lizzie hon, tell your mama I'll bring her a stick of margarine for the one she let me have last week. And some hot rolls just out of the oven."

"Yes, ma'am. I'll tell her."

We hadn't gone five steps before Judy said, "Well, I gotta go."

I came to a halt. "Wait a minute. I thought you said if I went with you to Jimmy's, you'd do anything I wanted."

Judy paused and I could tell she was thinking of how she was going to break her promise again. "Some other time, okay? I don't feel like doing anything right now." Both of us disappointed, we walked to my house in silence. I was beginning to feel used, but I needed a friend and Judy, despite her tendency to ditch me at times, seemed to be all I had.

"Look, come inside the house," I said. "My mother can fix us some sandwiches and we can sit in the garden and swing and think of something to do. You can even paint my nails." Judy didn't hesitate.

"Paint your nails? Are you serious? When's the last time you owned a bottle of nail polish? Oh, all right. Do you have grape?"

Mama was busy with some sewing, so I went into the kitchen, grabbed the Rainbow bread out the box and went to work on our sandwiches. Judy sat at our kitchen table jabbering about the fine qualities of Jimmy, which I half listened to. I'd known him for ten years and had never been apprised of these fine qualities, although he was pretty good with a knife and a stick of bamboo. I was putting the peanut butter back in the cabinet and starting for the fridge with the grape jelly when Judy spoke.

"Put those on a tray, and do you have any milk to go with those?" I poured two glasses, arranged our snack on a tray, and headed for the back door.

"Hey, slow down! You're not going anywhere until I polish those ugly nails of yours. Go on. Go get the polish." She pointed her polished finger at me while I stared at her for a second, reacting to her tone. She was right about one thing. I didn't actually own a bottle of polish, not even one, and I never had. So I slipped into Mama's room and borrowed a bottle of pink. Judy didn't waste any time slathering polish all over my nails, cuticles, and some that dripped onto the napkin under my hand. They didn't look like Mama's perfectly polished hands, but it kept Judy busy and present, in good spirits for the next half hour, proud of her attempt at turning me into a woman, albeit not a very glamorous one.

With my nails still wet, Judy agreed to carry the tray with milk and sandwiches out to the swings just past our screened in summer house. It would have made a perfect playhouse had my mother not stuffed it with all her garden equipment, but the little house was off limits for any projects I might dream up. Straightaway Judy's demeanor changed as she looked at it, and she became positively animated. She dismissed the fact that she had already passed it a hundred times before on our way to the swing set, and with rousing enthusiasm as if seeing it for the first time, she professed new employment for the small screened-in house.

"Lizzie! This is the perfect place for a dance party." In its former life perhaps this small garden house had known family cookouts on warm summer evenings—a father standing over a barbecue pit cooking a savory meal for his family, children laughing and playing around him, his wife setting out the accoutrements for their meal. Now the silent stillness of an old table, three old chairs—one of them with only three legs, a hoe, a pair of shears, a shovel leaning against the side, a rake, numerous clay pots, an old bird cage, three shelves full of garden tools, and several bags of soil and fertilizer swallowed up whatever it might have been.

"Lizzie? Did you hear me? I said—"

"I heard you."

"Well, what do you think? We could ask your mother if we could move some things out to make room to dance. I could bring my record player over and all my 45s. It'd be so much fun. Let's go ask your mother now." Judy put the tray on the ground near the swings and was halfway to our back door.

"No, I don't think so. Not enough room."

"Yes, you do. Come on. There's plenty of room without all that stuff in it."

"No." Judy whipped around, surprised at the boldness of my refusal, but the sparkle in her eyes was fading. She shuffled back to the swings before glancing briefly to inspect the contents of the room again, the embers of hope still burning.

"You're no fun at all. It was a great idea and this time you could dance, too," she said, not ready to give up, her hands still resting on the screen.

"Oh, yeah. Like the dance at school Friday. That was a blast."

"Well, it's your own fault. You could have asked someone to dance, you know."

"I'm not you, Judy. It doesn't work like that for everyone. Besides, my mother would probably say no. She's very territorial when it comes to her garden house," I lied. Mama would willingly, without question, give it over to Reggie later, but Judy seemed to believe me and sat down in the swing next to me.

"Look, Lizzie. You're never going to get a boyfriend without a little more effort on your part. If anyone could change her mind, you could."

"Maybe I don't want to get a boyfriend that way." I was too tired for her polemics, but I fell right into the act of defending myself anyway. "It feels like....setting a trap."

"So? What's wrong with that? You do what you have to do."

"Actually, if I do have a boyfriend, it'll be when I join the newspaper staff or the drama club at school." I grabbed my sandwich and milk from the tray to signal an end to the conversation.

"You must be joking. What kind of boy do you expect to meet in those clubs? They're all a bunch of fruitcakes if you ask me."

"Well, I didn't ask you, and I guess I just won't get a boyfriend!" I mumbled, stuffing a large bite of sandwich in my mouth. My mother poked her head out the back door, ending our dispute temporarily.

"Judy, your mother just rang. She asked that you come home quickly."

Two words escaped. "Oh, God," she whispered and ran to the front without even saying goodbye. Mama closed the door and walked down the steps.

"Everything okay with Judy? She was in a big hurry."

"Yeah, it's okay. She just remembered she has some chores to do," I hedged, knowing full well that her daddy was no doubt on his way home. Mama didn't stop until she came to the white Althea, took her sewing scissors from her apron pocket and cut a single bloom. I watched her inspect the roses and the lush bougainvillea whose thorny tentacles intermingled with the althea branches that needed trimming.

"Gracious. These are sharp. I guess it's time to get the shears out. Sometimes beauty can be painful." She put her fingers to her lips and before sitting in the swing beside me, she gently tucked the cut white Althea Rose of Sharon in my ponytail. I grinned as I reached back to feel the flower in my hair.

"How were your classes this week?" Mama asked, picking up the other half of my PB and J.

"Fine, I guess. Civics is pretty boring but all the girls think Mr. Hammond is cute. Judy says he's easy on the eyes." Mama laughed at our assessment of him. "He's new, isn't he?"

"Yes, he is. This is his first year, Lizzie, so I hope you'll give him a chance. How's your English class?"

"I was hoping you wouldn't ask. Mrs. Thompson is something else." Expecting full support for my just convictions, I said, "If we don't fold our papers just right or write a complete heading on our papers, that old lady said she'd put an F on it, like we were babies or something. She's so mean. She shouldn't be a teacher."

"I see. Well, first of all, Leanne Thompson isn't that old, not much older than I am. She's had a hard life, losing her husband last year and now taking care of her sick, aging mother. Lizzie, honey, let me give you a bit of advice. Every teacher wants things done her way and that's just how it is. I have rules in my classroom, too. If you're smart, you'll learn to rise to each of their expectations, no matter how frustrating or unimportant they may seem. Just put a heading on your paper, hon. It isn't really that much to ask, is it? And it's a good habit. Don't you want credit for your work? Why do you think artists sign their work?" I rolled my eyes and Mama laughed and gave me a hug.

I despised the thought of rising to anyone's expectations of me. What if they were wrong? What if they were different from what I wanted for myself? My mother, of course, had an answer for everything, and I had to admit, she was usually right. I gazed at her. In the shade of the leafy overhanging branches of the oak, I half expected to see a radiance glowing around her head, a perfectly round golden circle of light like the ones I had seen on Judy's Catholic saint cards. The renegade in me might disagree with her, but some angelic voice inside that longed for her approval answered obediently.

"Okay, I guess you're right." And then I was surprised to hear myself reciprocating in my new mature high school attitude. "How was your week, Mama? Are your students nice?"

"Mr. Reynolds has his hands full this year with the senior class, but the first week was quiet. Not much is going to happen to disturb the classrooms, I suppose, but I'm afraid I can't say as much for what could happen after school hours. Nevertheless, I'm counting on a peaceful year." Despite her somewhat contrived optimism, she didn't need to explain the possible outcome of political reform now underway. As discomforting to some as the news had been, it was relegated to only a brief report on the five o'clock news at the end of last year. The NAACP had been asked to assist the government in placing four Negro students in the only white high school in Carlton in order to comply with the new regulations on desegregation. President Johnson had signed it into law two years earlier.

"What're they like, Mama?"

She laughed at my naiveté, but she knew what I meant. "Teenagers, Lizzie. Quiet teenagers. A bit more serious than the rest of my students, but they're just kids, that's all. One of them, I think, is exceptionally bright—Reginald Washington. His mother works for Mrs. Griffith from church. That young man has—I can't explain it, really, such an intense look in his eyes when we open our books and read poetry. Keats at the moment, and Reginald's going to do quite well, I believe."

"Oh," I said blankly, trying to remember who Keats was. I had heard her mention his name before but that was all. We sat for another few minutes swinging gently, Mama asking questions about the new friends I had met and I giving her the assurances she needed to hear. Conversation dwindled and a sweet silence replaced the need for words as the fading light settled over us. Then Mama spoke.

"I do love this garden, especially at twilight." She was staring straight ahead of her, not looking at the garden at all. "There's a peacefulness all around that makes you think nothing can harm you." She looked over at me. I didn't say anything, but she could sense my doubt in the creases between my eyes. "You'll know what I mean one day, my darling." We sat quietly again, gliding back and forth on that old swing set until, abruptly rising, she said, "Well, sweet Lizzie, sitting in this swing is not going to get our supper cooked. Are you coming in now?"

"In a minute." Mama stood up and took my hand.

"Nice color. Let's get out the polish remover and clean it up just a bit, okay?" And she turned around, picked up the tray, and headed for the door without another word.

My head was crammed so full that I sat for a while longer. I boiled it down to doubt and confusion, not knowing what would happen to us all. Judy, Jimmy, Reginald Washington and the other Negro students. Me. The weight of uncertainty suddenly felt heavier, and I aimlessly moved back and forth in the swing, unable to get up. It was dark now. The Abbotts' dog began barking and a light on their back porch came on. Mr. Abbott yelled at Butch to pipe down and all was quiet again. My stomach was growling this time and I got up from the swing to go in and help with supper.

The visibility of a garden pest makes identification easier.
Look for symptoms first, as the gardener may have
only these clues to the problem she must address.

The Art of Gardening by Emily Mayfield

CHAPTER 5

1966 | Ninth grade was an exercise in becoming acclimated to change—
new surroundings, new people, and new ways of doing the same old things. I
learned to pay attention, put a proper heading on my paper, and like school
in general. That pleased Mama. Irksome as it was, I saw Judy in spurts,
mainly when Jimmy needed some time away from her and she needed an
ear to listen. With all that time on my hands after school, I signed up for
the newspaper staff, imagining some romantic, idealized life as a reporter
scurrying here and there interviewing people, gathering up the facts, and
writing articles that would dazzle. The editor, Henry Thomas, was a senior
who swore he would never have a freshman on his staff—after all, said he,
how could freshmen possibly know anything about anything? But for some
reason he made an exception for me. I hoped, though I never knew for
sure, that it had nothing to do with the fact that Louise Rowan, his English
teacher, was my mother. Whatever opened the door, my desire to stay there
rested on my ability to turn out quality work while dodging sarcastic gibes
from annoying upper classmen. Yet as much as Mama's reputation might

be connected to whatever I wrote or did or uttered, I refused to give in to the anxiety and instead prove myself worthy of the job I thought I had.

"So, Liz, I'm giving you an assignment." Henry caught me just as I was leaving my first staff meeting. "I'm putting you in charge of coordinating the creative writing contest we're sponsoring." For a moment I actually thought I'd be writing an article, and he must have seen the excitement on my face, but he continued as if I should be grateful enough with what he offered. "I know it's not an article, but it's really important that the word gets out to the English faculty as well as students and that the entries are collected as soon as possible. Can you do it?" His eyes connected with mine. Could I do it, or did he mean would I do it?

As long as I didn't have to get up and speak to a group of people, sure, I could do whatever he asked. "Of course I'll do it, Henry. I'm grateful to be on your staff. Thank you for giving me a chance." Although my response was tilted on the side of acquiescence, I felt indebted for his recognition of my ability to contribute, even if that task might seem insignificant to others. I had overheard Henry call one of the sophomores running all his errands his *gofer*. I assumed that was some kind of new slang, but I could figure out what it meant. Maybe I was one of those gofers, too, but I held my ground and pretended whatever he asked me to do was important, even if it didn't involve writing.

"No. Thank *you*. I knew you'd be good for this project. I'm glad I can count on you, Lizzie. You're really responsible….for a girl anyway," he laughed. "I'm just kidding. Stick with it, all right, and your assignment will come up. I promise. Hey, don't forget to remind your mother about the contest, okay?" He was right. I was a responsible girl, but did that define me? I wondered what Judy would say about a compliment like that from a boy. Not *pretty* or *cute* but *responsible*. No way was I going to tell her that. And, yes, there it was out in the open, the fear that fueled my anxiety. Don't forget to remind *your mother*.

I got home from school before Mama that day, dropped my books on the table, and went straight to the garden with a Popsicle. Two minutes later Judy and Jimmy whipped around the corner of our house. Jimmy, who was chasing after her, nearly knocked her over when Judy saw me and stopped abruptly.

"Hey," I said. Judy's face dropped and I realized then she hadn't expected me to be there.

"Oh. Hi, Lizzie. What are you doing home so early?" she scolded, her disappointment with my inconvenient presence on display.

"It's not that early, Judy. In fact, I had a newspaper staff meeting after school." I had intended to keep that a secret from her but I forgot myself and out it came. Maybe she'd let it go.

"Newspaper staff?"

I sighed. "Uh-huh. I'm on it. Was there something you wanted, or were y'all just coming over to hang out?"

"Course we were," she said eyeing the garden house. "Sure. We thought we'd come over and see what you were up to, right Jimmy?"

"Yeah. How's it goin', Lizzie?" Jimmy's face flushed as his hands slipped into his jeans pockets.

"Good," I said and continued licking the pink-red ice. Nobody spoke for what felt like a whole minute, Judy taking the other swing and Jimmy uncomfortably leaning against the side of the garden house watching us. "Want a Popsicle?"

"Nah. Push me, Jimmy." A word from Judy and he scurried around the swing set, put his hands on her back, and gave her a gentle shove. "Harder!"

"Judy," I warned, "I'm not sure this old swing set can take it. Better not push your luck." She slowed down, dragging her feet on the thin, well worn grass, and came to a halt.

"Okay. Well, we gotta go. Bye, Lizzie." She grabbed Jimmy's belt and he allowed himself to be convoyed down the path without looking back. Jimmy angled his head around. "See ya, Liz."

Six o'clock rolled by and Mama was still not home. Five minutes later the front door flew open and in she stepped, out of breath and arms loaded with bags from the A & P.

"Sorry I'm late, hon. I stayed after to listen to book reports and then I ran to the store for a few things. Salmon croquettes okay tonight?" I hated canned salmon. I started for the door.

"What else?" Mama was in the kitchen opening cabinets and banging pots around.

"What's that?" she yelled. I decided we were having mashed potatoes. I peeked back in just as she was peeling and dicing a couple of Irish potatoes and tossing them into a pot. "Liz, open that can of peas, hon."

"Whose book report did you hear?" I asked while I fought with the can opener, so old and dull it should have been discarded long ago. "Why do we still have this old thing?" I finally succeeded in opening the peas and decided it was a good time to calm down and practice my new grown-up conversation tactics again. It was, in truth, a good cover-up for hearing about the cute senior boys in her class. After all, that would be as close as I would get to knowing them.

"There was only one—Reginald Washington. You remember him. Well, he started talking about Voltaire's *Candide*, and then I started asking him questions—never had any seniors read Voltaire before, and I wasn't sure he could understand it. He said his favorite part of the book was the famous line about tending your garden when things get rough in your life. When I asked him why he liked those lines, he said the philosophy suited him. He's a very clever boy, Liz. Before long it was almost five, and we were still talking about the book. It's a real leap for him, but he did well. He got it. Put those peas in that smaller saucepan, not the big one."

"All that time for one book report. Must have been interesting. Tell me more about him."

"Well, let's see. He was a French writer of the eighteenth century, known for his satire, Liz. Voltaire was one of the great writers of the time who spoke uncomfortable truths and was imprisoned and even exiled for a while. He also was an avid gardener."

"No, Mama. Reginald Washington. What's he like?"

"Oh." She paused, retracing the steps into her head to find an answer to the more difficult question. "Reginald. He doesn't say much in class, but after school when we started discussing his book, he spoke as if he'd been waiting for this moment, storing it all up for this one afternoon. I was so moved and impressed with his ideas that when he left, I just sat at my desk. I felt—oh, to tell you the truth, I don't know what I felt. Odd, I guess. Maybe a little surprised."

"Good odd?"

"Yes, of course, but…. I suppose I don't know what I expected."

"What about the others? Are they doing good, too?"

"*Well*, Lizzie, not *good*. Use the adverb," she corrected with a slight frown but continued. "I think so. I have a girl named Mary Walker, but Mrs. Glenn has the other two. Mary keeps up and does her work just fine. The other students aren't saying anything, are they? Is there any talk of…."

"Of what?"

"Trouble?"

"Not that I know of. I haven't heard anything, but that doesn't mean much." The truth was, the whole community was holding their breath the first two weeks, waiting to see what might erupt in a segregated world where racial differences had, prior to this year, not been as issue, at least if you happened to be white. Now they were and those who were enraged kept their seething just below the surface. Change had been more difficult to accept for some of the town, so set in their beliefs that they actually believed colored people were satisfied with an inferior way of life. "I really don't talk to anybody about that sort of thing. I mean, I have friends and all. We sit together at lunch and I just listen but they talk about girl things, and boys, of course. Always boys."

Mama looked relieved. "Well, I'm glad to hear things are normal. How is newspaper club working out?" She was mashing a wad of salmon mix between her palms with hope in her eyes that my freshman year would be the success she envisioned and that I would somehow fit in.

"Fine."

"Fine? That's all? Are you writing anything?"

"Not yet, but there is this writing contest, and I'm supposed to see to it that everything goes smoothly. Henry asked me especially to be in charge."

Mama hesitated without looking at me. "Does that mean you'll have to speak to each class?"

"Not if I can help it. That's where I draw the line. Public speaking is out, not going to do it, ever. I'll quit first." Mama frowned sharply at me as I continued. "I just have to gather up all the entries." And then I remembered Henry's reminder. "Oh, and Henry Thomas asked me to mention the contest to you."

"Yes, I know all about it. All the English teachers got a note about it in our boxes today. I'm allowed to submit only two pieces. Lizzie, stir the peas and turn the fire down. Let's give it a minute or two more on low. So Henry's given you an assignment? Progress, dear one, progress. This is good."

"It's not really a writing assignment, Mama, but he promised I would have one soon." I had some doubt about that promise, but if Henry said the words aloud, maybe he would start to believe them. Writing an article, I decided, would be my focus for the year, possibly the only thing going for me in ninth grade.

The days crept by with nothing the least bit exciting to speak of until two events collided and my social education unexpectedly moved up a notch. The first one happened on my birthday. Despite my mother's resignation about the upshot of her own situation, she continued to encourage me to suck the marrow of life out of ninth grade, rendered this time in the hosting of a slumber party with a few friends to celebrate my fifteenth. Summerlike weather had crept into October but Mama wanted to light a fire and pop corn.

The fireplace was situated at the east end of the front room. It rarely got cold enough to light, but my mother loved the idea of it. A small wood burning fire complemented her English grandfather's little volume of poetry written in his own hand. She pictured her mother's father, a ship builder from Gloucester and the man she called Grandpa Bean—her nickname for a beloved grandfather whose surname was actually Breen, sitting at his desk near the fire in the cold Gloucestershire winter composing those lines. His poems weren't going to win any prizes, but, having devoted her life to language, she revered the notion that her own flesh and blood could put words as well as wooden hulls together. Proof of a heritage, a link to the past that seemed to countenance her existence, was all that mattered, so she sat in front of a cold fireplace every afternoon with a cigarette, a cup of dark roast Eight O'clock coffee, and the newspaper, intermittently staring at the tattered book resting on the mantle. It made her content with the life that had fallen into her lap.

I said I would think about popping corn, hoping she would forget about her offer. No one could have possibly appreciated how much that fire place meant to her anyway, and I was content with keeping it that way. Besides, it was warm enough without a fire, and I had planned for everyone to toss their sleeping bags on the living room floor, a big enough space with adequate distance from my mother's room.

Virginia Slater, Cindy Balkans, and Carolyn Ellis sat with me at lunch and said they could come, but I didn't consider them close friends. I wasn't much of a talker, unlike social butterfly Judy. I thought from the beginning that they said yes because Mama was a teacher at school and they were simply curious about where and how we lived, not to mention it was something different to do on a Friday night. Then there was Judy, overjoyed to be spending a night away from her mother's watchful eye and her father's unpredictable temper. Her enthusiasm prevented any measure of dread that might have been incubating in me, for she quickly orchestrated a game of Charades before the pizza arrived, after which she made everyone get up and dance to the records she had brought. Somewhere in her enthusiasm was a promise to teach them the mashed potato, and indeed she did. With the ritual of gifts, singing and blowing out the candles dripping all over the top of the cake, we waited for Judy to corral everyone into a circle around the table. Mama cut six pieces of that chocolate frosted divinity and handed one to each of us. Judy breezed through each phase of the party like an event planner, down to the minute. At eleven o'clock she announced it was time to crawl into our sleeping bags, and by then I couldn't have disagreed with her. Being the birthday girl yielded emotional fatigue even though Judy had been the center of attention most of the night.

I wasn't a light sleeper, but that night, when all I wanted was to escape from the social suffocation I'd agreed to, I lay in my bag wide awake. Eyes closed, I thought if I pretended sleep long enough, my body would catch on and cooperate—a soporific fake-it-till-you-make-it bargain with myself. Although I lay there trying to get comfortable for what felt like hours, I discovered later it was only eleven-fifteen. Judy, lying next to me on my left, began fidgeting. Soon her shadowy figure sat up and then disappeared behind me into the kitchen, and, according to the familiar squeak of the screen porch door, into the back yard. I didn't know how much time had elapsed, but when I was sure no one else was awake, I got up out of the unzipped bag, tiptoed into the kitchen, and looked at the clock. Eleven thirty. I made it to the utility room and ducked behind the washing machine, grabbing a flashlight off the shelf of laundry supplies and softly opening the back door. One, two, three steps down, and several more across the deck and I was squatting in the grass. I stayed there for a minute and looked around. The air was still. No lights, no sound except for a soft breeze rustling the leaves of the big oak and Althea. I inched my way to the nearest tree and hid. Then I heard it, a soft giggling followed by a *shh-hhh* in the direction of the garden house. On my hands and knees, I crept over to the little house, crouching behind the low wall until slowly, slowly I raised my body up to look through the screen. Moving shadows and soft breathing. I lifted the flashlight to the screen, cupping my left hand over my eyes. Click. On went the light. As I pointed it directly in front of me, up popped a head. It was Jimmy's. His eyes seemed to take in the light for a second as he squinted and shielded his face. I aimed the flashlight down a bit. There, lying on the bags of my mother's unopened cow manure was Judy, small white breasts gleaming in the light. She squealed and grabbed her pajama top. I flicked the flashlight off, ran as fast as I could down the dark but familiar path to the back door, and crawled into my sleeping bag, my heart racing and the flashlight still in my hand. I wriggled down into the bag, covering my face, and lay still, panting as quietly as possible until my breathing was normal again. I must have finally dropped off because the next thing I remember, a sliver of light was pouring in through the curtains in the front window and it was morning.

Mama had let us all sleep in that morning, but as soon as my eyes could fully open, I looked over at Judy's sleeping bag. She was back in it, sound asleep. I stood up, stretching my back, and went to look for Mama in the kitchen where she was sitting at the table reading the paper and drinking coffee. She folded the newspaper and put it aside when she saw me.

"Mornin'. Sleep well? Anybody else up?" She stood up and opened the waffle maker.

"No, not yet. The floor was hard but it was okay. What's for breakfast?" I already knew, but engaging in conversation would distract her long enough for me to return the flashlight to the shelf. Mama's specialty was Belgian waffles, so light and crisp you thought they might levitate right there on the plate. She said her secret, which she confessed she had copied out of the *Ladies Home Journal*, was carbonated water. Everyone was duly impressed with her culinary magic and said so before collecting their gear and, one by one, saying goodbye. When Judy was the only girl left, I asked her if she wanted to go outside and swing. She replied with a shrug. "Well, how about the park?" I suggested and she nodded. Judy didn't say a word the whole walk down the street, and when we opened the gate, she didn't even run to grab the inside swing. I let her have it anyway. Both of us struggling from insufficient sleep the night before, we slumped in our swings without moving.

"About last night," she eventually began. "You can probably guess Jimmy and I planned it, can't you."

"Is that why you sent us all to bed at eleven?" She smiled cautiously, staring at the ground. "If you're afraid I might blab it in the school newspaper, you don't have to worry."

"Thanks, Lizzie." She exhaled slowly as if she thought Henry would actually let me write something like that and I had done her a favor.

"Freshmen don't get writing assignments, but the sophomores do...." Her head snapped up with a dismayed look of concern, but I was laughing. "I'm kidding, silly. I'm not gonna tell anybody." Judy's tension eased a bit and with renewed energy, she increased her momentum and stretched out in the swing, almost parallel to the ground and looking up at the sky. We didn't say much after that, and I was glad. I would never have admitted it to Judy, but she was right. We were traveling at a different speed when it came to boys, and talking about it was the last thing I wanted to do. I didn't see her again until Christmas vacation. Judy was sent to live with her mother's sister in Morgan City with not so much as a phone call to tell me.

Many kinds of evergreen plants have their origins in the winter solstice traditions. Holly, ivy, fir, rosemary, and evergreen wreaths and trees provide lovely symbols of protection, remembrance, new growth, victory, and joy. Your own garden can provide you with Christmas greenery for decorating your home in the spirit of holiday symbolism.

The Art of Gardening by Emily Mayfield

CHAPTER 6

1975 | It was Christmas and the energy of the season invigorated all who walked through Mimi's door. Jack and Janie were enlisted at the beginning of December to decorate the shop with as many lights as Mimi could supply, especially for the seven foot live Christmas tree that graced the front. It was Jack's particular job to cut three trees from a farm east of Houston, and as tradition dictated, each family's tree, including the shop's, was duly festooned with twinkling lights and colorful glass ornaments. Mimi's childlike obsession with this holiday flourished in the panoply of seasonal gifts and decorations she displayed and sold in abundance. The season filled the coffers financially as well as spiritually, and it was a joyful time. No customer walked away without partaking of little cups of hot chocolate and a sugar cookie or two, which Janie took credit for icing and serving when Mimi needed her help. We were busy and I left tired but content at the close of each day. I drove to work that month, the cold Gulf air reinforcing the decision that I wouldn't be getting on my bicycle for another three months. If ever I thought of Mama and Christmases past, such longings were ameliorated by the time I walked through the shop door and was wafted away into the spicy world of Mimi's latest gift enticements—Christmas candles, potpourri, and soap, anything whose telltale ingredients were cinnamon and cloves, peppermint and evergreen.

Friday afternoons were especially cheerful even though the Christmas season meant Mimi needed me to come in to the shop every weekend. Still, there was an atmosphere of conviviality that seemed to compete with what I had known before, although there would never truly be an equivalent to the holidays spent with Mama. Often in quiet moments of being with my mother preparing the meal or opening presents lovingly selected, or in my mother's case, made in her unique creative way, the two of us felt an uncommon sense of peace in the paroxysm of the sixties that threatened to erupt at any time. Now each day my greatest crossroads, usually the latest weather report, seemed to converge with my casual approach to life, especially to whatever affected my decisions about transportation. This particular Christmas, however, my attempts to keep life simple went awry, and I found myself succumbing to the generosity of the Schwarz family.

Galveston's historical society had recently become energized in the midst of a crisis, the neglected and crumbling historical sites in a district situated around what was once an old thoroughfare called The Strand. Before the Hurricane of 1900 that left the island with an apocalyptic death toll and horrific physical destruction, the island had been a booming metropolitan city that boasted the charm and elegance of luxurious Victorian proportions. Now the cost of restoration surpassing millions, the committee ultimately answered the call by establishing a festival that would generate the necessary funds to refurbish the district and continue its ongoing maintenance ad infinitum. That annual two-day event, which became known as the Dickens-on-the-Strand Festival, sought to replicate Galveston's nineteenth century era in resplendent characters, costumes, music, and refreshments, and it became wildly popular. Mimi and Jack, being part of the business community, not only gave their financial support but also attended with family and friends in the two years since its founding. This would be the third year of its successful incumbency in the community, and Mimi insisted that her mother Mary and I accompany them as their guests. When Jack heard about Mimi's plan, he added another angle to her scheme. He would set up his new accountant Dennis Chandler, who had recently moved to the island and didn't know anyone, as my blind date. I thanked him but respectfully declined.

"Sorry, Lizzie. I've already asked him to come with us, and he's excited about meeting you. Think of it as helping out a friend. The more the merrier, plus it'll help to restore The Strand," he said with eagerness overblown. "And I might add, it would do you good to get out more."

"But....but, Jack!" I struggled for a reply that would disentangle me from this gentle, well intended conspiracy. No excuses, good or otherwise, would suffice for this family whose kindness had redeemed me, and I was struck speechless, so I caved and tried to make the best of it. This family had seen me through a difficult move from Carlton and I owed them a debt, the extent of which was known only to me.

The first weekend in December arrived sooner than I was prepared for. Kaleidoscopic lights washed over the city, transforming it into a watercolor palette of the most vivid hues and drawing swarms of tourists to the island revelry. On the downtown's main street, The Strand, musicians and vendors assembled, and at the appropriate time the mayor ceremoniously launched the opening of the Dickens festival. Guests who donned Victorian costumes, it was decided, could enter with half-price tickets, but I was content in my warm street clothes, without pretending to be someone else in front of a date I knew almost nothing about. Mimi and Jack, however, took the bait and volunteered, as business leaders of the community ought to do, to dress up in the personages of Victoria and Albert and preside over the old fashioned holiday fete. I must confess, the experience diverted me from the initial awkwardness of the blind date fabrication with enough amusement that I began to relax and enjoy the festival with Dennis. We might have lacked nothing for conversation in the backdrop of the sights and sounds of the day if only we could have heard each other.

"Lizzie," he yelled over the din of the music,"would you like to stop and have lunch at that café over there?" He pointed to a restaurant across the street that had set up tables and chairs outside as well as indoors. The thought of fried foods sold by street vendors unappealing, I nodded and mouthed the word *yes* as he guided me through the crowd. Just as we reached a table at the end of the café, a couple took the seats we had eyed and we looked at each other and laughed. Dennis nodded toward the interior where it would be somewhat quieter and warmer, too, and we entered, quickly grabbing a table that had just become available. I saved our places while he ordered burgers, fries, a beer and a coke at the counter.

"So," I said when he had returned with our order, "how long have you been working for Jack?"

"Not long, a few months. I graduated in May and spent some time traveling in Europe before I took a job at Jack's real estate company. He's great to work for, but living on the island is pretty laid back. I'm not used to that. No one in the office seems to have a consistent start time. They just show up, sometimes midmorning."

"Yes, living on the island does take a bit of getting used to. Did you go to school in Texas?" I asked.

"A & M. Yes, ma'am. I'm an Aggie," he laughed. "How about you? Did you go straight into the work force?"

"No, I went to college, too. You look surprised. I actually did my four years at Martha Faraday," I said. "You've probably never heard of it. It's a small college in the middle of Louisiana. I majored in history." Dennis was silent for too long a moment, so I continued. "I grew up in Carlton, but I decided to go to school in a different city, you know, get away and experience something new. I wanted a small, quiet college where I would have time to think about my life and what I wanted to do with it." I didn't know him well enough to explain the damage that the last five years' turmoil had done to me. Nevertheless, I suddenly felt inferior to the proud Aggie sitting across from me. I wanted to get up and leave, but he quickly spoke again.

"Let me get this straight. You have a degree in history but you've been working for the last two years in a *gift shop on the beach*?" Dennis stared at me with disbelief. Something in me snapped.

"As a matter of fact I have. What's wrong with giving some thought to what you want to do with your life?" A bold and daring sensation prickled my core with his stinging words. He smiled at my retort, leaned against the back of his chair with arms folded across his chest, and said, "Nothing, nothing at all," but I discovered something important about myself at that moment. I was where I was supposed to be, meeting the people I was destined to meet, and all of this strife was going to be distilled in the end like a lovely deep red restorative wine. Cheers to me and a happy new life that I knew must be waiting around the corner for me. It had to be. But wine could wait. All I wanted now was to go home and have a cup of tea with Mary. On our way back Dennis was calmer, friendlier than before and, to my surprise, he asked me out again. He had no idea of the storm brewing in me. Unable to think of an excuse fast enough, I agreed to have dinner and see a movie with him that week. He didn't apologize for the awkward comments that day on the Strand, but I decided I didn't need an apology. His arrogance actually strengthened my belief that I was on the right path. Despite his misguided impression of me, I nevertheless came to appreciate his company—he was clever and he made me laugh. By Christmas Eve he had gone home to spend the next few days with the Chandler family in Beaumont, and I was invited to the holiday dinner at Mary's with Mimi's family. Mary's son had made plans to spend Christmas with his wife's family again that year, which she accepted with a measure of sadness. I knew how much she missed her grandchildren.

Christmas Eve morning Mimi opened the shop for a few hours, but she told me I could leave early. I knocked on Mary's door, hoping for a cup of tea and maybe even breakfast, but what I really wanted was her company. She opened the door right away and happily invited me in. The living room was dressed in fresh greenery—none of the artificial plastic, over the doors, the piano and staircase railing, and her tree glowed with colorful lights and shiny balls, the tree she and I had meticulously decorated the week before. I had come to depend on the woman who was more than a landlady, not only for the friendship she offered, but also for her sound advice, the kind Mama might have offered. Mary brought the tray in and set it in front of me as I stood before the tree lost in self-absorption.

"Oh, sorry, Mary. I should have helped."

"No, no, not at all. I can manage. Sit down, pet." Before I could pour the milk in my tea, Mary asked about Dennis. "And how are you getting on with your lad?" Then she remembered his name, "Dennis," and poured herself a cup.

Mary's keen observation made it easy to start a conversation that needed to happen. "As you know, after the festival I wasn't sure I wanted to see him, ever again, but he asked me out and was friendly enough, so I guess you could say we're still on. Anyway, he's gone home to spend Christmas with his family."

"Ah, sure. Grand. Now what about your family? I know your mother's passed, bless her, but what about your grandparents? Will you be seeing them soon? Christmas is a time for family, I always say."

"I haven't seen them since my mother's funeral. It's okay. We weren't close," I said. "Besides, Mary, you're like my family. Doesn't that count?"

"Indeed. You're like a granddaughter to me. About Dennis—you're happy with him?"

Now we were getting closer to the tentative regard I had for Dennis, more like the disregard I felt and didn't want to discuss, yet I knew whatever I said to justify Mary's curiosity and, yes, even her concern for my well being, I'd be justifying it to myself as well. "The thing is, Mary, I do like him, I think—he's interesting and funny, but you know that spark you had the moment you saw Carl? I still haven't felt it."

"Is that so? Well, to be sure, it's one thing to enjoy a man's company and a completely different one to feel the quickened pulse," she said, "but I think there might be another reason you feel somewhat detached."

"Detached? Do I seem detached? What other reason? Do you know something I don't?"

"Would you be carrying a torch for someone else? I'll say no more, but it's something to think about, eh?" Mary abruptly ended talk about men and torches, but I wasn't going to let it drop.

"No, definitely no torches for anyone. And that's all there is to it. It's Christmas Eve, Mary. Play something—a carol—and sing. Please. You have such a beautiful voice. Let's sing Christmas carols." Her tunes always put me in a good mood. I loved Mary's life-giving music that had once brought hope to so many. No coaxing necessary, Mary moved to the piano, pulled out the bench and began to play strains of familiar carols.

"What would you like to hear?" she asked as her fingers were already gliding over the keys.

"White Christmas." Mary quickly shifted to the key of C and began to sing. I joined her, and when we came to the end, I put my arms around her and felt her moist cheeks. No need to ask why. I had no idea what it was like to have lived through such a war, having arrived on the scene after it was long over. For me the trauma would come years later when another war would divide a nation and exact its toll, closer to home than I expected. No battle had been fought on American soil, but I understood on the deepest level how it felt to lose people you loved. "Was that a war song?" I asked.

"Aye, it was, pet. It came out only a few weeks after the bombing of Pearl Harbor. It was the most popular song with the troops in Europe, and every time we played "White Christmas," it made people sad. But we played it anyway," she sighed. "It's what they all wanted to hear." Mary put her hands back on the piano keys for a livelier carol, displacing the gray mood that might threaten our holiday spirit.

Mary and I walked down the street to St. Cuthbert's for the Christmas Eve service. She said she hadn't been to church in a while, although for

Mary that could mean only a week or two, and she insisted on going. Singing carols had dredged up ethereal memories of the past, nostalgia so holy and pure that it could only be truly consummated inside a church. We found seats in the back, and even though the service lasted a little over an hour, we took our time walking home in the soft contented solitude of the clear, cool night, stars blinking overhead. Mary was tired and said she had an early day with Christmas dinner preparations—could I help her in the morning? Of course I would.

"Grand." Then she put her arm around me. "It's a wee bit early, but Happy Christmas, dearest Lizzie. Happy Christmas to you."

As temperatures drop, much activity is going on under the soil in preparation for winter dormancy. Perennials go into hibernation and may need mulching to protect them from winter's chill.

The Art of Gardening by Emily Mayfield

CHAPTER 7

1966 | "Pay attention, everyone," Henry called as the staff turned their attention to him. "Lizzie's collected two entries from each English teacher. That makes sixteen. Billy, Robert, and Sue—you're judging. Plan on staying this afternoon till we finish the top three prizes." Had I heard him correctly? Although I had little hope of being on the committee, judging this contest was an opportunity I had allowed myself to entertain. The three seniors rolled their eyes, groaning and shifting their weight uncomfortably when I raised my hand.

"Uh, Henry?" My voice was barely above a whisper. "If you need any help, I could judge." Poor Henry. He was speechless as he stared at me, wondering what he could possibly say to dismiss the quiet freshman with no experience but an unabashedly mellow kind of gumption.

"Thanks, Lizzie. Why don't you, uh, just stick around after the meeting, and, uh, we'll see what we have for you to do." Excited, I wondered if the silly grin inside was radiating from my face. The seniors turned and stared in disbelief.

"Henry, what are you doing? She's a—"

"Freshman. I know. But it'll be less work for you, my man." Henry seemed to be thinking on the spot and Billy groaned. I was in. With a sense of guarded jubilation, I found a seat where I would begin reading the essays in the folder Henry had given me. It was getting dark when, after three hours of reading, I packed up my books to leave.

A short walk from school and I was home, but a car I didn't recognize, parked in front of our house, caused me to pass our walkway and retrace my steps. When I opened the front door, Mama was sitting in the living room, not in her rocker but on the couch, and only inches away from her face was a man I didn't recognize. For an instant the incongruity displaced the familiarity of my home and I froze.

"Lizzie, come here, sweetie. I want you to meet an old friend of mine from New Orleans." I walked forward and leaned into the wingback near the door, cautiously hiding the lower half of my body. "Joseph, this is my daughter Elizabeth—Lizzie. Honey, this is Mr. Anson."

"How do you do, Elizabeth. You're in high school now, aren't you? I knew your mama and daddy when you were just a little girl—four or five years old?" He looked at Mama for assurance. "My, my, you're all grown up now." I smiled but suspicion immobilized me and he must have sensed my discomfort. "Well, Louise, I'd better be going. It was so good to see you again." He put his head closer to hers and whispered something I couldn't hear.

"So good to see you, too, Joseph." She smiled softly and stood up. "See you later." Joseph Anson got up to go but not before giving my mother a wink as he took her hand and held it a second too long. She walked him out to his car and when she returned, I followed her into the kitchen.

"Who was that?"

"Oh, just a friend from the old days. What did you think of him?"

"What does it matter? I don't even know who he is or why he was here." Even I heard the weary antagonism in my voice.

"Lizzie, is everything okay?"

"I guess," I said, the edginess growing as I grabbed the milk from the fridge.

"Well, let's not get carried away here. I knew Joseph many years ago and I liked him. He looked me up and asked if he could see me again. That's all."

"Okay," I responded, not feeling confrontational any more. I didn't have one ounce of energy left after spending the whole afternoon reading essays for the newspaper. I sprawled out on my bed and slept until supper. When I went in, Joseph Anson had returned and was sitting at the dining room table where Mama was serving him. That table was for special occasions. Why was he sitting there?

"Have a good nap, hon? I fried oysters tonight." She had obviously ignored the fact that I hated oysters, fried or otherwise. The chewy, gritty sensation in my mouth made me develop a strategy: take two bites and swallow before my nose or taste buds had time to react, and if that didn't work, spit them out in a napkin as covertly as possible. Right now Mama seemed happy, not just content with her situation, but actually happy, so I remained sanguine, answering politely when necessary.

"Don't put too many on my plate, Mama. Please." I had an extra napkin ready for the few she was about to dish up.

"So, Elizabeth. What do you do at your high school? This is your first year, right? You're a freshman?" What did he think kids did at school?

"Well, right now I'm on the newspaper staff."

"Ah, you're a writer."

"Not exactly. I do whatever the editor needs me to do, but I'm waiting for an assignment. Freshmen usually don't get bylines until the following year."

"Patience—that's all you need. You're just a freshman—and a girl. Don't take that the wrong way. It's just that, well, leadership roles usually go to young men. You're lucky to be a part of the staff, but if things don't happen in a few weeks, well, I bet your mother could make a call to the right person," Mr. Anson winked. I could see the discomfort on Mama's face. And then I forgot myself.

"We don't do it like that. Mama says you earn things in life based on your own merit and hard work. Even if you're a girl," I added. "Besides, I'm waiting to be assigned an article any day now."

Joseph Anson looked at my mother sharply, with a smile still on his face, which was a good thing for me since I had come close to being rude to Mama's guest. "Well, Louise. I guess she's a chip off the old block." Mama didn't say anything. She ate her fried oysters, but her sad, soulful eyes spoke of an understanding between us, and right then and there I made a silent promise to her to keep my mouth shut.

Mr. Anson would be a frequent guest at our table for the next two months, although I never understood how two people so different could be attracted to each other. But then, what did I know about men?

The last day of school before the Christmas holidays, the school choir had a carol sing-along after which the drama department presented a one-act holiday play. My heart raced. I discovered yet another untapped source of talent I might possibly draw upon and I was thrilled. Could I act? How hard could it be, this pretending to be someone else? It was what I did every day. Henry still hadn't given me an article, although, by a quiet, somewhat surreptitious request from him, I had taken the editing pen to the worst of the sophomore assignments. I had learned, if nothing else, the politics of upper classmen. Freshmen knew nothing, sophomores knew slightly more, juniors, who were almost human, were waiting on deck, and seniors ruled. The truth was irrelevant to Henry who needed my help, so I played along. I mean, what else did I have to do? With Judy gone, I had to fill my afternoons with something and it might as well be, as Mama had suggested more than once, something that would later look good on a college application.

My grandparents, Cecile and James Barker, lived in Mobile and we rarely saw them. Mama said it was because Granddad had a store and couldn't leave it. My grandmother did his accounting and never left his side, so when they called to tell us they were coming for Christmas, we scurried around in shock for two days getting the house ready for their unexpected visit. Mama hid her nervousness under the surface with a whirlwind cleaning spree, but she didn't fool me. I began to understand it the minute they came through the door and by the middle of Christmas Day, I, too, was ready for them to return to Mobile.

"Louise," my grandmother bellowed, "go help your father get everything unloaded from the car." I stood behind Mama listening to her own mother shouting orders to her as if she were a child.

"Merry Christmas, Grandmother," I said in my sweetest voice.

"It's not Christmas yet, dear. We have two more days. Elizabeth, get me a glass of tea, will you. I'm going to sit right here in this chair and rest my weary bones." I did as I was told and brought her a glass of Mama's mint and lemon tea. "Thank you, dear. Now be a good girl and go help your mother." I was dismissed. Where was my hug, the warm, welcoming words from loving grandparents—*I'm so glad to see you…. Has it really been two years….Look how big you've grown….Come tell me all about your new school.* I was starting to wonder why they had made the eleven hour drive and how Mama and I were going to survive what felt like a five-day confinement in the ice palace, almost a week of bitter chill filling the house with subtle traces of bullying.

Early on Christmas Eve morning before everyone had opened their eyes, I heard a soft knock at the front door. I listened again. No one had moved to answer it, so I crept into the living room and pulled the curtains back to look out the window. There was Judy standing on the front porch, with her hands in her coat pockets. I unlocked the front door and opened the screen. "Judy! Hi," I whispered, pulling her inside. "Come in but be quiet. My grandparents are here and they're still sleeping. What are you doing here?" We quickly moved into the kitchen and I shut the door. I spoke softly to avoid waking my mother and grandparents. "Did you walk over here in the cold? Why didn't you call me? Why didn't you tell me you were leaving?" I realized Judy had one volume—loud, and I motioned for her to follow me out the back door, across the deck to the swings in the middle of the yard, far enough from the back bedroom where my grandparents were still sleeping. Gray skies and a web of leafless branches overhead, we stood in the chilly but quiet solitude of the garden.

"Sorry. It's a long story. I'm back just for Christmas. At least that's what my mother is saying. But my daddy has been really nice to me. I think he feels bad about what happened."

"What did he do? I didn't know anything, except you were here one day and gone the next. Without even telling me, by the way."

"It happened so fast. Daddy lost his job and when I got home from school, he and Mother were arguing. I walked in on their fight, and I don't know—he thought I was looking at him funny. So he took off his belt again. This time my mother stood in front of me and screamed so loud I thought the neighbors would hear. Next morning she was on the phone with my aunt making arrangements for me to live with her. And that's what happened. Aunt Alice actually came and got me the next day."

"Oh, my gosh. I'm so sorry, Judy. Does your dad ever—"

"Ever what?"

"Does he ever hit....anybody else in your family?" Judy paused, deciding how to answer me.

"Most of the time I don't know what goes on between my parents. I just stay in my room. Anyway, enough about that. How's Jimmy?" she asked.

"I don't know. He's all right, I guess."

"You haven't seen him?"

"Sure, I see him, sometimes, walking to school, but you know Jimmy. He doesn't say much. Did you write to him? Did he write back?"

"I got one or two letters, at first. I kept writing to him but after a while.... nothing. I was hoping to see him over the holidays and see if everything's okay. You wouldn't want to go over there with me, would you?"

I never figured it out, but I couldn't tell Judy no. So there we were cutting across the Bertrands' yard once again to get to Jimmy. It was early morning and Christmas Eve at that, so he was bound to be home. I thought Judy was going to fall apart she was so nervous. When he came to the door, I could see his mouth full of teeth grinning through the screen, juxtaposed with Judy's sudden tears, her mouth scrunched up and quivering. I didn't hang around to watch the reunion, but I was glad I had gone with her. As much as Judy's behavior sometimes annoyed the bejeebers out of me, she had so much more to deal with than a girl ought to have. Even a splinter's width of happiness would have suited her, but she deserved more. We all did. I turned around and walked backwards for a couple of steps. Jimmy's long arms wrapped around her in a protective circle as he drew Judy to him, her pent up fears and disappointments melting into his shoulder. I walked back home alone, without feeling deserted for a change.

Mr. Anson joined our family gathering Christmas Eve night. Mama's table gleamed under the bounteous spread of cold cuts, cheese, baguettes, potato salad and seafood. Grandmother lifted her glass of wine followed by the clinking of crystal that seemed to go on and on. I watched from the kitchen, sipping a cherry coke and wishing it was just Mama and I again, happily alone like all our other Christmases. The evening was uneventful until Mr. Anson began teasing my mother about mistletoe, his personal contribution to the party. I decided to say goodnight early, not that anyone particularly minded, and after closing my bedroom door, I heard my grandparents turning in also. That left Mama and her gentleman alone in the living room. With mistletoe. I decided I needed a drink of water. Whether I tiptoed quietly or barreled down the hard wooden hallway floor, it wouldn't have mattered. Before I made it to the kitchen, there at the door were Mama and Mr. Anson, locked in a passionate embrace, the mistletoe tossed carelessly at their feet. They never saw me standing at the door watching them.

Observation of the garden in each growing season can offer beneficial knowledge as you commit to planting. Winter gardens look different from summer gardens in that they appear more exposed and reveal more than you intended.

The Art of Gardening by Emily Mayfield

CHAPTER 8

1967 | "Let's light a fire, Lizzie. The temperature's starting to dip again." Mama arranged the logs and lit bits of cardboard before I could think of something else I had to do. It turned out to be a good idea, one of the few times I could remember agreeing with her about the fireplace. She wanted to pull up a comfy chair from the other side of the living room for me, but I said I'd sit on the raised brick hearth where it was warmer. We ate our supper there, just the two of us, on trays from the kitchen.

"I think I'm going to join the drama club," I said between bites. "Judy is, too."

"Really? I didn't know Judy was back for good."

"She came back for Christmas and just stayed. Anyway, remember that Christmas play the drama club put on right before the holidays? I think I could do that—act I mean. It might be fun. Besides, I'm not exactly moving up the ranks in the newspaper."

"Well, you could always try it, Liz, but you are a freshman. Tradition is a hard habit to break. Better find out if you can join them without taking the class. Have you spoken to the counselor yet?"

"No, I wasn't sure about it then, but now I am."

"By the way, hon, you did a good job choosing the winners for the creative writing contest. I saw they came out in the newspaper last Friday."

"Maybe it's a good time to make my exit then. While they can remember a freshman did something right."

Mama thought that was funny and gave a little chuckle. "Could be. No one can say you didn't give it your all. And don't let anyone convince you that I had anything to do with it. I didn't. So which one of the pieces did you like best?"

I know Mama was hoping I'd say Reggie's essay on Keats, but I dreaded telling her the truth about the judging. Henry had originally announced first, second and third prizes would be awarded, but when Reggie's paper won first in the blind judging, he retracted it. All the judges knew Reggie's was the best, hands down, but he was, after all, a Negro, Henry had said regretfully, and it just wouldn't look right, a colored boy showing up all the white kids. And then he added it was for Reggie's protection, too. Anyway, Henry went on that people were bound to ask, wasn't it enough that he was allowed to go to our school? I didn't agree with all this business about what people would say, but I was a nobody, a freshman nobody. In the end Henry gave the top three equal billing and put Reggie's name last. Although Reginald Washington wouldn't be the star, anyone who had read his paper had to agree he had an enormous gift for writing.

"Reggie's essay was good," I said. "I especially liked the part where he quoted lines from Keats."

"Yes, I remember that part. It's why I selected his paper for the contest. 'Heard melodies are sweet, but those unheard are sweeter: therefore, ye soft pipes, play on.'"

"'Ode on a Grecian Urn,' right?" I hoped that wasn't the only reason she chose Reggie's essay.

Mama had put her tray down on the hearth and was staring into the flames, her hands wrapped around a warm mug of coffee. "Yes, that's right. I think maybe Keats could have been writing about all of us." A sadness seemed to come over her, but then she turned and gently brushed my hair back with her hand and said, "What melodies yet to be heard are stirring inside you, sweet Lizzie?"

"I have no idea, Mama, no idea at all." A good time to retreat, I picked up our trays and took them to the kitchen. I could barely stand to think about what I was doing with my life the next day or the next. "Think I'll go to my room and read for a while." Much like a cloister, my bedroom—two bookshelves, a chest of drawers, and a bed, was fit for a nun. Stark and devoid of mirrors or bulletin boards cluttered with the usual keepsakes of a teenage girl, it was my choice. It served as a refuge of privacy whose walls protected the unhappy if not cryptic truths known only to me.

The icy rain of January weather was so harsh I stayed after school just to get a ride home with my mother who was working in her room late that day to grade papers. I had been in a hurry that morning, giving no thought to the weather, and with my thin coat and no scarf or gloves, walking home was out of the question. I was working problems for algebra when she stopped what she was doing at her desk and stared at me over her reading glasses.

"Lizzie, I thought you were going to ask if you could work on the play." Had the thought just popped into her head as she was reading essays on *Hamlet*?

"I was."

"Well?"

"I just haven't done it yet," I said, still working on math. The idea of standing on a stage and speaking lines in front of hundreds of people suddenly made me ill. What was I thinking?

"Hon, I believe I heard Mr. Gordon in the teacher's lounge going on about a play rehearsal today. Forget the counselor. Why don't you walk over to the auditorium and see if they need help. Offer to do props or costumes, set, anything." And then as if she had read my mind, she said, "You don't have to act. Auditions are over and all the parts have already been cast. They're doing *Take Her; She's Mine*, a comedy I think. Could be fun." And then she looked down and continued grading papers. Mama believed if you wanted something or deserved something, and even if you might not deserve it, it didn't hurt to ask for it. Ask and you shall receive—it was her mantra of hope, a desire that always superseded her eventual acceptance of what was to be. I reluctantly closed my book, gathered up my belongings, and shuffled out the door and down the stairs to the auditorium. The heavy double doors swooshed open without a creak. It was dark inside except for the stage flooded with light, and I slipped into a seat at the back, gathering up my nerve and adjusting my eyes to the dark. After a few minutes of jittery, self-conscious tension, I felt my way down to the director, sat in the seat behind him and tapped him on the shoulder.

"Mr. Gordon, sir, I'm Lizzie Rowan and I was wondering—"

"Talk to me at the break," was all he said and before I could settle myself in the seat, I jumped up again and maneuvered the incline back to find another seat close by. It was only a few minutes before the house lights came on, but Mr. Gordon began spewing comments to the actors who emerged from the wings. This time I lurched into the aisle again, ready to approach him before the next act. I watched for any verbal cues that he was winding down, rushed in for the chance, a light tap on his shoulder and blurted out my request.

"Mr. Gordon, I'd like to work on props if you have an opening." Without looking at me, he spit out two words.

"Okay. See Reggie."

"Back stage, sir?" But it was too late. Act two had begun and I had to manage with the bounty of the director's brief approval guiding me with two words: *See Reggie*. The Reggie whose reputation preceded him, the Reggie who loved Keats and could write, the Reggie my mother the teacher adored. No matter how many new questions I might have, I was going to wait and find out, once I discovered how to get backstage. Worse, the house was bathed in shadowy darkness and I blindly felt my way down to the right exit along the velvety seat backs, into the hallway where crew members were standing around chatting. I spotted the friendliest face and spoke softly. "I'm looking for Reggie. I'm supposed to do props with him, I think." Four boys turned and stared at me without speaking. A tall blonde boy whose face was covered in acne pointed toward the stage door, and without another word I went inside. It was so dark I couldn't move, terrified I would bump into a table full of props that would go crashing to the floor and end my drama career. Then, out of nowhere, two eyes were looking into mine. "Are you Reggie?" I whispered.

"Yes?"

"I'm Lizzie. Mr. Gordon said to see you about working on props."

"Okay. Just watch me for now." I wanted to laugh but I dared not. If he turned away from me, he might disappear altogether. When my eyes had adjusted to the darkness, I could recognize his silhouette against the lighted stage. Although his black shirt and trousers seemed to meld into the depth of his dark skin and hair, his lean muscled body would be his trademark in the way one might recognize the configuration of a familiar word. When my eyes had adjusted to the dark, I could see well enough to observe exactly what he was doing, and I became his sidekick, mimicking every move. When the second act was over, Reggie talked so fast I caught only the tail end of his commands, which sounded like *pitcher and glass on the table....down right....move tray of letters* or did he say *remove* tray of letters? So I did everything I thought I heard. When the curtain went up, the actors stopped, confused, and Mr. Gordon began yelling for Reggie. House lights came on and Reggie stepped onto the apron.

"Reggie, what's the problem back there? Props aren't where they're supposed to be. The pitcher and glass need to be on the tray near the sofa, the letters on down right table. Can you take care of that, please," he sighed but Reggie was already on it.

"Yes, Mr. Gordon. Sorry about that, sir. I'll fix that right now," he answered, not once blaming the freshman girl who had actually made the mistake. The lights went down, the actors resumed their places, and Reggie was silent. I inched my way toward him, his back to me as he watched from the wing, and whispered, "I'm so sorry, Reggie. I was confused and I didn't hear everything you—"

"Forget it. It's okay," he whispered and we didn't speak of it again. Looking back now, I think it was then that I first thought how much I could love a boy who would sacrifice something for me. A small sacrifice perhaps, but still, he had spared me from embarrassment and I would never forget it. I stayed on props until the end of the show, following Reggie's lead and working hard to remember the correct placement. He was patient and never treated me as if I were beneath him. He must have known how that felt, determined to avoid the retaliation that undoubtedly could have been a constant worry. His keen sense of right and wrong prevented anything but kindness and responsibility to surface in the quagmire of struggling adolescent personalities, added to the current of the school's forced racial integration. By May, however, Reggie had been named outstanding crew member by the drama club, one more laurel added to his cluster of accomplishments. He was to graduate with honors and a resume that earned him enough scholarships in the fall to ensure a full ride to LSU. Reggie later confided to me in a rare moment of one-on-one that he intended to finish college and go to law school.

Toward the end I could get through the show moving items on and off effortlessly with Reggie. On the closing night of the play, he began tinkering so restlessly with props, even readjusting the ones I had set out, that he put me on edge. Had I disappointed him? Once I caught him staring at me.

"What?" I asked. "Did I do something wrong?"

"No. It's nothing. Just be ready to go. The last scene is quick."

"I'll be ready," I protested, irked that he was in a bad mood. He didn't respond. He just stood there looking away, lost in what was actually bothering him. When the play was over, the cast headed for the hallway where family and friends waited to heap adulation on them. Mr. Gordon met the crew backstage and told us we could wait and strike the set on Monday, that he'd see us at the cast party. I hadn't considered going until that moment, mainly because I hadn't heard anyone talk about it, Reggie being the only one who ever really spoke to me, and any exchanges we had were usually about props. I picked up my purse, followed him out the door, and found the courage to speak.

"Reggie, wait up. Are you going to the party?"

He just kept walking toward the exit. "No," he said without hesitating, and then he stopped and looked right at me. "Why? Are you?"

I began to feel uncomfortable with the conversation we were almost having. "I didn't know there was a party until a few minutes ago. Where is it?"

"It's here in the cafeteria. I saw the parents and some of the teachers setting everything up before the play tonight," he said.

"Oh, well, if it's here, why aren't you going?" He just shrugged his shoulders and continued walking. The cafeteria was at the other end of the hall. If you turned left, the big double doors led you to the front of the school, but a few feet on the right was the cafeteria. Reggie and I went left out the front.

"Hey. Boy." Jimmy's brother Randy was standing on the steps with two of his friends, blocking our way down. "You part of this fruitcake brigade? Long walk to your side of town. Lemme give you a ride home, after all that hard work," he smirked. I might have ignored his remarks if it had been anyone other than Randy, but he was my longtime neighbor and childhood images of him suddenly surfaced.

It was back in first grade when I began walking home each day with Randy's brother Jimmy, who was only a month older. I stayed at his house until my mother got home from the high school. When we needed to cross a street, Jimmy, a head taller than I was, had a habit of putting his hand on my head, fingers splayed across my scalp as if guiding me to safety. It felt steady and secure, and I loved going to his house. Their back room was air-conditioned, a luxury we didn't have. Randy often followed us home for the specific purpose of outmaneuvering his brother. He was three years older than Jimmy and as mean as he was willful. His favorite method of torture was to give his brother a frog when he least expected it, a painful bruise delivered with the third knuckle of his hand curled up for a quick jab to the arm. Jimmy dreaded walking home with him and we did everything we could to avoid it. I wasn't afraid of him, though, and threatened to tell his mother if he didn't stop, but he just laughed and found an even more fiendish way to annoy us.

Insects of all shapes and methods of mobility were never safe around Randy. Catch, torture, and destroy, all in view of an audience, of course—that was his modus operandi. One day, after pulling the wings off a mosquito hawk, I grabbed Jimmy's hand and ran, yelling, "I'm telling on you, Randy Bertrand! I'm telling your mama what you did!" And I did, too, for the little good it did. Jimmy and I marched right in to his house and told his mother the cruel and terrible thing his brother had done. Mrs. Bertrand closed her eyes and started to call him but the words were trapped inside her. She closed her eyes, put her hands to her face in irrevocable submission, and mumbled to no one in particular, "I don't know what I'm going to do with that boy. I really don't." Randy was only nine years old.

The next year when Jimmy and I matriculated to second grade, Randy had a reprieve and was allowed to pass on to the fifth. He still followed us, but when we tried to beat him home, he always caught up with us. October was warmer than usual that year as we watched the leaves turn. It felt like summer as we walked home in our short sleeves complaining of the heat but cautiously relieved that Randy was nowhere in sight. Jimmy and I were almost home, coming up to the corner of our street, when a small white curly haired dog ran across and began following us.

"Look, Jimmy!" The pooch began licking my hand and wagging a stubby little tail. "He doesn't have a collar, but he must belong to somebody. He's so cute and friendly," I said. Before Jimmy could answer, we heard a *Hey!* behind us. We turned around and there was Randy gaining on us at a fast pace. I was surprised to see him. Jimmy said he'd been made to stay behind to wash the teacher's board. It wasn't the first time he had received a punishment for hitting a classmate, but there he was after all. Randy had seen us pet the dog. He swooped on it, grabbing it with one hand under its belly and began whooping and clutching the animal under his arm.

"Play ball!" He didn't wait for Jimmy to respond, just threw the little white dog at his brother like a football, slamming it against his chest. Randy fell backwards and the dog flipped over and scrambled away yelping. "You were supposed to catch it, stupid!" Randy ran over to Jimmy, still on the ground, put his head in a chokehold and began rubbing the top of his brother's head vigorously with his knuckles. "And for being a stupid little brother, you get a Chinese haircut."

"Ow! That hurts! Stop or I'll tell!"

"Go ahead, you little weenie. See if I care." He released him and ran home ahead of us, but Randy, we discovered years later, had found a hiding place in the attic in the back of the Bertrands' garage, his safe house when he was forever in trouble. Grateful for a few minutes of peace, we decided to let him stay hidden, wherever he was. Jimmy had been amassing a hoard of comic books by then, and we spent the next hour in silence looking at them. Later that night I told Mama about the little white collarless dog and asked if we could keep him. She said she'd think about it, which really meant she'd give the pooch time to find his way home or time for me to forget about it so she wouldn't have to say no. We never saw that little dog again. I secretly hoped he'd found his owner, but I still worried about him. As the years passed we sometimes heard rumors about the cruelty Randy inflicted on neighborhood cats and dogs, not just insects, but I never actually saw him hurt anyone until late one night many years later. As time went on, I was glad we didn't have any pets.

Flashes of Randy's past indiscretions quickly dissipated when I spied a parent walking toward the steps and balancing a large tray of sandwiches covered tightly in Saran Wrap. "There's a cast party, Randy. We're helping with food." Neither of us looked back as I sidestepped Randy and his entourage. Reggie followed me. "Here," I said to Sally Wright's mother. "Let us take that to the cafeteria for you." Reggie obligingly scooped up the tray, and the speechless parent and I trotted along beside him. Whether he was too stunned or too proud, Reggie never mentioned the incident. He didn't have to. He knew exactly what Randy was up to. The consequence of treachery was not an experience I knew much about, but something deep in my unconscious recognized Randy's rage against everything Reggie stood for. I couldn't allow it, even though I had no idea why it was happening now or how I could prevent it from happening again. We made an appearance at the cast party, and, although Reggie didn't say much, he stayed by my side the entire night. At ten o'clock we said goodnight, and Mr. Gordon offered Reggie a ride home before he could make his long trek alone to the north side of town.

Morning glory seeds have hard shells that need softening. Prick them gently and soak them in water overnight so that they are more easily able to push their way through the soil. Once they do, their heart-shaped leaves will seek the scaffolding of a trellis facing the morning sun.

The Art of Gardening by Emily Mayfield

CHAPTER 9

1976 | January was a dreary month in Galveston, a between-time period. Christmas celebrations over and Easter break months away, the momentum at Mimi's languished to a lethargic pace, which gave me an unsafe amount of time to think about the somewhat vacuous career situation in which I'd found myself floundering. In short I was bored. Mary's tea breaks occupied enough of my time, however, and these simple digressions—engaging in conversation over a cup of tea, whiling away the hours in Mary's garden on milder days, or relaxing to her beloved old wartime tunes, preserved my sanity. Her warmth and her undeniable acceptance magnetized me in a way that encouraged a healthy amount of loitering, easily dissuading me from moving too fast. Her gift to me was also time to sort out my life. Dennis returned from Christmas and we were still hanging on as a couple, aptly defined by the insipid coordinating of activities that would provide membership in that societal boy-girl world. Although neither of us spoke of it, there was a nonverbal agreement between us that we would accommodate each other until the need for it eventually wore off. Late one night toward the end of March with Easter around the corner, it did. Dennis had decided on our previous date to the movies that he was in the mood for burgers, the kind he would prepare on the patio of his apartment, and so the next week he bought a small grill and invited me to dinner at his place. The arrival of a mild spring in Galveston afforded an evening outdoors, and we sat on his patio and ate our burgers until the evening chill sent us indoors in front of the television, a convenient escape from engaging in forced repartee. When the movie ended and I stood up to go, Dennis tugged on my jacket so hard that I lost my balance and indelicately tumbled onto his lap. We both laughed at first, but then he pulled me closer to him and began fumbling with the buttons of my blouse, all the while nuzzling my neck. In another time and place, I might have surrendered to a lover's arms, but this sudden surge of awkward romance appeared out of nowhere and I suddenly felt the ridiculousness of the moment. I wasn't crass enough to hurt his feelings, but I gently put my hand on his and pulled it away. As I tried to get up, I heard Reggie's voice playing in my head, like the distant, metallic voice on a tape recorder. *Your mother needs you. She sent me to tell you to come inside*—a phantom mother transcending flesh and speaking through her medium, rescuing me from boys with nefarious schemes. From a distance, wherever he was, Reggie continued to create a harmonious interface, coordinating my every thought.

"I'm sorry, Dennis, I like you. And I've enjoyed your company, the time we've been together. You've been a good friend. But......I'm afraid that's all we're ever going to be. I'm sorry if you thought there would be more, but I...I just don't feel that way. I do like you but...." Dennis rose from the couch, grabbed his keys and walked to the door, opened it, and waited for me to walk out. I was grateful to ride in silence to Mary's—what else could be said, and that was the last time I saw him. I barely slept that night, turning over and over the image of a boy unbuttoning my blouse. Only one other time had it happened. I was a naive sixteen year old, standing in my back yard wondering where Hollywood got the notion that undressing a girl was seductive. It would be some time before I changed my mind.

Early cool spring weather also brought in sickness. The next day I could hardly pull myself out of bed, suffering from an inflamed sore throat and a gut wrenching cough. When I missed my morning coffee with Mary, she knocked on my door. I finally was able to get up and over to the door. Mary took one look and said, "Oh, Lord Jesus, put your coat on, pet. I'm taking you to the doctor." Finding a doctor when I arrived on the island hadn't seemed necessary or even important at the time, so I had no idea what doctor she had in mind. As it turned out, Dr. Bonin had been Mimi's GP for years, and that's where we went, an office only a few blocks away. One antibiotic later and I was covered in blankets in my own bed downstairs with Mary bringing trays of tea and toast and soup every few hours.

Easter break arrived several weeks later, and Mary, who had been pouring over garden catalogues and was now determined to plant zinnias, salvias, and cosmos in the back garden, asked me to drive her to Houston to look for seeds. I knew we could find them in Galveston, but after the debacle with Dennis and bronchitis, I didn't mind the change of scenery, especially with Mary as a companion, so off we went. I found a garden center close to the freeway in the Heights area of Houston nestled among a myriad of similar ads in the Yellow Pages. It was easy to find and sunny weather provided a lovely drive. Mary seemed lost among the extensive rows of colorful flowers and sizeable display of greenery inside and even outside the entrance, so I left her to look and went inside to find packets of seeds. As I turned the corner past a rack of shovels and rakes, I saw, through an opening that led out to a covered pavilion for plants sensitive to light, a tall black man unloading plants from a dolly. *Reggie?* I ran through the opening and called out his name. He didn't turn around. Perhaps he hadn't heard me. I called again, louder, as I moved closer to look at his face.

"Is there something I can help you with, ma'am?" He was much older than I had thought, graying at the temples, glasses, wide jaw, and slightly stooped. My transparent disappointment took precedence over embarrassment.

"Oh," I said, startled at my mistake. "No. No, thanks. I'm looking for…. seed packets." *Seed packets?* The mind has a bizarre way of producing nonsense when alarmed unawares.

"Yes, ma'am. Those would be inside near the front."

"Thanks," I said, disheartened but also annoyed at my moronic response. I wanted out of there as quickly as possible. I whirled around to find Mary and look for the seeds, but there she was right behind me, watching.

"Not Reggie, eh? I'm sorry it wasn't your friend, pet."

"My friend?"

"Your friend, Reggie. You thought that man was your friend?"

"It's okay, Mary. I made a mistake. I haven't seen him in a while and it looked like him from here. It doesn't matter. I just thought I might like to say hello."

"Is that right?" Her sing-song response was telling.

"Yes, Mary. That's all there is to it. Let's get the seeds and go." I tried to recover from my blunder, but as usual, Mary's perceptive observation detected what I had been trying to hide. Reggie dominated my thoughts. His presence—the memory of his kindness and loyalty to me even in his absence, was firmly planted in my brain, and I couldn't stop thinking about him. As much as I wanted to be like him, I was a coward. I was trapped, without clear direction. Reggie was gone from my life, yet the thought of him was driving me mad.

By the end of the week, Good Friday being a holiday and the weather exceptionally warm for April, Easter weekend had inveigled hordes of tourists, largely students with beach blankets and beer, onto the sandy Gulf shore. This meant the shop was in constant motion. Mimi's jangling door drew in more lookers than buyers, but somehow she managed to sell more than enough that weekend, surpassing what she had sold in the previous three months. By Saturday night I was exhausted. My plan was to sleep in Easter morning and then join the Schwarz family for dinner at Mary's house. I woke up early, however, crawled out of bed and made my way up the stairs to coax a cup of coffee from Mary. When she answered the door, she was wearing a hat and Sunday clothes.

"Going somewhere?" I said. "I was really looking forward to a coffee."

"It's still early. Come in and I'll pour you a cup, and then you can go with me to mass. It's Easter Sunday, love." She took off her hat and headed for the kitchen.

"Yes, but, I don't know, Mary. I don't really have anything suitable to wear."

"Wear what you have on now, pet. Just put on a jacket and you'll be right as rain. I have a scarf you can tie on your head." Mary didn't take *no* well.

"But it's Easter, Mary. Everyone will be dressed up."

"Steady on, girl. Better to go than to worry about your clothes. Anyway, this is Galveston and no one cares what you wear." Clearly Mary was not going to back down, and by now I knew she was right about the island dress code.

"Okay, be right back. I need coffee though."

"Ah, sure. Grand. I'll pour you a nice cup."

I'm not a Catholic and going to church on Easter, now that Mama was gone, stopped being a priority. Yet, watching an Irish Catholic going through the motions that were sacred to her—the liturgy and flowers and incense and music, was the highlight of the day, and I was thankful to have joined her. We went straight to Mary's afterward and I helped her with dinner. I was setting the table when Mimi and Janie walked in, followed by Jack scowling in his obvious reluctance to join them.

"Hi, everyone. Happy Easter," I said. No one responded. Jack sat down and picked up the newspaper without a word.

"Hey, Lizzie. Need some help?" Mimi's eyes told me she had been crying, but I didn't ask.

"Sure. I'll ask Mary about napkins and see if she needs help in the kitchen." Mary handed me a dish of boiled potatoes as I walked through the door. "Mary, is everything okay with Mimi and Jack?" I whispered. "I think Mimi has been crying and Jack's giving everyone the silent treatment."

Mary closed her eyes, then looked up and whispered to herself, "Give me strength." When she looked at me again, she said, "It'll pass. Mimi wants him to buy her another shop but Jack won't consider it. Says Galveston has too many as it is. They'll be grand. Don't you worry. Let's eat." And as Mary would say, there was an end to it. Easter dinner was wonderful, although I passed up Mary's roast lamb. Every time I thought of the name *Mary* coupled with lamb, I felt sick. One should not be sad about food, so I devoured the vegetables and saved room for Mimi's chocolate cake, despite the frosty air at the table between Jack and his wife. Bubbly Janie was uncharacteristically quiet. Finally Mimi couldn't hold it back any longer.

"This weekend has been exhausting with so many customers in the shop, and now that summer is on its way, things are going to get even more hectic. Galveston could really use more gift shops near the beach, and the Hendersons want to sell their place just across the street. *Someone* isn't being very cooperative and I really don't understand why," she fretted. Jack continued eating without looking up, but I could see his jaw clinching. "Mom and Lizzie, don't you think it's a good idea?" Mary put her fork down with a force that came from a place I didn't recognize.

"Jesus, Mary, and Joseph, Mimi! It's Easter Sunday. Can we please have a little peace in this house!" Mary rarely raised her voice but when she invoked the holy family, the whole table fell into a silence. Finally Jack spoke up.

"Honey, Galveston may be in need of a hundred more shops, but we're already stretched too thin as it is. We'll discuss this later, okay?" Despite Mary's pronouncement, Mimi was about to open her mouth and tearfully continue arguing her case when the phone rang. Mary got up and went into the hallway to answer it.

"Jack," she frowned, "it's for you." Mary put her hand over the receiver and whispered, "It's Amy Ryan. Sounds serious, love." Apparently, Jack's best friend and business partner had been in a serious car accident coming back from Houston. His wife Amy wasn't injured, but Will had been hospitalized late last night and Amy was hoping Jack could meet them at the hospital. He put the phone in its cradle and, after explaining the details, turned to Mimi in the gentle voice of humility.

"Honey, would you come with me? Come with me, please." And as if she had already agreed, Jack turned to his mother-in-law. "Mary, can Janie stay with you this afternoon?"

"Of course. Go on and see about Will and Amy. She can help me in the garden, won't you, Janie. Lizzie, do you think you might be able to help us plant my morning glories this afternoon? Trouble is, I've soaked the seeds and really should plant them soon as possible. It won't take long. We can drop them in by the back fence with plenty of morning sun." Of course I would help. The garden was my favorite place of refuge and I identified right away with those hard little shells that needed softening. How else could I push my way through the proverbial soil and spread....whatever it was I had to spread? Will's accident and the fact that he needed Jack suddenly overruled the dispute between them and talk of a new shop ended. Mimi's husband needed her. I was all too familiar with that concept.

The days that followed passed in cheerful sprightliness, and before long it was May, which meant Janie's graduation from elementary school and her much anticipated move to junior high. I had become part of the Schwarz convoy, yet the security I felt, latched on to this family, also hinted at a barrenness of spirit within me, an intense longing for connectedness that hovered over me in my sleep as well as my wakefulness. As much as I wanted independence, the pinch of loneliness outranked with my daily thoughts without restraint, and I held on even tighter, especially to Mary.

Janie's graduation was scheduled to take place that Friday night. The Schwarz family piled into one car and Mary rode in mine as we pulled into the school's parking lot where other families were gathering to attend and celebrate their children's achievements. Janie, decked out in a new white pique dress and jacket and wearing low heels for the first time, nervously walked ahead of us and joined her friends, a sign of growing self-reliance in the plucky girl to whom I would forever be indebted for her defiant act of kindness. Two years ago, against her mother's wishes, she had given me Mary's address, and consequently I had a place to live and ultimately a family to fall in love with. The ceremony went smoothly undeterred by the heat and humidity in the gym, and then, as if suddenly feeling ill, I recalled another evening six years prior following a hot and humid graduation. The melancholy sickness of the moment thrust me into an inconsolable frame of mind, and I couldn't shake it off. I confessed to a debilitating headache and would need to beg off the rest of the evening celebrations. Mary had ridden with me—could they give her a lift back? I declined any assistance home and assured them I simply needed to lie down in the cool darkness of my room. I never told them, not even Mary, how heartsick I had become, remembering the events of that night six years before. It has been said that feelings of guilt never leave you until you finally forgive yourself, and I wasn't ready to do that.

Harmony is essential in gardening. Without it, conflict in color and design, especially in proximity, clashes with the senses. Despite our best endeavors, plants may suffer from adverse environmental conditions that only proper balance can restore.

The Art of Gardening by Emily Mayfield

CHAPTER 10

1967 | Judy had returned to Carlton, her father's irrepressible temperament at bay for a while, but most of the time I ended up sharing her with Jimmy, so attached were they to each other. I didn't mind tagging along with the lovebirds, however. It was better than watching Mama and Mr. Anson making fools of themselves. I used every excuse I could invent to leave the house. By May the three of us spent our Saturdays, sometimes all afternoon, on his back porch listening to the Beatles and the new Moody Blues and delving into Jimmy's comic book archives. My personal favorite was an illustrated *Oliver Twist*. I must have read it a hundred times, especially the part where Oliver gets a family, and while Judy and Jimmy thought I was engrossed in the story for the umpteenth time, they sat on his disheveled bed and made out shamelessly. Little did they know I could shift my gaze ever so slightly over the top as I turned the pages. I watched closely, fascinated by how they knew exactly what to do with their mouths and where to put their hands, neither of which moved very much. I had never even kissed a boy but if that was how it was done, I thought I could wait a lot longer. When I saw Jimmy's hand reach under her shirt, I realized, after the slumber party revelation, neither of them had any qualms about how far they might go in front of me. I jumped up and announced I needed to go home.

Jimmy's brother Randy was graduating from high school that particular Saturday, and Judy and I rode in the car with Mama, who had been asked to represent the senior faculty on the stage. The drone of idle chatter high and low, the undulating waves of fretful wailing from unhappy babies seemed to exacerbate the already stultifying air in the school's gymnasium that was bulging with what could possibly be the entire community. Jimmy said goodbye to Judy when we arrived and went to sit with the rest of his family who took up one whole row on the floor. As the school board never found it necessary to pipe air conditioning into the gym, we sat in the sweltering heat for two hours, sweat rolling down my backside. Several student council members stood at the entrances and passed out paper fans donated by McCray's Auto Parts in exchange for a bit of advertising, but all they did was move the hot air around. When it was finally all over, and the top scholarships had been announced, including Reggie's substantial gift from the NAACP that drew scant but noticeable murmurs from the crowd, I was ready to go home and take a bath. Judy on the other hand had other plans when Jimmy's mother met us outside and invited us over for impromptu burgers. Randy was going party hopping, out to a series of celebrations with his friends, but his grandparents were staying over for the weekend, reason enough for Mr. Bertrand to fire up the grill. So Mama and Judy and I walked over to Jimmy's house for a hamburger social. As usual the three of us gravitated to the back porch away from the adults sitting on the hot patio. No one objected to our absence.

"Let's play poker. Jimmy, go get your cards." Judy was on a roll again, bossing everyone around, but Jimmy just flopped out on his bed as if he hadn't heard her. "Jimmy," she scolded, "what's the matter with you? I said I wanna play poker."

"I dunno. That's boring." I couldn't believe my ears. There was Jimmy, who never disagreed with anything Judy wanted, usurping her. This was just the beginning of a night that would turn ugly.

"Bored?" she said. "How could you possibly be bored? I'm here and we can play an exciting game of poker. What's to be bored about?"

Jimmy grunted and rested his hands behind his head, stretching out his legs. "I didn't say I was bored. I said poker was boring."

"Okay, then, what do you suggest?" Jimmy didn't answer her, but he got up and unexpectedly pulled a box out from under the bed, retrieving a pack of cards and a large, salt-glazed jar full of pennies so heavy he had to drag it out with both hands. I was more fascinated by the craftsmanship of the jar—its unusual orange-peel glaze. When I asked him where he got it, he ignored me and, as if poker had suddenly become appealing, said, "I'll deal." Without another word we sat on the floor in a circle and Jimmy dealt us each five cards. For the next half hour we played penny ante poker until Mr. Bertrand called us to come outside and eat. It was getting dark and the mosquitoes drove everyone inside, the adults in the living room and the three of us settling on the porch again.

When Judy had eaten half her burger, she said, "I know how we can liven things up a bit." We both deferred to her to see what wild scheme she had concocted, as the juice rolled down my right hand. "How's about a game of strip poker?" Judy was beaming.

"I don't think so," I mumbled with my mouth crammed full, but Jimmy didn't wait for me to finish.

"You're on. Finish eating and I'll check on my parents." Jimmy disappeared and I glowered at Judy as if she had lost her mind. I finished chewing.

"Listen, Judy. You may want to bare everything you've got for your boyfriend, but I don't. If you two are going to take your clothes off, I'm going home."

"Oh, spoil sport. It's just for fun. Besides, Jimmy's bored and it'll get him going." Jimmy was back, closing the door and grinning.

"Lizzie doesn't want to play. She won't agree to take anything off," she laughed, but Jimmy's grin disappeared.

"Okay," he said. The old Jimmy was back, his usual agreeable self. I sometimes wondered if he ever seriously considered what *he* wanted. We played the usual penny ante with our clothes on for the next two hours while Judy slowly amassed the majority of the coins from the jar. Earlier Mama had peeked in to tell me she was going home and not to stay too long. At eleven something, the screen door popped open to reveal a swaggering Randy swinging a bat.

"Hey, what are you doing with my Mickey Mantle?" Suddenly Jimmy came to life. It was his prize possession, given to him by his grandfather two years earlier, a souvenir from Bat Day at Yankee Stadium. Few things really stirred Jimmy to reaction; this beloved bat seemed to be one of them.

"Been playin' ball, little brother. I needed the best to play ball with......a zombie!" he burst out, trying to scare us. He was stumbling toward the door to the house. "Old man 'sleep?"

"I dunno. Go see for yourself." Randy dropped the bat where he was standing, fumbling around for the door knob. When Jimmy picked it up, blood on the bat covered the palms of his hands. He looked down and then at the bat and back to his hands as if the two had no rational connection. By the time Jimmy looked up, his brother was gone.

"What the hell—" Jimmy thought he could feel a thin crack in the bat. "What did you hit with my bat?" He followed Randy into the house for an explanation. When Jimmy returned with his bat wiped clean, he pushed it under the bed and sank into his bed. The door opened again and Randy's face appeared around the side.

"Yeah, he's out. C'mon. You wanna take a little ride down to the school? Bet you'll never see anything like this again." Whether bewildered or merely disappointed, Jimmy was speechless, and for the first time, so was Judy. "Come on, let's go. Get in the car." Jimmy looked at us with a blank face and Randy nodded, "They can come, too, but y'all better not get scared." Randy looked at Judy. "You scared of zombies, little girl?" That was the bait, sufficient to entice her instantly but I hung back.

"I don't know, Judy. I don't want to get in trouble. Maybe we should go home." Judy flashed her wild eyes at me. It wasn't a look of pleading this time. It was unadulterated temerity, something akin to an infatuation with danger. It energized her. Before any further objections, I found myself sitting in the front seat of Randy's Chevrolet. Judy had nudged Jimmy into the back seat where they were already making out, and I sat up front wondering how I managed to be sitting next to a drunk behind the wheel. Fortunately the high school was down the street, and as he drove through the dark parking lot near the tennis courts, I could just make out the shadowy movement of what I presumed to be seniors still celebrating. I have to admit I was as curious as I was terrified of what my mother would say, afraid of the ghoulish presence we might witness there in the dark. I didn't believe in zombies and yet fear that was vague could also be real. Randy stopped the car with a jerk and ordered us out. All thoughts of reason vanished temporarily, and I was filled with pity for the "zombie"—most likely some poor innocent animal that had been in the wrong place, meeting his untimely beating at the hands of crazed seniors. With all that blood on Jimmy's bat, it had to have been a large animal, probably a stray dog. My mind traveled back to a nine year old Randy obsessed with torturing animals. I cringed as I slid down in my seat, hoping to be invisible and forgotten. Suddenly the door jerked open and Judy grabbed my arms.

"You'll thank me for this one day. Tonight is one night I'm not going to let you chicken out on us." With my usual compliance toward her, I allowed Judy to drag me through the crowd, pushing our way to the inner circle. Surrounded by teenagers, a dark mass was slumped over on the ground, almost prone. It was too big to be a dog, or even a wild animal, and when a single flame from a cigarette lighter illuminated the dark figure, I gasped as if the click of the lighter sucked all the air out of me. The boy fell over on his back and I recognized his face through the bloodied eyes swollen and closed. Randy stood over him and, along with another boy on the other side of him, kicked his ribs and swore. The boy winced, emitting the deep guttural sound that accompanies sudden severe pain, but when two thin slits of eyes opened again, he seemed to be looking straight at me. I turned to find Judy. She was laughing. The whole thing was so surreal I thought I must be dreaming. A dream in which stoical Jimmy stood behind her with his protective and loving arms around her waist, completing the picture with the strange irony of the moment. Fifty or more people, some couples I knew, stood packed shoulder to shoulder to watch the violent Roman-like spectacle. I tried to make out the faces of the kids across from me and recognized two boys and a girl from the play on which I had worked props with Reggie. Suddenly Randy began yelling.

"C'mon, nigger. Get your black ass up. I said get up! We ain't done yet. You really thought you goin' to LSU? A white boy's school? Don't matter how smart you think you are, nobody wants stinkin' niggers pollutin' our schools," and he kicked him so hard this time that the boy on the ground groaned, turned on his side, and coughed up blood that spattered on the shoes of two boys standing nearby. He looked briefly at his assailant and passed out. I feared he was dead. The boys had quickly backed away from the bloody spray but remained to watch Randy overpower the colored boy. He no longer had possession of the bat that had already struck down his victim, and so three sets of fists and feet struck him again and again, turning him over, now and aiming his blows at the boy's back and head.

"Hey, Randy." Someone stepped forward. "Maybe he needs a drink— you know, wet his whistle." The suggestion came from a tall senior I didn't know standing in back of my neighbor as he handed him an opened soda can. Randy, in his inebriated state, held the can up for the crowd to see and asked for someone's lighter. Two girls looked at each other and gasped, terrified of what he might do, and murmurs rippled through the crowd.

"No, man, it's piss. Piss ain't flammable," he laughed, looking around at his friends and grabbing his crotch. Randy smirked, throwing his head back as if he understood all along, and poured the contents on the battered boy's mouth and face, instantly reviving him as he jerked about. It was too dark to see the color, but from the smell I knew right away the putrid thing Randy had done. When I recalled the image later—and still recall it every single day of my life—it seemed that each disgusting deed, one more terrible than the next, added to the revulsion of that nightmare . But I knew the awful reality the instant I saw the battered face of Reginald Washington. How I managed to remove myself from the tangled mass of curiously morbid onlookers remains unclear, yet I struggled to push my way past the crowd and run as fast as I could to the other side of the tennis courts near the street. I couldn't breathe, choking I was crying so hard. I stopped, held on to the chain link fence, and vomited all over my shoes. My head was throbbing from the unbearable pressure, and, wiping my mouth on my shirt, I sank to the ground praying for relief, my fingers still painfully gripping the wire of the fence. I could see in my mind Reggie's body curled up on the ground, and once again I began shaking and sobbing. I finally steadied myself and ran to the sidewalk when I heard a siren's high pitched shrieking. A patrol car was coming toward me and I crouched behind a tree until it passed. I ran the rest of the way home.

The back door was unlocked so I crept through the darkened hall and got into bed. Every inch of my body ached, and each time I woke up and remembered, the sobbing reclaimed me. Once I cried out so loud I had to stifle the sound with a pillow so Mama wouldn't hear. It must have been midmorning when she opened the door.

"Lizzie, honey, are you going to stay in that bed all day?" I heard her but I couldn't find the energy to answer. "Lizzie? Are you sick, hon?" She came closer to the bed. Even her gentle touch sent shocks of pain through my body. I was feverish and when I turned over, Mama had returned with a thermometer. The mind's power to control the body has always fascinated me, like bending spoons just by thinking it. My sickened heart had an iron grip on my mind and body, bending them into an unrecognizable shape. Was he dead? Did Reggie survive the unexpected brutality that altered his joyous day of accomplishment, or was he left in a high school parking lot to spend his last bloody, gasping breaths dying? The uncertainty of his fate propelled currents of grief down, down to the deepest recesses where guilt resides. I hadn't been willing to help him. Not once had I tried to stop Randy. I hadn't even *tried*.

The thermometer read 101 and I was instructed not to get out of bed. Mama would bring me a cup of milky tea and later a bowl of her chicken noodle soup. She would check on me when she got back, she said.

"Where you going?" I managed to whisper.

"I'm going to visit Reginald Washington at the hospital and see what I can do for his mother. Apparently several boys beat him up last night and left him for dead. We don't know who it was yet, but I imagine we'll find out. Thank God, someone had the decency to call the police. I just don't know what we've come to. He's such a nice boy, a decent boy." Mama's voice was tired. "I thought we had managed to get through this year without this sort of thing."

All of a sudden I found my voice. "Will he be all right?"

"I don't know, sweetie. All I have is the little information Mr. Reynolds gave me. He called all of Reginald's teachers this morning. Now try to get some rest. I'll bring your tea in a minute, and then I need to go. I won't be too long." I closed my eyes and tried to sleep but the words *decency to call the police* were the shackles that would imprison me for the next ten years. Even in my feeble state, I found more tears until I must have fallen asleep. The next thing I knew, Mama had returned and was setting a tray of soup and crackers on my bed.

Walkways and paths leading to a garden accommodate
foot traffic and improve the general landscape, offering
opportunities for viewing gardens at close range.

The Art of Gardening by Emily Mayfield

CHAPTER 11

1967 | School had ended with a whir of fans, sleeveless shirts and pony-
tails, and a rush to the local community swimming pool. Despite the
cataclysm of the ill-fated post-graduation night, everyone left school for
summer vacation. Talk of Reggie subsided as other concerns replaced him,
and he was no longer a major subject of gossip. While it was strangely all
but forgotten with the general public, continual feelings of guilt immobilized me. With Mama's gentle but steady prodding, Judy and I signed up to
take diving lessons at the recreation center, but on the Sunday afternoon
before the class was to begin, Judy wanted to go to the pool and practice.
She met me on the corner and we walked in silence until I spoke up.

"We never talked about that night, you know."

"That night?"

"Graduation night. What happened after I left?" I asked.

"Yeah, about that. What happened to *you* is the question. I turned
around and you were gone. You have a bad habit of that, by the way."

"So, what happened?"

"Nothing really. We left as fast as we could when we heard the police. Jimmy pulled Randy back to the car and grabbed his keys 'cause Randy was too drunk to drive," Judy laughed. "I ran after them, but that's about all I remember."

"I heard the siren but everything was a blur after that. I guess an ambulance took Reggie to the hospital. No one was arrested?" I pretended I knew very little about that night.

"No, Lizzie," she said with her usual disgust at what she considered my simple-minded approach to life. "Look, girl, you better not tell anyone. I mean it. Stay out of it. You'll get all of us in trouble—including yourself, don't forget. Anyway, it's a little late to say anything now. You're in it all the way up to your eyeballs. Besides, we didn't actually do anything wrong. Just because we happened to be there—." I didn't answer her, just kept walking until we reached the pool. It wasn't clear to me then, but as time passed I began to understand Judy's views of right and wrong. Being a by-stander was a neutral position that claimed neither the weight of contrition nor the pleasure of watching without getting caught. There would be no more discussion—what was done was done, but for me the suffering would be interminable. Case closed for Judy, she dropped her shirt and towel on a chair and stood close to the water's edge in diving position, hands overhead. "Ready?"

"I can't practice something I don't know how to do. What if I do it wrong?" I said.

"Lizzie," she stopped on the side of the pool and glared, putting her hands on her hips to show her exasperation. "Why do you always have to be so perfect? Can't you just let go and have fun? Look, I'm gonna dive off the side—no flips or anything—and then you dive off. Okay?" She didn't wait for a reply but pointed her hands toward the sun, curved her spine, and bent her knees to push off into the water. When her head bobbed up seconds later, she was smiling triumphantly. "Ooo, it's so cold! It feels great. Now you." If Judy could do it so easily, I thought, I may as well try. With feigned confidence, I stood on the edge of the pool in plain sight of everyone there. My navy one piece called attention to the curves I had recently developed, a prominence of breasts that I'd just as soon no one noticed. I leaned my body over the side, arms stretched out in front of me as Judy had done, and plopped in. The first attempt felt awkward and the loud slap against my belly announced an embarrassing lack of gracefulness to the weekend crowd at the pool, but the water did feel good against my warm skin. I swam over to Judy who was already pulling herself up the side and out of the water.

"Move over. I'm going again!" she exclaimed. Judy stood on tiptoe this time, bending even more to get a good arch. I couldn't say for sure, but I think I felt the thud when she hit her head on the bottom of the pool. When she emerged, a big red splotch on her forehead was turning into a bump. "Oh, my God, that hurt," she said, gurgling a mouthful of chlorine water.

"Are you okay?" I dragged my heavy body slowly through the water to get to her.

"No, I think I need to get out and sit down a minute." I looked over at the life guard and motioned for him to come over. He took his time descending from his perch to shuffle his flip-flopped feet over to Judy, who was now lying on a poolside chaise longue.

"What's the problem? Hit your head?" She nodded. "You shouldn't be diving off the side, you know. That's what diving boards are for," he scowled, eyes hidden behind his mirrored sun glasses. "Didn't you read the sign," he said pointing to a placard behind us.

"We were practicing for our diving class tomorrow," I explained sheepishly.

"Not gonna be one. Sorry. I'm the instructor and not enough people signed up. You'll have to take the Tuesday-Thursday class with Bobby. Just show up and tell him you were in the Monday group." And then he turned around and walked back to his post. At that moment I understood why not enough people had signed up for his class.

"Can you walk?" I asked Judy as I watched him sidle back to his station unconcerned.

"I think so, but I'm starting to get a headache."

"Really, Judy, maybe you should go home and tell your mother to call the doctor," I suggested. The bump seemed to be getting bigger. "A headache after hitting the bottom like that could be serious."

"I'm sure it's nothing. Probably nothing. Besides, my mother's not home. She went to visit her sister and she won't be back until Wednesday. I'm definitely not telling Daddy," she added.

"You want Mama to look at it? She'll know what to do. She knows everything." We walked slowly down the sidewalk to our house and soon Mama was inspecting Judy's forehead and asking questions. When she was satisfied Judy wasn't in immediate and grave danger, she put her in the car and took her home. I rode in the back seat with them, but Mama told me to stay in the car as she walked Judy up the steps. When her daddy came to the door, he opened it for Judy to go in. I could see Mama engaged in some sort of conversation with him, and then it seemed like he shut the door while Mama was still talking. She turned and walked as gracefully as ever back to the car.

"He's been drinking again," was all she said and started the car to go home. I didn't know how much Mama knew about Judy's father and what he had done to her, but I wasn't going to tell her. I still felt a sense of loyalty to Judy regardless of her inability to reciprocate. That's how it went—up and down, like the swings at the park. I seriously wondered when Judy eventually flew out the seat of our friendship where she would land.

On Tuesday I showed up for diving lessons. I looked around at three boys half asleep on pool chairs and took a seat. Judy wasn't there, but that wasn't really a surprise, even if she hadn't banged her head. No one said much and when Bobby the instructor arrived, he told us to jump in the pool to wake up. Then we lined up and marched around the pool to the low board. When he called roll and realized I was not on the list, I spoke up. "You don't have me on your list. Lizzie Rowan. I was in the Monday class."

"Right," he said, glancing at his clipboard. "What's the name again?"

"Lizzie Rowan."

"Rowan, huh? How do you spell that?" I told him and he wrote it on his chart. When I got home after the lesson, I called Judy but no one answered.

"Maybe she decided to take it easy. That was a pretty nasty bump. Could give her a pretty nasty headache, too. I encouraged Lizzie's father to have a doctor examine her just to be safe." I looked at Mama and rolled my eyes, no point in responding to that.

"I don't think diving is my thing, Mama."

"Liz, you've been in the class one day. How do you know until you give it a chance?"

"It doesn't feel right. I was the only girl—Judy wasn't...." I stopped her before she could ask. "And she probably isn't going to. She always does this to me. Besides, I just can't get it right, Mama. Do you know what it's like to keep doing belly flops in front of a bunch of boys?" Whether she felt sorry for me or simply tired of coming up with ways to keep me occupied, that was the end of diving lessons. Although I was aware of playing hopscotch with my life, jumping from one square to another without a real plan, I couldn't see a way out.

The one thing I had going for me was also the one thing I dreaded, the rate at which the days seemed to be forging ahead. It was already the middle of August. I was moving away from the events of May and hurtling into my sophomore year, yet I had not moved an inch toward forgiving myself. I had a bad attitude in general and I was well aware of it. I hated myself. I hated everything. I wanted to hate Judy, too, but she was the only friend I had, and so I succumbed to her antics as well as her little betrayals. Mama attributed my moodiness to hormones, and maybe that didn't help, but I knew the truth. Shame gnaws away relentlessly at its host, and in my case, the shame of keeping secrets. No one had been punished, the matter was shelved, and nobody at school talked about it anymore, not even Judy, yet Reggie invaded my thoughts every day and there wasn't a soul I could tell. Added to the mix was Judy's secret.

The drama club produced two plays that year, Synge's "Riders to the Sea," a one act for the state competition in the spring in which I had a bit part, and *Take Her, She's Mine,* where I had worked on props under Reggie at the beginning of the year. Although I'd gotten the hang of it, I thought that part of my high school career, working in theatre, was finished.

"What do you plan to do with yourself before school starts, hon?" Mama, who never wasted anything, was making chicken salad with the leftover chicken from supper.

"I think I'll just stay inside and read for two weeks. Besides, I can keep you company now that Mr. Anson doesn't come around anymore." Mama tilted her head and shot me a warning glance. It was clear she didn't want me to bring it up again. Joseph Anson's job had taken him to Tulsa, and he wanted Mama to quit her job and move us to Oklahoma to be with him. Mama wished him a safe journey and that was the end of that. Life went back to being as normal as it had been before, or as normal as it could be under the circumstances.

"Now, Lizzie," she began in her sweet scolding way. "I'm glad you plan to read all those books, but you really shouldn't go into hiding. It's not healthy and you still have plenty of summer left. Go down to the recreation center and sign up for a class." *No, Mama, going into hiding is exactly what I'd like to do.* "We'll think of something. I wish I could have sent you to church camp, but I just didn't have—"

"Forget camp, Mama. I wouldn't have gone anyway. I'm fine. Besides, I have two shelves and a long list of books at the library that I'd been waiting to read. I've been through all of Jimmy's illustrated classics, so now I going to read the originals. I'm thinking I have enough time to start with Dickens and finish before I go back." I knew there would be no argument there, and I was right. She dropped the subject, for a few days anyway.

Mama was in the kitchen again, cooking figs this time. She'd never preserved anything before, but she was determined not to let all those figs in the back yard go to waste. The tree had stood in the far left corner of the garden for years, long before we moved in, and its branches of large green foliage couldn't hide the clusters of brown figs peeking out from every branch. She'd given away as many as she could to the Abbotts and the Bertrands, but every branch of the tree yielded a profusion of fruit that continued to ripen daily. Cardinals and blue jays could leave gashes in every other fig and we still had more than we could use. At that moment, however, I wasn't thinking about figs.

I slumped over the kitchen table and rested my cheek on my fist. I was bored. I'd read three of my new books and Judy was never at home, but more than that I was suffering from a restless spirit ignited by the guilt I couldn't shake off. I couldn't even talk about it with the one person who might help me. Mama was quiet for a minute before speaking. I thought she was going to come up with another brilliant way to occupy my time, but she was concentrating on figs.

"Oh, dear, I don't have enough jars. Liz, run up to the store—." Before she could finish she looked up at me and saw how miserable I was. "I know," she said, taking off her apron and turning off the burner. "Why don't we take a ride down the street to the A & P together? We can have a nice little chat and figure out something else for you to do. And you can get a cold Barq's. Let me get my purse."

The thing I remember most about the A & P was the smell of freshly ground coffee the minute you walked through the door. I didn't particularly like the taste of it, but somehow the aroma of coffee beans grinding was tantalizing, which made me love going to the store. Also, it was air conditioned.

"Afternoon, Mrs. Rowan. How's everything?"

"Fine, just fine, Mr. Harper. I'm putting up some figs and I've run out of mason jars."

"Last aisle on the right. Next to the pickles."

Aisle seven was a mess. Right in front of the pickle shelf was a stock boy sprawled out on the floor surrounded by a big case of pickles and several broken pickle jars, liquid streaming everywhere. Mama rushed over to the boy who was trying to get up from the accident.

"Oh, for heaven's sake!" Mama stooped over the young man. "Reginald? Are you all right, son? What happened?" And then she turned to me. "Lizzie, run get Mr. Harper," but I just stood there staring at Reggie, unable to move. "Now, Lizzie! Go!"

The investment of loving care in your garden can be realized in the maintenance of healthy soil and good cultivation with the regular addition of fertilizer, compost, and mulch. The resulting growth of healthy plants is the bounteous dividend.

The Art of Gardening by Emily Mayfield

CHAPTER 12

1967 | By the time Mr. Harper and I reached aisle seven, Mama and Reggie were standing amidst the broken glass talking. At least, Mama was talking and Reggie was hanging his head with his thumbs hooked in his back pockets.

"All right, get the mop and clean it up before somebody slips and falls. Then we'll really have a problem. And pick up all that glass." Mr. Harper was shaking his head and swearing under his breath.

Without waiting for Reggie to speak, Mama intervened "Les, could I have a word?" She led Mr. Harper a few feet away to the end of the aisle out of earshot. I looked at Reggie.

"What happened? Did you faint?" I said softly. Reggie just shook his head and began piling up the larger pieces of shattered jars without looking at me. Another stock boy arrived and swept up the smaller pieces, and the two of them worked together in silence to clean up the avalanche of ruined pickles. I looked over at Mama who appeared to be arguing her case while Mr. Harper just kept on shaking his head. I tried to picture Reggie at school, his lithe body gliding over the darkened stage, his strong arms balancing a tray of sandwiches. Reggie, who had won the writing contest and several scholarships to LSU, was now a stock boy in a grocery store, and apparently not a very good one.

It wasn't until we got in the car that Mama spoke. She had neglected to buy the jars for her fig preserves still in the pot on the stove. She sat there for a moment and then said, "Lizzie, wait here. I'll be right back." And she was, too, but she hadn't run back in to get the jars. She'd gone to fetch Reggie. Mama opened the car door empty-handed and in stepped the humiliated stock boy. When she drove in the direction of our house, I knew she wasn't giving him a ride home and I felt panic rising in my throat.

"Reginald, you don't have to start today, of course, but at least you'll know where we live. It's just around this corner. The little yellow house on the right here." Mama slowed down so Reggie could get a good look but then she turned into the driveway.

"Thank you, Mrs. Rowan," he whispered, trailing off as if he were too tired to say any more.

"I'll take you home now." Then she turned and said, "Liz, I didn't get the jars. Could you—"

"All right, Mama," I said, desperately wanting out of the car. She got a five from her pocketbook and handed it to me.

"Just six. Six jars. Bring me the change, please. I won't be long." So I walked down the sidewalk, back to the store while Mama backed into the street and drove off the other way.

I was reading on my bed with the door open when I heard her come in and walk down the hall straight to my room.

"Lizzie, are you all right?"

"I'm okay. What about Reggie? What happened? Back there in the store." Mama sat on the edge of the bed and let out a long sigh.

"Where to begin. I suppose it's time we talked about this." *Oh, no,* I thought. *Please, God, don't let her know.* "Reginald has been recovering from….from the incident in May," she said. "He should have been at LSU on a scholarship, but he was in the hospital with severe bruising and complications from trauma to the head for two months. College is not an option for him right now. Instead of a promising future, the only job he was able to get was stocking shelves for Mr. Harper at the A & P, and he was hired only a week ago. He had a seizure, Lizzie, and, well, you saw what happened."

"Did Mr. Harper fire him?" I asked. Mama clearly wasn't going to mention my role on graduation night, and I tried to hide my relief.

"I guess he felt he had to. Reginald was too great a liability," she nodded.

"A liability?"

"There are people in this town, Liz, who may feel….who may be afraid of a Negro stock boy who could be prone to unpredictable seizures."

"You mean Mr. Harper," I said.

"Yes, and others. People who shop there."

"You mean he thought he'd lose his customers? Is that why he fired him?"

"I'm afraid so," Mama said. "It's such a disappointment, really, to see Reginald come to this. He had such a bright future." Mama shook her head but then she looked up. "I've asked him to come here twice a week and work in the yard. I could use some help and he needs the money. It's temporary. He needs a full time job, but it will help him get on his feet while he finds something more permanent." Her usual resignation seemed to have vanished, so I knew she meant business.

"Wait. Reggie's going to work in the garden for you, Mama? What's wrong with me? We don't need any help. You have me." I didn't know if it were surprise or fear I was feeling—probably both, but the idea of seeing Reggie there in our back yard twice a week brought back the agony of the guilt I'd been trying to stuff with little success into the farthest corner of my brain.

"Come on, Liz. It'll mean less weed pulling for you," she smiled, unaware that even her small attempt at humor was completely lost on me.

"What if he has seizures here in our back yard and you're not home?" I knew now she would hear the panic in my voice.

"Lizzie, honey, you mustn't be afraid. Reginald believes working in the garden won't be a problem. He says he rarely has them anymore—Mr. Harper needed him to do a double shift and he was tired." She put her arm around me as she sat next to me on the bed. "Liz, he needs another chance. We all deserve at least that." Yes. Good, kind, smart, innocent Reginald deserved another chance, and as much as I wanted him to have one, I wasn't ready to be his benefactor.

A garden can be a wildlife habitat, and it is here that people often experience their closest encounters with nature. Just as plants experience crises, sometimes the wildlife attracted to your garden may need assistance.

The Art of Gardening by Emily Mayfield

CHAPTER 13

1967 | Reggie worked the rest of the summer and into the fall in our back yard, not twice a week as Mama had promised but every day, and the absence of seizures made me feel they might be gone for good. My doubts about him weren't over, however. My privacy had been utterly violated, the garden now off limits for me as dictated by a self-imposed boundary. The days grew hotter and I missed sitting in the swing less and less, but I often found myself watching him from my window. He moved all over the yard as confidently as he had done on the stage, watering the irises Mama had planted, pulling every last weed from the bed, cutting back the invasion of bougainvillea overshadowing even the tall cannas. I kept my distance, though, and so did he, diverting his eyes and looking straight ahead as if he had never known me. One afternoon in late June, I saw him stop under the big oak on his way to put up the tools. Something had captured his attention. He knelt down in the dirt and scooped up a tiny brown bundle with both hands, bringing it close to his face as if nearsighted and examining it, tilting his head one way and then the other. Before long he was walking quickly toward the house. Mama wasn't at home, but Reggie began banging on the back door loudly with his fist. I pretended I didn't hear him, but he just kept pounding on the door even harder.

"What's the matter?" I asked, finally opening the screen door. He thrust his hand to me palm up to display a thin brown furry creature. I looked at him and then his hands. His sudden good will left me speechless.

I continued to stare at it until he said, "It's a squirrel."

"Oh," I said. "How do you know?"

Reggie eyes squinted at me as if he hadn't understood the question. "How do I know what?"

I leaned over and examined the tiny creature again. "Yeah, I guess it is a squirrel. How'd you find it?" I said innocently, acting like I hadn't been watching him all along.

"Just lyin' under that oak tree over there. It must have fallen out of the nest, but I didn't check." I could almost see a laugh behind his eyes, so I was careful not to say anything else stupid, just in case he was serious.

"Well, what're you going to do with it?"

"Don't know yet but he must be hungry." Reggie smiled like he wanted to laugh with childlike delight, so happy to have discovered this living creature that needed his help.

"How do you know it's a boy? Maybe it's a girl squirrel." He stopped smiling and he became his serious self again.

"I turned him over and looked at his underside," he said so matter-of-factly that I believed him.

"Oh, okay," I said. "Well, come on in. What's he eat?" Reggie didn't say anything but faltered at the door before stepping inside the house and into the kitchen. I detected his reluctance by the way his forehead wrinkled and his eyes widened as he moved toward me, oddly unsure of himself. I thought about how different he looked in the bright kitchen light, face to face alone in the house with me. I couldn't stop watching his every move.

"Water."

"You want a drink of water?"

"You asked what we should feed him," Reggie replied.

"Right. Water. Is that all? Can't we make him some porridge?" Reggie looked down at me with his liquid brown eyes and spoke as if explaining the situation to a child.

"He's a squirrel, not a baby."

"We can put some milk in it and feed him with an eye dropper. I think we have one," I said, pretending I hadn't heard him. I wasn't sure about this plan of his, but I didn't have anything better to do and Mama wasn't at home to make the decision. I turned to go look for it.

"Wait. Before we give him the wrong thing, let me find out what he actually eats. My sister cleans at the library and I can ask her to see if the librarian can look it up. Let's just give him some water for now, make sure he's hydrated." Reggie constantly surprised me. He had said *we*.

"Hydrated. Hmm." Reggie's descent from scholar to yard man made me forget how smart he was—reduced to planting and pulling weeds when he should have been sitting in a college classroom. For now, I was glad he was standing in our kitchen, saving a baby squirrel and asking me to help.

"No, I can walk to the library this afternoon. I'll look it up. We probably shouldn't wait so long to feed him. I have a shoe box in my room that I don't need. Mama would have a fit if she saw him on the table."

"No, of course not. We don't want to upset Mrs. Rowan," he quickly added.

I found the empty shoe box that had held my new red tennis shoes. I thought we probably had an eye dropper in the cabinet in the bathroom. When I returned Reggie hadn't moved, the baby squirrel still squirming in his hand. I gave him the box and a dish towel, and he placed the animal in it with his big gentle hands. Without speaking he took the eye dropper from me, and I watched him retrieve drops from the cup. Then he handed me the dropper, expecting me to do it. Reggie opened the baby squirrel's mouth and I aimed and squirted. I missed the first time and Reggie smiled and began to relax. The feeding went on for a few minutes before the front door announced Mama was home. She must have heard us in the kitchen because she yelled, "What's going on in there? Are you and Judy making cookies again?" Mama stepped into the kitchen, saw Reggie and me, and gave a startled, "Oh."

"Hi, Mama. Reggie rescued a baby squirrel in the back yard. We're hydrating it."

"Mrs. Rowan," he nodded. "I was just leaving." Reggie was about to walk out when I stopped him.

"Hey, where do you think you're going? You're not leaving me here to take care of this thing by myself."

Mama glanced over at our project. "She's right about that, Reginald. I'm surprised Lizzie's been any help at all. She's a bit squeamish."

"I am not. I'm the one who fed him with the eye dropper," I said in defense even though I knew I wouldn't have done it if Reggie hadn't made me.

Mama looked like she didn't know what to say. When she did speak, she must have decided a gentle reprimand was in order. "That's not my clean dish towel under that wild animal, is it?"

"We had to use something. Besides, he's not a wild animal. He's a baby, and baby squirrels get cold," I informed her, glancing over at Reggie for approval but he was stone-faced. Mama smiled and put a pot of water on the stove for her coffee.

Reggie was invited to stay for supper—an act of kindness that our neighbors would never understand, but I knew he wouldn't accept. He made an excuse about having to go home, but before he left he said, "Mrs. Rowan, that old bird cage you have in the shed—it would be a good place to keep him, at least until he's big enough to let go."

"What? We have to let him go? We can't just keep him as a pet?" I protested, unable to think that far ahead.

"He's part of the garden. He belongs there. He's not meant to be caged," he replied.

Mama continued putting up her bag of groceries. "You're welcomed to it, Reginald. Who's going to be the guardian of this infant?"

Without hesitating I said, "I am." Reggie didn't dispute my claim to the little fellow, didn't say a word, as if we had planned it that way. I stepped out the back door and watched him pull out the neglected cage from under a discarded old table and haul it to the steps, where he cleaned it off with a rag and carried it inside. He picked up the squirrel and went for the opening of the cage. His hand was too big.

"You have to do it," he said. "Put the dish rag in first." My heart raced at the thought of touching the little creature, but I knew it was too late to back out. Involuntarily extending my hand toward the box, I curled my fingers around the baby squirrel's little body and retrieved the cloth to make a nest in the cage. I slowly passed him through the cage door and set him down gently. Mama's hand was still on a can of asparagus, reaching for the top shelf, frozen, when she finally closed her mouth and put away the rest of the groceries.

"What are you going to name him?" Mama asked. Agreeing to look after a baby squirrel was my limit, so I turned to Reggie.

"Rocky. We'll call him Rocky," he said.

"Rocky? That's not very original for someone who won a writing contest," I said. Mama quickly dispatched a cautionary look of disapproval.

"Rocky suits him. He's had a rocky start in life. It's a good name," he said.

"Yeah, I guess so. We can call him Rocky if you want." Reggie started for the back door, turned around and nodded at Mama.

"See you tomorrow," I said. He didn't answer me and I watched him leave without telling me goodbye. It was his way. Reggie had uttered more that day than I had heard him say the whole four weeks we had worked together on the play. It was sort of like having a new friend, a private one secluded in the secrecy of Mama's garden.

"Better put him out there in the garden house. Looks like you'll be busy for a while." I was, too. Reggie and I spent the rest of the summer watching Rocky become an adult. Part of me didn't want to tell Judy, but I finally called her to come over and see our new pet. It turned out she was spending the last two weeks of summer at her aunt's house in Morgan City, and once again Judy hadn't called to tell me.

Two months into summer and Reggie seemed restless, wandering around the garden looking for the odd stray weed or tool that needed putting away, roses that needed deadheading. His fretful fidgeting led him to our back door one morning.

"Hey. Everything okay?" I asked.

"Uh, I'd like to speak to Mrs. Rowan if it's not too much trouble."

I turned around and yelled, "Mama! Reggie wants to talk to you," but she was already in the kitchen close by.

"Good morning, Reginald. Would you like something to drink? Come on in," she said.

"No, ma'am," he answered, not budging from where he stood outside the door. Mama didn't push it, acknowledging his reticence about coming inside. "Thank you, but I was hoping you had a book on gardening that I could borrow. I'd like to read up on a few things so I can do a better job out here." That was Reggie, always aiming for some higher level of himself. I needed to pay better attention to how he did it.

"Of course. What a good idea. I believe I have just what you're looking for, Reginald. Let me get it for you," and within a minute she was back at the door handing Reggie a large hardback book whose cover read *The Art of Gardening* by Emily Mayfield. "This should help. Lots of gardening advice but some landscaping ideas, too. You can keep it as long as you need it."

Reggie simply said, "Thank you, Mrs. Rowan" and headed to the garden house. Two hours later he was still there sitting at a table pouring over Mama's book. Mama made a pitcher of lemonade and poured two glasses, one for me and one for Reggie. I took them outside, happy for a good excuse to see what he was doing

"Hey. Mama thought you might be hot." Reggie looked up at me not so much with surprise as with curiosity. I handed him the drink and sat down on the chair next to him. I knew it would make him uncomfortable, but my own curiosity defeated my better judgment. "So," I said grappling for my next line. "Have you learned anything new?" Surely he knew my thirst for knowledge about gardening had not reached that point of concern since I had demonstrated no interest whatsoever in plants. It was the only opening that would make my presence relevant. Reggie, however, closed the book and moved it to one side while he took a long drink of the lemonade. When he put down the glass again, he said, "Mrs. Rowan has entrusted me with her garden, and I want to make it a showplace. I'm going to give her a plan, a design I've been thinking about, and ask her to let me get started. I think this book can help me achieve that." I shouldn't have been surprised at his eagerness to please my mother, looking back on it. I pressed him further.

"Can you tell me more about it? Do you have something in mind right now?" I tried to match his enthusiasm without the hesitation that might communicate any misgivings about his newly hatched plan. It must have worked because Reggie opened the book again and turned to several beautiful photographs of garden ideas he hoped to achieve in our back yard. He said he wouldn't begin planting until March, but he wanted to have a plan ready to go. I don't know if it was Reggie's contagious excitement about planning the garden or the unabashed friendship offered in our joint squirrel venture, but I will always remember that day when more than a new garden took root.

The garden must rest through winter's siege. The gardener can alleviate undesirable results by pruning perennials that will blacken and turn to mush. Remove excess debris to avoid crown rot. Give your plants the best possible chance of creating a long-lasting display when spring rolls around.

The Art of Gardening by Emily Mayfield

CHAPTER 14

1967 | It was September and my sophomore year of high school had commenced. Reggie was busy getting the garden ready for winter, cutting back what was needed. Zinnias, cosmos, and marigolds had strained under the hot July sun. While fall wasn't particularly devastating to plant life in the garden, in a few months, a cold snap, one night of freezing weather, could destroy his remaining handiwork, and he was determined to face it with the utmost in preparation. Meanwhile, Mama was working on three new dresses from the Vogue pattern book—madras was the thing and for the first time, all I could think about was how I looked. Judy was coming around more often, too, which I attributed to my makeover attempt. It was amazing what new clothes and a little lipstick could do for my self-esteem, which Judy previously had taken pleasure in blitzing weekly. It was the last Friday in September and I hadn't spoken to her at school that day except for a quick hello at lunch, but there she was standing at my door after school.

"Hey. Come in." Judy took several steps inside and quietly stood there as if waiting for something to happen. "Uh, did we make plans that I forgot about?" I asked.

"Oh, did you forget again?" she said in a mocking tone. "No, just kidding. I was bored and thought I'd walk over and see what you were up to."

"Oh, okay. Come in. Want something to eat?" Judy followed me into the kitchen and sat down at the little table at the end. She didn't answer but stared straight ahead as if she had no intention of responding. Her moodiness was normal, so I ignored it and went about my business. I looked in the fridge and saw a bowl of tuna salad, pulled it out and started making sandwiches.

"Oh, no thanks. I'm not hungry." It finally dawned on me that Judy hadn't come over to hang out. She had something on her mind and I was going to get it out of her. I poured myself a glass of milk, sat down across from her at the table and took a bite of my sandwich.

"So, how are things? You and Jimmy okay?" I started digging.

"Yeah, everything's good." That was all. Judy was quiet again as she stared at the loose thread she was twisting around her finger.

"Okay, so what's …." Before I could finish, Judy burst into tears. "Hey, what's the matter? You can tell me." I handed her a napkin and she pulled her sleeves back revealing the same ugly bruises up and down her arms that I had seen before. "Oh, my God, Judy. Not again. Your father." I took a deep breath. I had hoped for Judy's sake this business had stopped. "What are you going to do? This time you really need to tell someone."

"I already did. I didn't have any choice. When I dressed out for PE today, Coach Allison pulled me aside and asked me about them."

"So what did you tell her?" Judy was quiet again. "Did you tell her about your father? That this wasn't the first time?" Judy got up without looking at me, but I grabbed her shoulder and stopped her. "Judy, what's going on? You can't leave now. Tell me what she said." Judy sat down again and put her head in her arms and cried. She was talking between gulps and tears.

"Judy, I can't understand you. What did you tell Coach Allison?" It was then that Judy stopped crying. She shot straight up and yelled at me.

"I told her it was Reginald, okay! I told her your yard boy attacked me. Are you satisfied?" And then in a voice that sounded exhausted, she said, "I need to go home." I was so stunned I let her walk to the front door. I was standing in the kitchen when she returned and stood in the doorway. "You've got to back me up, Lizzie. If I tell the school it's my daddy, they'll tell him what I said, and then you know what he'll do to me? Can you imagine what he'll do to me? You've seen it. Please, Lizzie. Help me."

"I don't know, Judy. I just don't know."

"You don't know? You'd put *him* above *me*? A colored boy?" she cried. "I thought you were my friend! Well, I've told Coach it was Reginald Washington, and if you can't understand, then I'm sorry for you!" The front door slammed and I sat at the table with my half eaten sandwich. It was still uneaten when Mama walked in minutes later.

"You're home early. Was that Judy I saw walking down the street? Oh, you found a snack. Good. I'm starving. Had to grade papers during lunch. I'm thinking spaghetti tonight." Suddenly Mama frowned and walked over to see what I was eating. "Oh, dear, you're not having that tuna, are you? It's old, hon. I meant to throw it out last night."

"Ugh!" I got up and stomped over to the trash can, dumping my sandwich and yelling over my shoulder, "Then why didn't you do it?"

"Lizzie, come back in here." When I kept walking, she rushed over to me and gently grabbed my arm. "What is this really all about?" I pulled away from her but stopped at the door with my hands on either side of the frame to support my defeated self.

"Nothing. I'm just tired, that's all." Mama didn't respond, and I went to my room, shut the door, and spread out my disillusionment on the bed. What was it that made me so angry at the prospect of Judy publicly accusing Reggie of assault? Wasn't it that he had suffered enough? But what was he to me? And why couldn't I tell my mother about Judy's father and how his abuse left massive purple bruises on her body and soul? The one question

I didn't want to answer but knew I had to was why I was so weak that once again I could not stand up for him. After all that we had been through, Reggie was my friend. I cared about what happened to him. When I went back into the kitchen to humble myself, Mama was boiling spaghetti.

"Sorry for yelling." Mama was quiet. "Can we talk?" I said in a voice teetering on tears.

"Yes, if you can talk without yelling." It wasn't an icy response, but she didn't look up, just kept stirring the sauce she had started. I sat down at the table and looked at my hands, hoping to thaw out the air in the room with my contrition.

"What do you do when you know someone is lying and that lie is going to hurt someone else, really badly?" Mama looked at me and before she could speak I spurted out Judy's story as fast as I could, most of it anyway.

Mama was pretty sure Coach Allison wasn't going to call the authorities until she had spoken to Mr. Reynolds who was at a principal's conference until Monday. To begin with, she was more interested in what I knew about Judy's situation.

"Hold on. I can't imagine Reginald hurting anyone, but you're saying Judy admitted she was blaming Reginald to protect her father?"

"More or less. Judy's scared of what her father might do next, Mama. She told Coach Allison Reggie did it when she called her in her office and asked about them."

"Liz, Reginald's never hit you, has he?" Mama seemed more confused than ever.

"No! Reggie would never!"

"Okay, okay, just getting the facts straight. Is there anything else you're not telling me?" I had promised Judy I would keep her secret, all our secrets, and now Mama was asking me to snitch. It's odd how the truth keeps rearing its head when things seem to be going along just fine. This was how it was to be with Judy. I had to give a report on spiders in science once, but Judy, who went before me, made the class laugh so hard I got hiccups that wouldn't go away. I had practiced my report the night before, terrified of speaking in public, but I had memorized most of it. When my turn came, I hiccupped right through the speech and into the next class. I paid for it, though, when the teacher thought I was simply trying to be as funny as Judy had been, and gave me a C on the project. Judy was a millstone that I agreed to carry, to weigh me down and even crush me at times. If only we could have kept her well guarded secret a while longer. Beating your daughter black and blue could have easily remained a private affair in Carlton, the harsh reality remaining underground indefinitely. As appealing as gossip might be, it had consequences. Most people, however, were of the belief that what went on inside their own homes was strictly their business and no one else's. Even neighborhood rumors seemed to die down quickly, but pinning a crime on a black boy, and not just any black boy, changed everything.

"I promised Judy I wouldn't tell." I knew what was coming next.

"It's a funny thing about promises." Mama talked and stirred the spaghetti sauce as if explaining the how-to on a cooking show. "The harmless ones are meant to reveal a pleasant surprise, but what about the ones that harbor malice, the ones that stay hidden and betray not only the person keeping the secret but the ones who own it?" I waited for the tag line. "Reggie has been through enough. Why should he keep paying the price for the misdeeds of others?" When she put it like that, a heavy weight should have been lifted, but in truth, Judy's secret was only one of many, and I wasn't about to reveal the most heinous of secrets, graduation night.

"It was her father, Mama, never Reggie." Mama didn't seem surprised when I finally got the whole story out. She reached for a little address book in her purse and headed for the phone.

"Hello, Peggy? It's Louise Rowan." By the time Mama finished her conversation with Coach Allison, she had agreed to call Judy's mother and set up a meeting with the three of them the next morning. The following Monday, Judy went out of her way to ignore me, but Reggie was never informed about the bullet he had dodged. It was not until December that I found out from the school rumor mill that Judy's father had moved out.

A garden that complements a range of wildlife habitats introduces plants that serve as food sources, enhancing biodiversity that will boost the entire gardening experience.

The Art of Gardening by Emily Mayfield

CHAPTER 15

1967 | Judy didn't speak to me for months, and as we slowly drifted apart, life seemed to go on with no other consequence than empty days of loneliness. One weekend when the sunny chill in the air belied the arrival of spring, I discovered a warm but empty coffee pot, a quiet kitchen and Mama already in the garden. She had left the back door open, her way of inviting the morning air into the house. Standing several feet from the chinaberry tree in the far right corner of the yard, I found her looking up into the branches.

"Mornin'. What are you doing out here so early? You can't be planting. That's Reggie's job."

"Shhh…," she whispered. "Come over here. Quietly." The closer I got to her, the more I could hear first and then see that our old chinaberry tree was covered with yellow birds, chirping noisily.

"Wow! The tree's full of 'em. What are they?" I asked, surprised at the sudden appearance in our back yard of a mass of yellow birds I had never seen before.

"Goldfinches. Hundreds of goldfinches. They've just begun migrating and they've honored us with a visit," Mama softly murmured as if humming a lullaby. She put her arm around my shoulder and pulled me close as if we were experiencing a moment of pure love. I was caught up in her rapture.

"It's like a gift," I added. "Too bad they're goldfinches and not real gold."

"Elizabeth!" Mama whispered, jerking my shoulder toward her in gentle reprimand. "Not everything can be bought, my darling. And some things are more valuable than gold."

"Like what?" I laughed, finally old enough to enjoy the fundamental benefits of consumerism and the money it took to engage in it. I soon realized the birds weren't bothered by us and couldn't have cared less that we were disturbing their reverie.

"Like poetry—Yeats, Wordsworth, Dylan Thomas. Like having people in your life who care about you. Friends. Reginald."

"Reggie? What does he have to do with this?" Mama had casually slipped him in, but I knew what she meant. Although I had never acknowledged it, we were both indebted to him. My conflicted loyalty and complicated feelings about him simply wouldn't let me admit it out loud.

Mama had arranged for Reggie to continue yard work every day, and he became a fixture, not that I took his presence for granted, but there was an ease in the way we began to communicate. Because I had decided to try out for the school play and had subsequently been given the part, however, I rarely paid much attention to him or he to me, or so I thought.

Mr. Gordon had selected Inge's *The Dark at the Top of the Stairs* as the high school's first spring production. He must have liked my audition well enough to give me the part of Flirt Conroy because several girls had tried out specifically hoping to get that role, but here I was with it, script in hand night and day memorizing her lines. I had discovered that acting and public speaking were entirely different endeavors. With acting, I could be someone else, so no matter what people thought of me, I wasn't Lizzie Rowan up there speaking, leaving a vulnerable part of myself to criticism.

Flirt Conroy was, though, but she wasn't real so it didn't matter. I was never going to be a public speaker. Too dangerous. But I could act. When rehearsals finally began, the crew and cast met together in the auditorium to listen to Mr. Gordon lay out the schedule. I looked around to see who would be in the same space for the next six weeks, and in the very back row sat Judy and Jimmy, obviously part of the crew since the cast had been announced the week before. I wondered how long it would be before Judy and I were friends again. As it turned out, they were both working props, which meant I would eventually bump in to them, and I did. I was gathering up my books to go home when I heard my name.

"Lizzie, wait up!" I turned around to see Judy running after me. "Hey. I just wanted to tell you how good you are as Flirt. Never would have imagined you would want to play a role like that," she snickered. "She's so sassy! Total opposite of you. Are you walking home? Jimmy and I are going to stop and get a cherry coke if you wanna go with us."

"No, thanks. I still have some homework to finish. I'm glad you're doing props. Never would have thought you were interested in theatre. All those fruitcakes, you know." Her smile disappeared upon hearing my artful one-upmanship, but she quickly regained her composure. My response time to Judy wasn't perfect but it was slowly improving.

"Well, you never know. I'm full of surprises. Besides, it was really Jimmy's idea. I'm just going along with it." She smiled and walked back to Jimmy who was waiting for her. The weeks flew by and the production was going well, light crew and prop people working in harmony. That afternoon we had our first dress rehearsal for the matinee the next day.

Mama was in the kitchen finishing dinner when I opened the front door, exhausted and in need of comfort food.

"Liz, honey, come in here and get your snack while I talk to you." Now that was a suggestion I was happy to hear.

"What's on your mind, Mama?"

"I need to take tomorrow off, so I've told Mr. Reynolds I'll need a sub. I can drive you to school if you don't want to walk, but I need to take Reginald to the Social Security office and it might take a while."

"Why? Why does he need to go there? Can't he take the bus?" I said as I scooted over beside her to reach for the peanut butter.

"Mrs. Washington and her grown daughter moved to Los Angeles two weeks ago, and in the middle of the night apparently, and had Reginald's benefits moved to their new address. Reginald said he told them clearly he didn't want to move with them, but they changed the address anyway. I'm going with him to the Social Security office to see if we can get the problem sorted out."

"Reggie gets Social Security benefits? What exactly is that and why?"

"Do you remember when Reginald was in the hospital after the accident?"

"It wasn't an accident."

"Well, at the time he was diagnosed with seizures, not epilepsy, but seizures that couldn't be explained by the doctor. "

"You mean seizures from being beaten and left for dead?" I snarled.

"Let it go, Lizzie. What happened to Reginald was unfortunate, but he's made the best of it. Some things in life can't be changed overnight. Anyway, his situation is a bit more complicated than that, and he needs those benefits to get back on his feet. He lost his scholarships but that's no longer an issue. He needs money to live. I can't pay him enough for his work in the garden, at least not enough to get by. Anyway, I just wanted you to know where I'd be tomorrow." I shrugged and started to walk to the living room and plop my weary self down in front of the television when I suddenly remembered the matinee.

"Wait a minute. Does that mean you're not coming to see me in the play tomorrow?"

"No. Lizzie, I'm sorry, honey. Reggie really needs my help. He just can't make it without this income. I'm sure you can understand." I should have been able to understand but I didn't, not then. It would be years before

I appreciated the other complications in Reggie's life. But for now she was giving her time to Reggie instead of me and it wasn't fair. I needed her, too, but her consideration of Reggie came first and I didn't like it one bit.

The play was a success and Mama did come to see it that opening night. Friends streamed backstage to congratulate the cast and, feeling like a star, I was on top of the world. The stage and wings, spilling out into the hall, were packed body to body with students and family members, and it was difficult to move much less find people. I recognized one voice, however, amidst the happy confusion. It was Judy's but she wasn't talking directly to me.

"Oh, Lizzie? Actually, we're not friends anymore." Judy was right behind me gossiping with several girls in our class. "Her situation at home is kind of weird," she continued. "I mean, that mother of hers—you know the senior English teacher—she's got something unnatural going on with...." She lowered her voice but I could still hear her. "....that nigger who works for her. I don't want any part of that. I'm afraid to go to her house now." When I turned around and looked at her, she stared straight at me to see if I had heard, then smugly glowered with an about-face toward her friends. I found Mama in the crowd after changing out of my costume and asked if we could go; I said I had a headache. On the way home Mama's abundant praise for my performance satiated my wounded ego and I squeezed her hand, hiding the tears that she didn't need to know about. I showered and dressed for bed quickly, but Mama opened my door to tell me goodnight.

"Lizzie, you were wonderful tonight."

"You told me that twenty times, Mama. I'm really tired." I turned my back to her and mashed my face into the pillow wet with tears. She came to the bed and sat down.

"I'm sorry I didn't see your matinee. What would you have had me do, hon? Today Reggie needed me more. He has no one to help him. One day you'll understand it's not about loving one person over another." When I didn't answer her, she kissed the back of my head and said, "Night, sweetheart" and closed the door. My frustration wasn't about choices or favoring someone else or craving my mother's attention, although I saw the validity in everything she said. It was always about Reggie, my defiance toward him that seemed almost bellicose in its tenacity, yet I was drawn to him, this bewitching mousetrap of a man whose daily allure continued to ensnare me. I despised myself for it and longed to be free from it, yet I wasn't sure if that freedom was from Reggie or myself.

The careful gardener pays attention to weather and adapts the needs of the garden to the local climate, not only *making life easier for herself but also gaining an awareness of how to achieve success in the garden.*

The Art of Gardening by Emily Mayfield

CHAPTER 16

1967 | The pain of adolescence, a consequence of my naïve response to two lonely years of high school, was slowly sloughing away. Despite the protective shell I had formed around me, Judy's presence at school appeared to be linked in some way to every agonizing event, and I spent far too much time thinking about it as well as my inability to make friends easily. There didn't seem to be a replacement for Judy anywhere on the horizon. Every day Mama added another suggestion to a growing list of possible activities to keep me occupied. I reluctantly succumbed to the latest, the community stamp club. Other than needing one to mail a letter, I knew nothing special about postal stamps, ordinary or rare, but the stamp club met every other Saturday, and I decided it was far better than waiting for someone to call me with plans. In truth, that was never going to happen. Mr. Hammond, the freshman civics teacher, sponsored the stamp club, and his handsome face might have been another somewhat motivating factor. I was now fifteen without a clue about what to do with my life. With excitement on the day of its organization, Mama woke me up early, relieved to see me engaged in something besides holing myself up in my room reading or anesthetizing myself with Saturday morning cartoons. She hurried me out the door and drove us across town to the school board office where the meeting was to be held. This edifice of education, a large faded red brick building with tall windows on all four sides, had ripened to an anachronism in a town that had watched its boundaries move west over time. The building that had long been the dominion of school board activities for over a hundred years now maintained its rigid place right on the edge of what was now considered colored town, and one street over not one white person lived or shopped or carried on with the necessities of daily life.

Mama said she could drop me off, did I mind walking home? She would be at the typing teacher Mrs. Turner's baby shower. She pointed out the directions as she drove, and I reassured her it wouldn't be a problem. I often walked to the downtown library, which was about the same distance. When we arrived, we said our goodbyes and I made my way down the sidewalk. A handwritten poster right inside the door led potential stamp club members to the first conference room at the end of the hall where Mr. Hammond stood at a table just inside the door greeting students who were arriving. I smiled shyly at him, signed my name on the piece of paper, and took a seat in an empty row of chairs. At exactly ten o'clock, Mr. Hammond turned on his slide projector and gave a brief history of stamps. I must admit, I have always held a fascination for history—what little I knew, but after twenty minutes of the history of stamps, I couldn't stand it anymore. Instead of listening to his talk, I passed the time by looking around the audience, seven potential members, all boys, trying to decide which one I would connect with, knowing full well I wouldn't be friends with any of them. I was still sitting on a row with no other students, so it was easy to slip out, leaning heavily on the justification that life was too short to be bored or alone and wondering if Mama would buy that excuse.

Stepping out into the cool November day, I suddenly felt the torrential downpour of worthlessness. In a moment of stark recognition, I now believed I was never going to fit in anywhere. With blind frenzy, urgently needing the momentum for flight, I started walking, and it was not until I looked up from the sidewalk at my surroundings that I realized I was lost with no recall of where I had been or how long I had been walking. I didn't recognize anything—buildings, trees, any sort of landmark. Had I gone right or left? Did I turn the corner? How many corners? Why couldn't I remember Mama's directions in reverse, and why hadn't I paid better attention? The sun was almost directly overhead, which afforded no help. How long had I been traveling this way? I decided to stop and head in the opposite direction, but potential landmarks were as unfamiliar as before. One thing was certain. I was the only white person on the street. Benoit's Pharmacy stood at the next corner across the street where I could stop in and ask for help. A colored man in a white coat and glasses stood behind the pharmaceuticals counter at the back of the store, his kind face drawing me to him and building a sense of hope in my chances of getting directions home. I approached the counter with the confidence that he would be able to help, and not seeing any other customers at the back, I reassured myself that no one would take me for a silly white girl who couldn't find her way. When I reached the counter, however, a tall lean black man was kneeling on the floor several feet away looking at Band-Aids. I knew before he saw me that it was Reggie.

"Yes, ma'am. May I help you?" said the man in the white coat.

"Uh….Yes, sir. I, uh, was looking for bandages. And can you tell me how to get to Oak Street?" I felt stupid adding the directions part and I immediately stared at my feet, more concerned about what Reggie might think than the pharmacist I had just asked for help.

"Well, let's see now. Bandages are right down there to your left, and yes, I can give you directions to Oak Street." He began waving his arms in the air as he pointed the way home. "I believe if you'll walk left as you leave the store, then turn right at the corner and left again after the second block, then walk straight ahead, you'll hit Bentner Avenue. From there just go straight ahead and Oak Street will the second one after the park."

I watched his hands dancing about as he explained how I might find the street I was looking for, but watching him was such a distraction that it kept me from listening. He lost me completely after the first turn, but I thanked him and moved over to the bandages.

"Count to ten and meet me outside. Count slowly," Reggie whispered, and he got up and left. I counted to ten before heading for the door, hoping Reggie indeed was waiting to guide me home, but he wasn't there. I looked to the right and left. I couldn't find him until I walked to the corner and in the distance, turning left at the next corner, I saw him walking slowly, glancing once over his shoulder at me. He was leading me home. It occurred to me after I began following him that he didn't want to be seen with me, but that was okay. Reggie understood how to live in a world of which I had almost no knowledge, intuitive or learned, but no matter, I was grateful for his help. Twenty minutes later he was on Bentner Avenue, and I expected him to head back to his own house, but he didn't. He walked me all the way home.

We didn't talk that day. He headed for the garden where I thought he had some work to do, but when I went outside to thank him, he was gone. I went to my room and lay on the bed, thinking about the seemingly coincidental turn of events, not just the morning's walk home but every episode in the adventures between us, from the moment I appeared backstage to work on props. The fact that this boy seemed to show up when I needed him was steadily making its way to my consciousness although it would take another decade for me to decipher its meaning.

By the time Mama's car pulled into the drive, I must have fallen asleep, and it was not until after six that she called me to supper.

"My goodness, hon. That stamp club meeting and the walk home must have been exhausting. Ready for supper? I made a roast." Mama headed back to the kitchen and began setting the little corner table, and I followed her.

"I didn't stay. And I got lost coming home. Reggie showed me the way back."

"Oh? You saw Reggie?"

"Yeah. He just happened to be at the drug store near the School Board Office." Mama smiled and put slices of roast beef, carrots and potatoes on my plate. "I'd probably still be on the road walking to Timbuktu if he hadn't been there when I needed him. No peas, please."

"Milk?"

Mama put a big spoonful of peas on my plate and poured me a glass of milk. "He does seem to have that uncanny ability to know things, doesn't he. So I assume stamp club is a no-go? What's next on your list?"

"I don't know, Mama, and I don't want to think about it, much less talk about it tonight." We sat down to supper and didn't mention Reggie again, but I couldn't get the image of him out of my head. That night I tried reading to help me get to sleep, but I could see him in the distance leading me home in every other sentence I tried to read. When I woke up the next morning the book was nestled under my arm, and Reggie was still on my mind.

A clever plan for color in your garden is essential for mood and atmosphere. Deep bright colors create excitement, while soft, pastel colors suggest tranquility.

The Art of Gardening by Emily Mayfield

CHAPTER 17

1976 | As time passes in a beach town, only fashion seems to change, and not even that is worth noting it's so minor. The year was 1976 but it could have been twenty years earlier. Once again it was summer, and Galveston's same old hot, noisy, crowded beaches gave me a reason to stay inside. Mary had lived on the Texas coast since 1946 and had no intention of ever succumbing to cold weather again. Memories of winters on the Irish Sea still made her shiver, whereas wintertime in Galveston lasted three months and really only one month hastened her into a heavy coat. She loved the warmth of summer and pottered around in the garden as often as she could, leaving the windows of her house open to the warm sea air. By June the jasmine's heavy white blossoms no longer perfumed the arc of the arbor leading to her garden, but her beds were adorned with an array of colorful roses and zinnias in shades of deep purples, yellows, pinks and reds. On her fire bush bright red blossoms were ablaze. One late afternoon Mary invited me to tea on the patio in full view of the garden. The warm air was more uncomfortable than she would admit, but that day she was determined to serve tea and conversation on the patio.

"Mary, you've always loved music, right?"

"Ah, yes, love. Always have. It's been my life these many years."

"Well, a man came into the shop this morning and asked if he could put up a sign in our window, an advertisement for a musical. Seems they're bringing the road show of *Camelot* to The Grand. I thought you might like to go. My treat, of course. What do you say?" When I first saw the poster announcing the production of *Camelot*, something inside my stomach did flips, every part of my body reacting badly to memories of a day long ago. But I relished taking her to the theatre, my dear friend Mary, whose love of music never failed to leave me gratified and free from pain, even for a moment. I could get past the memories if Mary were sitting next to me.

"That would be lovely, pet. I would very much like to do that. I've never been to The Grand. My Carl never liked plays and musicals, but.... yes, I would like that. Thank you, Lizzie." I stood up and began to gather up the tea things, so pleased with our plans for the musical. At eye level a tiny greenish bird hovered over the fire bush.

"Oh, Mary! Look! There's a hummingbird right behind you." Mary turned around slowly.

"First one this year, I do believe," she whispered.

"'...and the flight of it so fast you can't see it and you know it's there only by the faint whir of its wings.'"

"What's that, pet?"

"Just a poem, one of Mama's favorites. It's about love."

"Aye, it would be, wouldn't it." I agreed and we moved to the cool air of her kitchen.

Mary's wardrobe had changed since her days in England. I had seen old photographs of her singing in the band, lovely pictures of her in long satin dresses and elbow length gloves. Now men's trousers and loose fitting shirts, suitable for gardening, comprised her attire, but when she opened the door that evening, I was certain the ghosts of her past still lingered in her closet. She was lovely in her creamy silk shirtwaist, the full skirt flowing around her calves that stretched her legs into a pair of heels. Pearl earbobs peeked out from little gray wisps of hair neatly tucked in a bun. The effect was stunning, a prodigiously marvelous change, and a broad grin spread over my face.

"Mary! You look fantastic. You're obviously ready to go. I look shabby compared to your elegance. Hope you don't mind being seen with me," I laughed. My surprise must have embarrassed her a little. She said she'd check the back door and get her bag. I followed her down the stairs and we drove to the theatre with intermittent small talk, happy to get out and enjoy an evening of music.

I had been able to purchase seats close to the front and the score was as beautiful as I had remembered, haunting and soul wrenching for me but divinely bewitching for Mary, the one outcome I desired for the woman who had done so much for me. Like the crescendo of *Camelot's* finale, Arthur took the stage heartsick but not broken, and my spirits sank, too, as the play reawakened another drama—Tom and Reggie and a badly behaved teenage girl whose retribution backfired, the way it usually does with ill-conceived actions. I could still feel the pang of embarrassment, and yet Reggie had shown up to repair the damage.

Mary chattered away as we walked to the car until her unrequited exuberance over the musical needed an explanation.

"Didn't you like the play? You're very quiet," she said.

"It was wonderful. It's just that going to the theatre after several years has brought back some memories that I wanted to forget."

"Aye, the past can dredge up painful moments but joyful ones, too," she said. "Is this one about your Reggie?"

"My Reggie?" I laughed. "My Reggie. Well, he was never my Reggie, but yes, I guess I was thinking of him. Something happened when I was in high school, Mary. I was in the chorus of *Camelot*."

"Were you now!"

"Yes, and during production I didn't behave well, in the end, and I guess I've never gotten over it."

"Ah, Lizzie. Whatever happened, make peace with it, pet. If I tormented myself over all the mistakes I've made in life, I'd never get out of bed in the morning. Don't hold on to it. Love the girl you are now." Mary was right. I knew she was right, but Reggie's friendship had been far-reaching, paramount to my survival in his ponderous way of accepting my faults, and there were many. He had stepped in and filled the gap for the man who left so early in my life. Not like a father. Something deeper. Long after he was gone, I thought how easy it was to love a person who made you love yourself just by standing in his light.

I walked Mary up the stairs.

"Come in for a glass of sherry." I declined, saying I would see her tomorrow. She thanked me for the evening and I went downstairs, falling into bed without washing up. I turned out the light, begging for sleep to rescue me, but floating downward, haunting and distant, a tune drifted from Mary's piano and then I heard her lovely voice. "I'll be seeing you in all the old familiar places…. that this heart of mine embraces all day through…." I closed my eyes and listened to the words. Was Mary sending me a message?

By the end of June Mimi and Jack surprised everyone with the announcement of a baby, a late in life surprise for a couple that after twelve years had completely given up trying to have another one after Janie. Mary chalked it up to a miracle and hurried off to church to light a candle. Jack and Mimi were delighted, Mimi was now grateful not to have another shop to worry about with a baby on the way, and Janie was happy albeit uncertain of her new status in the family. This new family member was expected to arrive some time the following January, but for now another unexpected arrival—Mary's son Charlie, added to her delirium, her fervor creating a celebratory air.

Charlie planned to arrive late in the afternoon at Hobby Airport in Houston, so Jack volunteered to fight the traffic and transport him to Mary's where the family was gathering for a welcoming party. I was invited, although I felt slightly out of place. Mary simply ignored my reticence and put me to work in the kitchen.

Charlie had a wife and two young sons back in Arkansas, but they didn't accompany him as his primary reason for traveling to Texas was business. Seeing his mother and sister was little more than a convenient second thought. Nevertheless, Mary was happy to see him and made plans for the family to visit Carl's grave before anyone suggested anything else. She had no objections to other plans, but after all, she said, it had been ten years since they had laid him to rest and proper homage on this anniversary must be paid. Mary asked me to help choose flowers from her garden.

The zinnias were gigantic and plentiful in a wide array of colors, and we prepared a lovely bouquet. Charlie went to the local florist and purchased his, but not without a jab at Mary's homegrown ones. I decided I didn't much care for Charlie after that, but I would never have said so. I was relieved that no one asked me to go with them to the cemetery. Charlie didn't stay long as he said he was already running behind schedule for his business trip to Austin. Carl was still on Mary's mind, however, and I suggested we plant a herb garden in his memory. She loved the idea, and that night we planned what to include and where with the help of a book on herbs that I had found in the book stall near Mimi's. Mary was also interested in their healing properties and I added that the book even explained the symbolism of each one. We finished the garden with the herbs we purchased in Houston several days later, and Mary immediately began using them in her kitchen. I was invited to dinner on Saturday. The scent of rosemary chicken permeated her house and even beyond. I could smell this culinary masterpiece from downstairs, and I soon made my way up to her kitchen.

"Rosemary."

"Right you are. Rosemary for remembrance."

"Your Carl would have approved."

"Yes, he loved roast chicken and never let me forget. Asked for it every Sunday."

I savored Mary's quick Irish wit that night as much as her roast chicken. Her clever quips and love of family complemented the spirit that prevailed in her. A herb garden would add to this bountiful life, replete with symbols of remembrance and hope for the future.

By the end of June I was riding my bike three or four miles a day on the beachfront drive, having given up running in sweltering heat. The sandy beaches were packed with tourists and colorful umbrellas and occasional joggers braving the heat. I circled back around to return to my street when I saw a young woman slip off the curb and tumble onto the walkway. She was grabbing her ankle and moaning when I cycled up to her.

"Hey, are you okay? Can I offer you a hand? Do you think you sprained your ankle?"

"I'm not sure. All I know is it hurts like hell! Can't believe I was so clumsy."

"Look, why don't you let me give you a lift on my bike, at least across the street to that gift shop. Over there, Mimi's," I pointed. "I work there and you can use the phone."

"Wouldn't do any good. I have no idea who to call. I don't have any family here." I thought a minute before plunging in with my offer.

"I have a car and I know a good doctor. Will you let me help? I'm Lizzie Rowan."

She let me pull her up, and I helped her onto my bicycle and walked it across the street. She introduced herself as Anne Marie Blandford and said she had just finished her first year as a third grade teacher at the local elementary school. That was the extent of our conversation when disembarking from my bicycle became too painful to talk. Mimi was minding the store that morning, waiting for me to take my shift, but when she saw us, she ran out the front and helped Anne Marie inside.

"I need to get my car, Mimi. This is Anne Marie. She's sprained her ankle." The words spewed out like bullets. "Do you think you could call Dr. Bonin and tell the nurse we're on our way?" I didn't wait for an answer, just ran out the door and cycled down the street three blocks to Mary's. By the time I got back, Mimi had Anne Marie at the curb waiting for me.

"Don't worry about your shift, Lizzie. I've got it. Just take care of Anne Marie."

Three hours later—Dr. Bonin had to fit us in after his other patients, Anne Marie and I were on our way to her apartment.

"Look, Lizzie, I can't thank you enough for what you did for me. I'm not sure what I would have done if you hadn't come along—my Good Samaritan. Let me at least buy you lunch."

"I'll take you up on that offer! I'm starving. And Mimi said I don't have to come in this afternoon. So, I'm with you all the way. What are you hungry for?" Anne Marie said she never passed up seafood, so we stopped at a little café down from Mimi's that served the best shrimp and oyster poboys on the island. I knew we would be instant friends. She hated oysters as much as I did.

The price the gardener pays for the joy of watching butterflies emerge is the tolerance of the caterpillars' plant diet. Invest in caterpillar-food plants that extend a welcome to this wildlife addition to your garden, and accept the destruction of your plant in exchange for the miraculous metamorphosis of these winged creatures.

The Art of Gardening by Emily Mayfield

CHAPTER 18

1968 | Reggie continued to be a regular feature in the garden, and although I spoke to him often our conversations had grown casual, distant at times as we took each other's presence for granted. Rocky was a full-blown adult squirrel and, as far as I could tell, still lived in the oak in the back yard. I often saw Reggie talking to him, offering him pecans from his pockets, but he never invited me to join his secret society of man and beast. Our inconstant friendship was bridled by the waning of emotions one day and the burgeoning increase the next. It sometimes drove me mad. I was sixteen now, full of inconsistent hormones that led to mood swings only a mother could tolerate. It was in this unfortunate state that I met Tom, a college boy who worked lights for the Community Center play that I was in. I had agreed to be in the chorus of their production of *Camelot* after Mr. Gordon gave the director my name. Tom had joined the cast and crew at the café next door for hamburgers the first week of rehearsals, and I was smitten. I subsequently saw him often and not just at rehearsals. If some-one had a party, it was Tom who escorted me, and he came to the house every weekend to have dinner and watch television, under Mama's unso-licited supervision. I started to introduce Tom to Reggie one evening, but he kept digging in the dirt as if he didn't have time for me. I knew he was watching us every time Tom came over. I told myself Reggie had nothing to do with Tom. Why should I care if Reggie approved or not? And so my relationship with Tom took off at a dizzying speed, too hasty for my own good, and for the duration of the play everyone knew we were an item. One night right after a rehearsal, he disappeared, leaving me perplexed since he was my ride home. As Benny, Tom's partner in the light booth, was walking to his car, I called out to him.

"Hey, Benny. Have you seen Tom?"

"Yeah, he just left. Why? Did he forget to put something up?"

"No, but he always gives me a ride home. Did he really just leave?" Benny slowly closed the car door and started walking over to me. He had that look on his face that betrayed bad news.

"Don't worry. I'll give you a ride." And then he stopped abruptly and looked at me. "Uh, listen, Lizzie. Don't tell him I told you, but he left with Laura."

"Laura? The Laura in the chorus? Why? He didn't tell me anything about that."

"No, he wouldn't, if you know what I mean." I actually didn't know what he meant at first, and I certainly wasn't ready to drop it. And why would he tell me this?

"I'm afraid I don't know what you mean, Benny. Just spit it out. Please."

"Oh, come on. You're old enough to know what a guy wants with a girl like Laura. Don't be naïve, Lizzie. Get in the car and I'll drive you home."

"A girl like Laura? What's wrong with Laura? What do you mean? She's my friend."

"Your friend, huh? Not any more, I guess. Come on."

And then it hit me. Tom had ditched me for a night with Laura and obviously Laura had agreed. And was it going to be just one night? That old feeling of betrayal was creeping in again. Benny drove me home. I didn't cry once until I walked through the door and vowed I'd never trust a boy again. Then the floodgates opened. When I finally stopped crying, I was angry, so angry I threw a stack of books across the room one by one, crashing against the wall in one miserable thud after another. When Mama pushed open the door, more than a dozen books were strewn across the floor, blocking the doorway, some open and some upended. I feigned sleep to avoid an explanation. She never mentioned it, and I surmised she chalked it up to my new stage of adolescent moodiness. The next day ignoring Tom during the production wasn't difficult, and I found satisfaction at least in that. I never wanted to see him again.

Saturday morning had finally arrived with my usual routine intact, sitting in the swing and basically thinking about the week that had just transpired. It wasn't Reggie's day to work in the garden but there he was, darting around the driveway to the back yard as if in a hurry.

"What are you doing here?" I said surprised to see him.

"I'm not staying long. Just wanted to check on the butterflies. They should be coming out soon." He kept walking toward the back of the summer house where the butterfly weed had been stripped of its leaves by a number of caterpillars. I was glad to see him again, and Reggie soon called me to come over and look. I ran to the back where the milkweed grew.

"Just in time. Look! This one's already started coming out of its chrysalis." Reggie's voice overflowed with energetic anticipation. We stood there and watched as the black legs stretched and turned as it attempted to squeeze itself out its thin translucent shell, the bottom of which had ripped open. But the butterfly wasn't coming out. It was struggling, and after almost twenty minutes it had made no more progress than before. Impatient with the monarch and Reggie, too, and unable to stand there and watch it a minute longer, I told Reggie to call me when something happened. I went inside the house, but ten minutes later curiosity drove me to the back door again. Reggie hadn't called me yet and he was leaving.

"Well, did it come out? You were supposed to come get me."

"No," was his only response, and he kept walking to his truck. I ran out to look for myself. The butterfly was partially hanging from its chrysalis, the intricate wings still folded firmly inside its tomb, but the writhing had stopped. It wasn't going to come out, ever. Something had gone wrong. It had struggled for its life before it gave up, too exhausted to go on perhaps, or was it nature's way of eliminating what was imperfect to begin with? The injustice of working so hard for nothing overwhelmed me, and I stood frozen, unable to take it all in. I don't remember how long I stayed there feeling helpless and incomprehensibly alone, but the next thing I knew I was in my bed cradled in the sublime escape of sleep.

Not long after the disappointment of the chrysalis, when the theatre department's performances had closed and my stage gig came to an end, I went back to sitting in the swing, working on a rapidly melting cherry Popsicle. Tom, who was becoming a bittersweet memory, appeared in the drive around the side of the house as if nothing had happened and sauntered up to me, grinning as if I would be glad to see him. I threw the remainder of my Popsicle in the bushes and wiped my mouth, hoping he wouldn't notice my red tongue.

"Hey, Lizzie," he crooned, sitting down next to me. I was silent for a minute, thinking of a response that would be appropriately stern.

Hey, Lizzie? Are you serious, I thought. What I wanted to say was, *How could you do this to me? I thought you liked me.* I wasn't in the habit of using profanities, but I thought of a few choice words I could have thrown in his face. But if I did, I'd feel worse. I wanted him to be sorry for the humiliation he had put me through but more than that, I wanted him to like me again. And he had shown up after all, hadn't he?

"Aw, come on, Lizzie, you're not still mad, are you? Look, it didn't mean anything. I just gave her a ride." He conveniently left out the part where he had taken Laura home after a jaunt in the back seat of his car.

I had overheard his friends the next day at the theatre. Tom hadn't gone home until late that night. Pretending to be indifferent, I got up and walked behind the summer house to look at the butterfly weed. Six more chrysalises had already formed, so I bent down to look at them. Tom followed me.

"What're you lookin' at?" he said.

"Monarch butterflies will emerge soon. They're in the chrysalis stage. One tried to come out, but he didn't make it. But there's more, and I think they'll be okay." My matter of fact tone wasn't intended to put him off. I just didn't want to talk about what happened between Tom and Laura. And I might have been showing off.

"Oh, good for them." Tom got closer and soon his hands were around my waist and he was pulling me toward him, picking me up and pinning me against the back wall of the summer house. "You're the one I want, and you want me, too, don't you." Fortunately no one could see us, but then he pushed me so hard against the wall that I gasped. He was like a wild man, kissing me hard and unbuttoning my blouse, until in his impatience, he simply ripped my shirt open the rest of the way. Several buttons went flying across the grass. He pulled my bra down and grabbed my breast as his wet mouth moved across my neck and chest.

"Stop! What are you doing? Let me go!" I tried to keep my voice down as I struggled to push him away.

"You don't really want me to do that, do you." By the time we were on the ground and the weight of Tom's body was bearing down on me, I heard movement, like the shuffling of tools in the summer house. Of all the emotions stirring in my head, anger should have had the right of way, but I was filled with fear. I couldn't let Mama see me like this. I wasn't yelling, but Tom still held his hand over my mouth. The noise stopped yet my heart was pounding. Within seconds, Tom heard someone coming and let me get up. I turned around and pretended to look for caterpillars while I tried my best to pull myself together. But it wasn't Mama who came around the corner and stopped right in front of us. It was Reggie.

"Lizzie, your mama needs you. She sent me out here to tell you to come in," he said as quietly and unintimidating as a man could be with a shovel in his hand. He walked away as quickly as he had appeared. Tom, startled at the paralyzing sight of Reggie, didn't budge, but before he left he leaned toward me and whispered, "We're not done yet." I got myself sorted out, pulled my buttonless shirt together, and waited until I thought Tom was gone before returning to the house.

"You all right?" Reggie, standing in the doorway of the summer house, startled me. Tom was gone, but I averted my eyes as I moved quickly to the back door.

"Yes," I hissed and hurried to the house, but I could hear Reggie say, "You deserve better, Lizzie." I walked into the house to find it empty. Mama had not returned from school yet. Reggie was still working in the garden when she found him weeding a bed of irises. A few minutes later she came in and called me to the kitchen.

"So Tom came over this afternoon? Hon, you know my rule about having boys over when I'm not home."

"Reggie told you? He told you? What makes him think he's my keeper!" I was ready to explode, throw something at Reggie and hurt him. He had rescued me from Tom, but that information was meant to be our secret, every part of it. I ran to my room and slammed the door. Mama let me stay there until supper was ready, and when I did come out we ate together in silence. I couldn't get rid of the anger. Throughout the next day it grew uncontrollably like a malignancy, my fury soon becoming a maelstrom I would later regret. I picked up the pruning shears on the shelf just inside the garden house and aimed them at every chrysalis I could see. When all six of them had been snipped and lay vanquished on the ground, I dropped the shears in the dirt and ran into the house, my anger unabated.

It didn't take long for Reggie to see what had happened or to know exactly who had done it. His disappointment gave him the courage to knock on our back door and ask to see me. He didn't wait for me to open the door but spoke directly through the screen.

"What did you do?" he said. Reggie's voice, heavy with the fatigue of anguish, pronounced my sentence in that one question, and I defended my guilt. I stayed behind the screen door as if to protect myself from his wrath.

"What does it look like? I cut them down, every last one." Reggie shook his head. "They're just insects, Reggie, for God's sake. What difference does it make?"

"Girl, you have got some growin' up to do."

"Oh, really. Well, what gives you the right to tell my mother anything about what I do? Who said you could meddle in my business?"

Reggie stepped closer to the door and lowered his voice. "He's scum, Lizzie. And he'll end up hurting you."

"And what do you care whether I grow up or not!" I knew what Tom had done was wrong, but I would never admit it, especially not to Reggie.

"They might be on the ground, Lizzie, but they can still come out."

"So? Who cares?" He walked away and I slammed the door. Once again there I was, running inside and throwing myself on the bed for another cry to wash away the guilt and shame that would continue to exhaust my relationship with him. No doubt Mama had heard us but she left me alone. I tried to think of what she might have said. *The paths we take are invariably full of uncertainty. The one thing we do know is that we're going to make mistakes all along the way.* Right. Blah, blah, blah. Forever the philosopher, she was, and right then I hated her for it. Then I could hear her say, *Sometimes we hurt the people we love, but sometimes we get it right.* Was I even aware of what I was doing and how I was hurting people and why? The fact was, I wanted other people to feel the pain that was forced on me, yet I knew that I often brought it on myself. I was the cause and I had to fix it. *Stop feeling sorry for yourself and do the right thing.*

At the time I couldn't recognize the right thing. Everything I did seemed to turn out bad for someone—Reggie, Mama, Judy, Tom, myself. When I asked Mama, she would be quiet for a moment, and then she would say that she couldn't answer that question, no one could. I wanted to scream. "I don't know enough! I don't know how to live in this world. I'm drowning here, Mama, I'm drowning." But no one came to put her arms around me and pull me out of the mire. The next morning I confessed to Mama what I had done to the chrysalises.

"So that's what he was doing with my tape in the garden this morning. He was here earlier—came to the back door as I was pouring my coffee. Don't worry. I guess he was out there taping them to the stalks or the side of the garden house. You want to tell me what happened?"

"I was angry. Why did he have to show me that poor butterfly that was dying inside the chrysalis? That was horrible, Mama. Horrible. And then, I know I was wrong but he absolutely had no right to tell you about Tom. So I cut them down. I was so angry. I didn't know what else to do."

"Yes, well, Tom is welcome here, only when I'm home. But I'm sure Reggie didn't plan to show you the poor butterfly struggling and dying. He has no control over that. In fact, he probably was just as surprised and sad as you were. It's nature's way. He's a good man, Liz, ahead of his time and right now few people can appreciate what he's been through. Struggling isn't new to him."

"Is that why you help him?"

"Don't you think he's worth helping?" I knew he was but I didn't answer her. "The butterflies will be all right. Reggie's seen to it."

"Yeah, that's what he told me. No matter what I did to them, he said they could still come out." We didn't discuss Tom after that. It was just as well. I never saw him again.

A number of trees, shrubs and vines can be propagated with root cuttings. Although they are slow to develop, by preparing the parent plant ahead of time, you can reestablish the plant with plenty of roots ready for the new growing season.

The Art of Gardening by Emily Mayfield

CHAPTER 19

1977 | Almost no one buys beach souvenirs or gifts of any kind in January, especially after Christmas. With few customers walking through the door, Mimi put me to work dusting and polishing the old furniture in the back of the store again, the ones she referred to as antiques, with selling them an anticipated eventuality, so by the time I got home with orange chicken and fried rice take-out from the Chinese shop around the corner, all I wanted was a warm bed. Anne Marie was busy with lesson plans and getting nine year olds acclimated to her classroom again after the long Christmas break, so I mainly saw her on weekends. We had become good friends in the months following her accident, and since neither of us seemed to be occupied with a boyfriend, we kept each other company. I was completely inexperienced in the landscape of girl friends, but I was pretty sure that Anne Marie defined the virtues of a true and loyal friend.

When I opened the door, a blast of cold air greeted me instead. I checked the thermostat and ran upstairs.

"Mary, I think something's wrong with the heating system downstairs. Can you come and look at it?" It didn't take her long to discover the heater was indeed malfunctioning.

"It's freezing in here!"

"To be sure. You'll sleep in the spare room tonight, and I'll get someone out to look at it in the morning. Cuppa tea now." I grabbed what I needed for the next day and followed her upstairs, grateful once again for my guardian angel. That night we sat in front of the television, I with my Chinese dinner and Mary with her soup and sandwich. The newest member of the family, a little girl christened Mary Elizabeth Morgan after Mimi's mother, had arrived the first week of January. Mary made sure to let everyone know she would be preoccupied with a new television series called *Roots* every night that week. I didn't know much about it, but Mary, who rarely watched television, had read the book and felt it worthy of a week's investment of her evenings. I asked what it was about and she simply said, "Wait and see." I saw. In the evolution of slavery, African men and boys captured by slave traders were whipped and shackled and chained in the ship's hold, suffocating with heat and filth, morality and regard for life postponed by investors in human capital anxious to be rid of their cargo. Halfway through the second episode, I got up to get a glass of water. I leaned against the kitchen sink, wondering if I would be sick. A dark cloud of sadness had settled over me and I wanted to cry. Mary came to the doorway when I didn't return. "Everything all right?" I blew my nose and said I was fine, but Mary reached out and put her hand on my shoulder. "You'll have to put a brave face on it, pet. It isn't easy watching the cold-blooded brutality we give to each other, but we can turn the telly off if you like." Mary had been waiting to see this program, and no matter how disturbed I might be, I reassured her that I needed to watch it, had spent too many years in the dark, and we sat down again and finished the episode.

When it was over, neither of us said anything, but after a minute without any prompting she proclaimed, "Well, there it is, man's inhumanity to man. The poets had it right, you know. Bobby Burns, bless him. "Man's inhumanity to man makes countless thousands mourn."

"My mother was an English teacher, Mary, and that phrase—man's inhumanity to man, popped up quite often in literature."

"Oh, there was plenty of injustice where I come from, pet, don't you worry. Times were hard especially during the rebellion. When I was just a wee girl, the English believed that it was God's judgment that sent the potato famine to Ireland, to teach us a lesson they said, but it started long before that."

"What lesson?"

"For simply being Irish, I suppose. You know, sometimes feuds go on for centuries and no one can remember why. Maybe we complained too much? We Irish are known for our extremes. Jolly one minute, sad the next."

"Oh, you mean mothers grieving over sons and husbands lost at sea." I remembered being part of the crew for Synge's play. "Or Darby O'Gill and the little people." Hollywood, although it tried, was no match for the melancholy of Irish writers. Mary didn't comment and I suddenly regretted making such a foolish comparison when suffering, real not some theatrical version, had taken place.

"A man named Trevelyan—Sir Charles, as he was known, said the famine was an effective mechanism for reducing surplus population. Can you imagine."

"Mary, no! What kind of person would say such a thing?"

"Yes, shocking, isn't it, but 'tis true. Relationships between England and Ireland weren't good when I was a girl, and they got worse by the time I was fourteen. I met Michael Collins, the man himself, or so my mother said. I wasn't paying much attention. In a shop in Dublin, it was, with Mammy who was buying sausages, as I recall, and a man stepped back right on to my foot. He apologized and tossed me a coin from his pocket. After he walked out the shop, my mother bent over to me and whispered, "*That* was Michael Collins." When I looked back at him as he left, everyone else in the shop was looking at him, too. So I suppose it must have been."

"Who's Michael Collins," I asked.

"Ah, the most famous member of the Irish Republican Army, that's who. He was a hero to the Irish people. And God knows they needed a hero."

"Is he still? A hero?" I asked.

"Ah, no, he's gone now, but I suppose he is. He certainly was at the end of the rebellion."

"How did things end, I mean with the fighting?"

"Ireland became independent, the large southern part, that is. The north remained with Great Britain. All right. That's enough history for one night. I'll make some cocoa." Mary started to get up.

"But Mary, what about today? What's it like now?" Mary was still standing as if she didn't want to talk about it, but she gave in to my curiosity.

"Well, things are improving, but it's been a long time coming. Only a decade ago, it wasn't unusual to see signs on boarding houses—no blacks, no Irish, no dogs."

"That's awful. But Mary, what about you? You traveled all over England singing during the war. Did people try to hurt you? Were they disrespectful to you?"

"No, but even if they did, any show of disapproval would have been subtle."

"But you were still the lead singer and you said they loved the band," I asserted in Mary's defense as I followed her to the kitchen where she filled a kettle and lit a fire beneath it, forgetting the cocoa.

"I was paid, mind you. Make no mistake, love, and that was a godsend in those days when everything was rationed. And I met my Carl, didn't I. We kept up the spirits of those brave men and women during some very dark times. We never knew who was coming back from fighting, and some even wondered if we'd be speaking German when it was all over. The music took their minds off their troubles, at least for the night. And I was making money singing, so it wasn't all bad. No one needed to know my name, and because of that I didn't face the troubles that many others did." I was struck by Mary's awareness of hardships in her youth when I knew so little about my own history. How could I have been so sheltered? I sat down at the little turquoise table near the stove.

"I was in high school when Martin Luther King was assassinated, but no one at school even mentioned it, not even the teachers. I barely knew who he was. I found out only when Reggie told me."

"No one talked about it much here either at the time. People fear change. They think if no one talks about something, it didn't happen," Mary replied.

"I wish I had been more understanding when Reggie told me. He was pretty upset about it, and I acted like it wasn't that important. I was so stupid then."

"Reggie must have meant a lot to you. Where is he now?"

"Yes, I guess he did. I haven't seen him in a long time—years, in fact." I wasn't ready to say more about Reginald Washington, and the conversation was turning gloomy, so I quickly changed the subject, eyeing a tin resting in front of me. "Mary, do you still have some of those ginger biscuits you made yesterday?" I said, patting the tin of cookies. Surely she would go along with my act of evasion, lame though it was.

"Of course I do. Did you think I was going to eat them all myself!" Mary laughed and the kettle began to whistle. "Let's have some tea with those biscuits."

"All this talk has made me hungry," I said. I wasn't good at equivocating, although I too often found myself in need of evading people, but I was tired. It was getting late, so I took another cup of tea and cookies to the spare room she had prepared for me, set them on a table, and sprawled out on her starched and ironed sheets. The next morning a call to the repairman took care of the heating in my room, but I returned to watch the last two episodes of *Roots* with her the following nights. Our conversation still fresh in my head about oppression and injustice and suppressing the truth, Reggie's image drifted in and out. I wasn't the naïve girl he once shielded, and it made me sad that he would never know that. When the series ended,

I thanked Mary for letting me watch it with her and as I was leaving, she grinned playfully and said, "Yes, go dream about your Kunta Kente and make the world a better place." I tossed my best frown at her but "Good night, pet" was her reply.

Planting a rose bush requires a sunny location with fertile, well-drained soil and a large hole. Fertilize, water, and mulch your rose bush once it is planted to retain moisture and add protection in winter. Give your plants what they need and you will be rewarded with magnificent blooms.

The Art of Gardening by Emily Mayfield

CHAPTER 20

1968 | It was later than usual that spring when Mama decided she wanted four new rose bushes near the garden house. Reggie agreed to plant them, but I could tell he was worried about squeezing anything new into the carefully laid out garden he had designed the year before. Alongside the right fence that separated our back yard from the Abbotts—their dog Butch had demolished their own yard digging holes, Reggie had planted bulbs— tulips, daffodils, day lilies, irises, and cannas. They punctuated the massive bougainvillea as well as a stand of trees—oak and althea, and wove in and out among them. The back of the garden was boxed in with a hedge of bamboo and four kumquat trees, remnants of the previous owner, but he created a free-standing bed in front of them that boasted seven rose bushes and a sea of colorful zinnias. Finally, a large, sprawling fig tree stood in the left corner of the garden opposite the old chinaberry. On either side Reggie planted vegetables just for Mama's kitchen—tomatoes, cucumbers, and peppers. Mama, of course, was delighted and called him her garden alchemist. Tall red and yellow blossoms of butterfly weed lined the back of the summer garden house. Reggie strategically placed several seed trays that were visited frequently by all the local birds and even the migrating ones, ignoring him as if the gardener were a natural part of this magnificent sanctuary. Reggie prepared the ground for roses right below the screen windows of the garden house close to the old swing set, out of place perhaps in his green paradise, but it was my refuge and I insisted that it stay put.

I sat and watched. He glanced up at me several times but said nothing. Finally he spoke. "You might as well come over here and help me." He would dig the hole, he said, and he wanted me to cut the bottom and sides of the plastic pot with shears, then place the plant in the hole. On the second rose bush pot, his hand brushed mine and I flinched, enough for him to notice. He looked up to see my reaction, our faces coming so close they almost touched. Reggie stood up and put his heels on the plant base to firm the soil around it and turned his back to me, circumventing the impossible liaison that might have developed between us.

It was April 5, 1968. An uneventful day for me—nothing extraordinary had occurred at school, which in my mind was already winding down to summer, but for Reggie, the previous day of April 4th was a day he would always remember. He worked so quietly that I finally asked him what was wrong. He shrugged without answering, but by now I thought enough time had passed that we were friends who could be honest with each other, the invisible line between us notwithstanding.

"Look, if you're not going to talk to me, I might as well go inside." That was enough to evoke a quick response from him and he spoke up.

"Did you hear what happened last night?" Now we were getting somewhere, but I had no idea what he was talking about, so I shook my head and stood there waiting for more information. "Nobody at school talking about Dr. King?" He spoke with a tone of incredulity. How could I not know what had happened, he wondered. Didn't I know history had been made that day? Reggie rarely stepped foot out of the real world—he knew the danger of it, but that day he rose above his own protective parameters. His utopian desire for people to be more than they were had superseded the facts.

"Well, Mama did mention something about it this morning—saw it on the news, but it was just a regular day at school. Nobody, not even the teachers, talked about it today."

"Dr. King was assassinated last night and nobody thought to mention it?"

"Oh. Well." Reggie's words didn't register fast enough for me to process the severe upshot of this revelation. In my gut I knew he was right, but I didn't know what to say. I suppose at this point nothing I could say would have satisfied or improved upon my want of proper regard for the day. "That's.... awful, Reggie. I'm really sorry. I guess the teachers at least should have said something. I don't know. Maybe the topic was too sensitive." Reggie closed his eyes as he shook his head, disappointed in my lame response, once again out of ignorance. Breaking up the clods of dirt in the bed, I attempted to bury the only explanation I had, insufficient as it was.

"You really don't understand, do you. Martin Luther King. The civil rights activist. One of the men who made sure I could go to Carlton High. And vote. You know that thing where you cast a ballot for something or somebody. You have heard of civil rights? And yes, it was awful, more than you know." I realized Reggie was upset when he resorted to sarcasm, which was virtually unknown to him.

"Yes, I'm not stupid. I know what voting means, but I'm sorry, Reggie, I really am. He didn't deserve that, but I'm not good about keeping up with what's going on. The truth is, I don't really understand it all. Maybe I should, but I just don't get it." Reggie kept digging another hole and we didn't speak for several minutes. "Did it make you sad, the death of Mr. King?" I asked.

"Reverend. The Reverend Dr. Martin Luther King," he said, in a tone that sounded like Mama correcting my grammar. "Did it make me sad?" He paused for a minute and looked at me. "I know it's hard for you to understand this, but my people have been hungry for any crumbs of hope—of any justice we could get. For decades, Lizzie. That's a long time to wait, don't you think? And while they were waiting, they had to endure hardships, things you couldn't survive for one day." Reggie stopped and handed me the third rose bush and pointed to the newly dug hole. "My mama used to tell me stories about my great-great-great grandfather. He was a slave on a cotton plantation, not far from where my uncle lives north of here. When the war was coming to an end and it looked like the Confederates were going to lose, his owner and other slave owners, too, took all their slaves, at least those who weren't sick or too frail to travel, and crossed over into Texas. They left the elderly and sick to fend for themselves. Apparently there was a call for workers to help fortify Galveston when a Union ship was headed there to take the island. Slave owners weren't too happy about lending their slaves, but they did it. My great-great-great grandfather was one of them. He got his freedom after that and went back to find his family when the war ended. And he did, too. He worked hard enough to buy the land that my uncle still owns." Reggie was on a roll. He hadn't opened up like that since we met. I was stunned. His story wasn't included in my version of history, but I listened until he was finished. I wanted to set him straight with Civil War facts but I didn't know them that well, and I'd already made a fool of myself. We had just studied that in history and there wasn't even a paragraph in our book about the war being fought in Texas, nothing about Galveston. Was it just some kind of legend being passed down, some made up version of history that families tell each other? Reggie looked at me as if he could see straight into my head at all my thoughts and then resumed digging in the dirt that seemed to swallow up his story and put it to rest.

"Hand me that yellow rose over there. Please." Reggie had moved on. There would be no more discussion about Dr. King or his grandfather's slave days, as if I had won the argument, but if I had won, why didn't I feel like I'd won? Reggie took the rose out of the pot and placed it in the hole, asking me to hold it while he filled the empty spaces with soil. We worked together quietly until suddenly a handful of dirt landed on my hands.

"Hey! What'd you do that for!"

"Do what?" He was struggling to stifle a triumphant grin.

"Oh, okay, buddy. Take this." I picked up a trowel, scooped up some dirt and tossed it at him. He threw a handful back and I got up—throwing dirt as I ran. Before I knew what was happening, Reggie grabbed my arm and I stopped. For a moment the concept of time didn't exist. There was no past, no future, only that nanosecond of the present when Reggie froze, his warm hand wrapped around my arm, his breath on my face, both of us puzzled if not anticipating what would come next.

I looked at him and spoke so boldly that I hardly recognized my own voice. "So, Reggie Washington, are you gonna kiss me?" Reggie quickly dropped my arm and returned to planting the rose, finishing it by himself in silence. I couldn't move, couldn't command my legs to move forward, until somehow I was able to walk the few steps back to the house. I later lay on my bed humiliated, and yet I replayed it like the Hollywood movie I wanted it to be, Cary Grant taking the leading lady in his arms and planting a kiss on her adoring lips. But it didn't happen like that, and imagining that it might wasn't what actually made me shudder. Reggie must have been stunned by my advances, praying no one had seen us, a white girl asking a black boy to kiss her.

He didn't come back. When the second day of his absence from the garden had passed, I asked Mama why. As pedestrian as putting up cans of vegetables on the kitchen shelf, she explained that Reggie would be working elsewhere for a while. Mr. Jackson from the Green Thumb nursery had asked about his work when she was buying the roses. He was curious about who was going to help her plant them, and she told him about Reggie and how he came to do yard work every day. On her praise and recommendation, Mr. Jackson asked if he could hire him to help out at the nursery, just until his son, who had been injured in a football game, could come back to work. Reggie was supposed to start on Monday of the next week, but he asked if he could come earlier. He would get a weekly salary, more than Mama could pay him.

"Will he ever come back and work in our yard?" I asked, hiding the residual pangs of regret over my last foot-in-mouth blunder. The thought of not seeing Reggie again suddenly toppled me.

"Yes, when he can. He'll come and mow the grass once a week, I think. This job is temporary. Reginald will be back as soon as he can." I changed the subject, camouflaging not only the anxiety of not seeing Reggie but also the relief that he wasn't gone for good.

"What's that plant called where the butterflies laid all those eggs?"

My mother smiled at my newfound curiosity about plants. "People call it milkweed or butterfly weed."

"That's all. Doesn't it have a Latin name or something more sophisticated?"

"It does, but I can't remember what it is. I do know its genus name is derived from the Greek god Asclepius, god of healing."

"And they call it a *weed*? A plant that heals ought to have a name more dignified than a weed."

"Yes, you're right. What a shame something so lovely and important should be given the name that nobody wants in the garden."

I never thought I'd have an attachment to an insect, but I raced to the back yard every day to see the new butterfly weed Mama helped me plant next to Reggie's old ones. I wanted to see if the butterflies would come and lay their eggs for me, too, and if they did, what would Reggie think of me then? Monarchs had become a pastime, each little green chrysalis reminding me of him and the refuge he seemed to find in our garden. Or was I spinning a protective chrysalis around myself? I had no doubt he was relieved to have some space and time away from me. Still, I missed him.

An informal pond is a classic feature for a small garden and contributes to the landscape. A fountain that helps to move the water adds life to an otherwise static space. Floating water lilies provide oxygen as well as beauty to this complex ecosystem. A fish pond will also attract birds and other wildlife as it becomes a natural habitat in your own back garden.

The Art of Gardening by Emily Mayfield

CHAPTER 21

1968 | Reggie eventually returned from The Green Thumb as predicted. Furthermore, he went straight to Mama to speak to her about a new project for the garden, and she invited him to sit down at the kitchen table to explain it. Trying to be inconspicuous, I stood just inside the door to listen, and while Mama didn't appear to notice, Reggie glanced at me only once, casting a look that acknowledged my presence and perhaps even accepted me into the plans. He began to describe a pond that he could construct between the new flower bed and the bamboo hedge in the far back center of the garden. He said he had already asked Mr. Jackson if he could work for supplies, and having recently stood in for his son for three weeks, the owner of The Green Thumb was willing to let him have a liner and a simple fountain that he could easily rig up. He could get the water lilies and irises later, along with four bags of river rocks and five goldfish.

"And who's going to dig this big hole in my back yard?" Mama asked, but she already knew Reggie would be willing to dedicate the long hours needed to complete it. I was so excited at the thought of a pool with a fountain splashing coolly over the surface and fish darting round and round that I stepped childlike out into the kitchen and interjected myself into their conversation.

"I can help, Mama. I can help Reggie. Oh, please, Mama, please let us have a pond!"

Surprised at my sudden entrance, Mama turned around with her jaw slightly open, not expecting my enthusiastic interest in the hard physical labor this project would require. "Lizzie, honey, do you even know how to use a shovel?"

"How hard can it be? You shove it in the ground, pick up some dirt, and dump it off to the side. And you keep doing it until you get the size hole you want. No big deal." I looked at Reggie for approval. "Right, Reggie? So I can help you dig the pond? You'll definitely need some help, right?" He didn't say anything, just grinned so wide I could see all of his teeth.

It was the middle of summer and the timing was perfect for helping Reggie construct his pond. No school work or interfering Judy to get in the way, and I had already finished seven books on my summer reading list. Reggie ended up doing most of the digging as he realized it was taking me twice as long and with too little progress, so I was relegated to handing him tools, but I brought him lunch and lemonade and offered conversation for two weeks. When the hole was three and a half feet deep, Reggie placed the liner inside, installed the fountain and filled up the hole using the hose. The next morning he stopped by The Green Thumb and picked up the water lilies. It was too late to plant irises, but he left room for them on the edges of the pond and said he would plant them in early spring. Arranging the water plants in boxes at the bottom of the pond was more complicated than Reggie originally thought. I could see his mind traversing every inch of the little pond in silence, executing each one with the precision necessary for providing not only the design he was after but also enough oxygen for the fish to survive. I went inside to read when I understood he didn't want to be disturbed. It was a little after five when I went out again to check on his progress, but he had already gone home, and six water lilies floated on the surface.

I was watching Saturday morning cartoons and eating breakfast when I heard a knock at the back screen door. Mama was in the kitchen, so she answered it first.

"Lizzie," she called, "come and see these beautiful fish for our new pond." Besides my name, all I heard was fish. I left my bowl of cereal in front of the television and went running to the kitchen. There stood Reggie with five large bags of goldfish.

"Well done, Reggie. The crowning touch. They're lovely," she said. "Let's go outside, Liz, and watch Reggie launch these beauties," and without hesitating Mama followed him out into the garden with me trailing behind. The five goldfish quickly took to the pond and swam in circles, coming to the surface and swimming off again. I was enchanted.

The next morning before breakfast, even before getting dressed I ran outside to look at the pond. I counted the fish—one, two, three. Wait. One, two, three? What happened to four and five? I assumed they must have been swimming in the dark depth of the pond. I waited and counted again, but once more only three fish swam their watery circular route. I ran inside to share the unfortunate news.

"I was afraid that might happen. Either a cat or a raccoon has helped himself to a meal," Mama speculated.

"That's not fair! Those poor fish. That's just not fair! We have to do something!"

"Well, that's really up to Reggie. This is his project, hon. He'll probably be over later today to check on the pond. We can talk to him then. Come on in and get ready for church."

Concentrating on the sermon was impossible, and when I got home I lay on my bed and tried to read. Nothing helped. I couldn't take my mind off the missing fish, and Reggie still hadn't shown up. It was almost dark when he did and the minute I heard him at the back door I met him outside.

"Where've you been? I've been going crazy all day over this pond. Something got two of our fish last night." Reggie didn't answer, just walked calmly across the garden to the pond.

"Yeah, must have been a raccoon," he decided after giving it a good look. "Could have been a cat, but I suspect it was a raccoon." And he walked back to the house to knock on the screen door, but Mama was already there in the laundry room.

"Mrs. Rowan, would you mind if I staked out the pond tonight? I'd like to see exactly what's getting the fish and try to come up with a plan."

"Of course, Reginald, but are you sure you want to sit up all night out there? Won't you get tired?" Once again, I jumped in.

"I could keep him company, Mama, and if he falls asleep, I could wake him up."

"Definitely not," she snapped.

"Why not? I really want to see a raccoon," I admitted. "I've never seen a live one before. And Reggie might need something, a snack or something."

"No." And Mama turned around and began her load of laundry as if to say *it's finished, don't ask again.* I stayed outside to talk to Reggie. How could *no* be the final decision?

"I wouldn't get tired or make noises, you know." I was jubilant at the idea of being part of a stakeout but I kept my cool. "Are you going to kill the raccoon that ate our fish?" I asked defiantly. Reggie swung his head around and looked at me with his wide eyes.

"Kill him? No. I don't think that's necessary. That old raccoon is just doing what nature intended him to do. He was just being a raccoon. No, I'm not gonna kill him. I just want to make sure he's the one getting the fish. I have a better solution in mind. I'm going back home now, but tell your mama I'll be back around nine o'clock."

"I'll be waiting for you," I said. Reggie gave me a warning look but I just smiled as I walked inside. He might not know it with any degree of certainty, but I was not going to be left out of this adventure.

Mama and I had supper and I even volunteered to do the washing up, but I had every intention of secretly beating Reggie to the pond. I put a robe over my clothes, said goodnight to Mama and announced I would be in my room reading for a while and closed my door. A few minutes before nine, I quietly opened it again to check on Mama. Her door was closed and no light was on, so I assumed she had already gone to bed. Without a sound, I slipped out through the laundry room, grabbing a flashlight, the paper bag of food I had hidden, and an old quilt to sit on. I headed for the back of the garden and looked around for a spot to spread out the quilt when I heard my name.

"Lizzie, what are you doing?" I aimed the light in the direction of the voice. There was Reggie, squatting on one knee behind the fig tree. I joined him. "Did your Mama say you could be out here?"

"You're early. Look, I brought a quilt to sit on."

"Go back inside, Lizzie. Are you trying to get me in trouble again?"

"No. What do you mean *again*? Of course I can be out here."

"Your mama said it was all right?"

"Sure." Reggie didn't say any more about it, but he sighed like he knew the truth.

"Okay, but turn off that light and be quiet."

"Can't he smell us, or sense humans are in the garden? Won't he know we're here?"

"Maybe, but he's probably thinking more about getting the fish than getting caught, especially if he can't see us."

"Okay," I said settling down on the quilt. "I brought us a soda and sandwich," and I pulled the paper bag open for Reggie to look. He didn't seem interested. "What're we going to do while we wait?"

"Just wait. That's what a stakeout is," he whispered. "Be quiet. Just sit here and watch. Don't talk. And stop rustling that bag." I understood that we had to be quiet, but the urge to say what I'd been wanting to tell Reggie was even greater than my desire to see a live raccoon. Now was as good a time as any.

"Listen, Reggie, I need to tell you something."

"Shhh. Not now."

"Reggie!" This time I didn't whisper and he responded with a *shhh*. I lowered my voice and continued. "About that last time we were in the garden and you threw dirt on me."

"You mean when you threw dirt on me," he whispered.

"You started it." Reggie didn't answer. "Okay, when we were throwing dirt on each other. All I want to say is…. I'm sorry about the thing I said after."

"What thing?"

"You know. The kissing thing. I didn't really mean it, you know. I was just kidding, but it was stupid, and I wanted to say sorry if it made you feel uncomfortable. That's all." Reggie didn't answer, just stared at the pond and sat in silence. After a while he shifted positions to get more comfortable. I never mentioned it again, but I couldn't say for sure that either of us would ever forget it.

We sat there for what felt like hours before gravity got the better of me, and I leaned on Reggie's arm and fell asleep. He must have moved me over because when I woke up my whole body was sprawled out on the side of the quilt with my feet in the grass. "Look!" he whispered. Reggie nudged me and I sat up, still groggy. Scampering across the garden on agile feet were a mama raccoon and her two little ones. Time had stopped. Here in the garden, on this ephemeral night, I was cradled in the arms of the universe—earth and sky and air and water—the ballast of the moment, and I was sharing it with—if I dared name him, my best friend. On many occasions for the rest of my life I would once again recall this magical night. Neither of us spoke but let the raccoon and her charge fish for their supper. When she reached into the water to retrieve another goldfish, I let out a gasping little cry, and the mama looked up and ran, her babies following behind. Reggie didn't bother scolding me, but by noon the next day he was back at the pond with five more fish and a roll of chicken wire to cover the top of the pond. I never told Mama, and Reggie, who knew I didn't have permission to be out that night, never betrayed my secret.

At times one may feel the garden is more like a graveyard. Even an experienced gardener can have problems with failing plants. If they fail to thrive, you may need to loosen the soil down to two feet and add compost. It may seem like starting over as you double-dig the entire garden, but this method will revive the garden and plants will have a better chance of success.

The Art of Gardening by Emily Mayfield

CHAPTER 22

1968 | The Bertrands' three sons couldn't have been more different from each other, a study in Daedalean contradiction. Jimmy, their youngest son, and I traversed the halls of elementary school and junior high together beginning with Miss Mason's first grade class, and the rooms seemed to shrink as we grew up. We were never going to be more than friends, but I was grateful to have a buddy with a male perspective, not having had a father around. The eldest son, Philip, joined the Marine Corp right after high school and was stationed at Camp Pendleton in San Diego, working in an office and writing home every week according to his mother, but even when he was at school in Carlton, our paths rarely crossed. Like everyone else, I heard stories of Philip's popularity and his participation in school and how it established for him an extensive social life. All of us knew and loved Philip's sense of loyalty mingled with his ardor for fun. Randy

Bertrand was the middle child and the antithesis of his two brothers, sullen and quietly enigmatic except when he was angry, which was more and more frequent now that his older brother was gone. Randy worshipped Philip, wished to be like him even though he didn't even come close. Randy never understood what it took to be a Philip—honest and fair, loving and respectful, willing to serve a cause greater than himself. In a state of disequilibrium after graduating from high school, he eventually enrolled in the Lois B. Winston Junior College in town that fall. It was a small educational institution that trained students in job skills as well as basic courses requisite for a two-year degree, in addition to hours that could apply to a degree at a larger college. Prior to that, Randy worked at several part time jobs, but he couldn't manage to hold anything down for long. He was let go from the Burger King when his boss discovered he didn't make his friends pay for their orders. His tenure at Andy's Hardware lasted less than a week. Randy's impertinence with customers who couldn't make up their minds about what size nails or how much paint to buy turned into rudeness reported to the manager almost daily. Embarrassed by the subsequent widespread reputation of his son in the small town atmosphere of Carlton, Mr. Bertrand pulled some strings and got him a position as a clerk in the accounting office where he worked so he could keep an eye on him. Two days into the job he simply got up and walked out for lunch and never came back. Secretarial skills, he said, were women's work. When Mr. Bertrand had had enough, insisting vociferously enough to motivate even Randy that he go to school and do something useful with his life, he enrolled in the junior college, barely maintaining his place there and resuming his disappointing habit of substandard grades.

Despite the fact that Reggie was now working in close proximity to the boy who had attempted to kill him, their paths rarely crossed. Reggie quickly became cognizant of my neighbor's daily comings and goings, and—no need to say anything to Mama or me, he established his own working timeline to avoid another confrontation. He was always gone by the time Randy came home. One day in November he lost track of time finishing a stone walkway through the garden, part of his new beautification plan.

Warm weather incongruously accompanied stockpiles of leaves in every yard that autumn. Randy had just come home from class one afternoon as I was sitting on a swing with a cold lemonade. The stone pavers, according to Reggie, were too heavy for me to handle, so I spent my time watching him and raking up the never ending piles that left blisters on the soft pads of my palms. When I heard Randy and his brother Jimmy yelling at each other in the driveway, I jumped up from the swing, Reggie safely behind, and ran to see what the ruckus was all about. There was Jimmy on the ground with blood oozing from his nose, Randy standing over him with clinched fists. I looked at Randy, then Jimmy, and then Randy again before running to the lanky body sprawled on the pavement. The minute Reggie saw him, he stopped, anchored to the ground where he was standing.

"Jimmy, are you okay?" I said bending down to look. "Randy, don't just stand there! Help him! Get a cloth or something to stop the bleeding." But Randy wasn't listening. He was staring at Reggie, fists still clenched and the muscles in his jaw taut and red.

"Mind your own business." Randy rubbed his knuckles, turned around and walked inside. Jimmy tried lifting his head and shoulders off the ground but fell back with a groan.

"Hold on, Jimmy. Be back in a minute. Just be still." Reggie walked away as I went inside our kitchen and grabbed a dish cloth and some ice. When I returned a minute later, he was gone and Jimmy was wobbling toward his house. "Hey! Come back here! At least take this cloth with you. I put some ice in it." Jimmy limped over to the steps of the screened porch on the side of his house, sat down, and took the cloth covered ice cubes to his nose, wincing as he touched his face.

"Why did Randy hit you? What was that all about?" I asked, taking a seat next to him.

"He hates school," he mumbled.

"So?" I could relate to this from time to time but I continued listening.

"I mi'ta said…so'thing he di'n like." Jimmy was stumbling over his words as sound echoed through his nose. "He…al'ays bellyaching…having……work hard, work a' all. I end up do'ng……all his chores. Dumb ass freeloa'er."

"Oh. You called him that?"

"Yeah, an' a fuckin' mo'ster who bea's up everybody."

"Oh, yeah. That might have done it. Maybe that wasn't such a good idea, Jimmy."

"I don' care. I's the truth. Man, m' nose hur's. I thin' he broke it." Jimmy and I sat there for a few minutes in silence until I spoke up.

"I hardly see you anymore. You doing okay?" Jimmy didn't look at me. "I mean, other than Randy beating you up."

"Yeah, I guess."

"I miss you. We never talk anymore."

"Sorr', Lizzie. Y' know…." He didn't need to say any more. There was nothing else to say. Judy was in the picture and that didn't leave room for another girl in his life, not even an old friend. Jimmy sat there with the ice pack on his nose while I listened to his intermittent groans until the sun went down and Mrs. Bertrand opened the door.

"Hon, didn't you hear me calling you? Hey, Lizzie. Supper's ready, son, come on in now." His mother saw his bloody swollen face when we stood up. "Good heavens! What happened to you?"

"Ran'y." And he slowly got up and walked through the open door.

"See you later, Jimmy. Hope it's not broken," I called back, and Mrs. Bertrand stood there in the door as if she wanted to say something to me.

"Oh, dear." She exhaled a sigh and finished, "Randy's not happy about going to school. I don't know what is ever going to become of that boy." And then as if realizing that she had said more than she intended, she added, "Well, night, hon." Mrs. Bertrand shook her head and closed the screen door. I could hear her yelling at Randy as I crossed the driveway back into my own yard. I sat in the swing until dark, thinking about the range of hostility between Randy and Jimmy and Randy and Reggie. The brothers would get over their dispute eventually, but it was the first time since graduation that I witnessed the prodigious hatred in Randy's eyes as he glared at Reggie. A sudden reflex of fear and premonition struck me in such a tangible way that I lurched up from the swing and ran inside.

Then the call came. The Viet Nam war was in full swing and Philip was being shipped out, which meant Viet Nam. No one knew exactly where in Nam, but the news they had been dreading had indeed arrived. It was disheartening not only for the Bertrands but for all their neighbors and friends. In early June of that summer of 1968, the country had received the news of Bobby Kennedy's assassination, and with an end to an election hopeful—at least for some, continued protests and the burning of American cities were reported on the nightly news, which Mama and I had begun watching. So the idea of Philip, the pride and joy of the neighborhood, being sent to war was a grim punch to the gut. By his wife's account, Mr. Bertrand was glued to the local newspaper and the television set every night, but Mrs. Bertrand didn't want to know. She equated long periods of silence with good news for her family.

The arrival of the Christmas holidays dispensed palliative relief. Mama and I planned to spend it alone this time, happily just the two of us. My grandparents had decided to take the cruise to the Bahamas that they'd always talked about, and they chose the middle of December for their holiday fantasy. They would return home two days before Christmas Day, but Grandmother decided two trips in one month meant far too much time away from the store. I dared not complain. Their previous visits to Carlton invariably cast a dark spell over the house, and even Mama breathed a sigh of relief when after only four days they packed up and returned home. We drove down to the Green Thumb one Saturday to select a medium size tree to set up and decorate in a corner near the fire place. Reggie was working part time inside the garden center, and today he was at the far end of the store arranging a long line of poinsettias. When our eyes met, he graciously nodded and kept working.

It was seventy-three degrees outside but Mama started a fire with a bundle of wood she had purchased along with our tree and turned on the radio now playing nonstop Christmas music. I pulled out several boxes of decorations from the hall closet. One box contained flat felt ornaments that Mama and I had made one year when the art teacher at school, who was throwing away felt scraps from her overstuffed supply closet, said Mama could have them. At the time she didn't really have any plans for them, just hated to see the colorful scraps go to waste, but when I had a look at them, I immediately thought of Christmas. A jack-in-the-box, a black and white panda with a red bow, Christmas trees and wreaths—we spent an entire Saturday morning cutting and gluing felt so that after several hours we had new ornaments for our little Christmas tree. That was years ago, but every time I looked at those little pieces of felt, I was transported to that lovely day of peace, no stress or resistance or regret, only love.

I slept late Christmas morning, and despite a blue jay's spasmodic squawks interrupting my slumber, I fell in and out of dreamland until the lure of sizzling bacon pulled me into the kitchen.

"Merry Christmas, hon. Ready for breakfast?"

"Hmm. Smells heavenly." Something different caught my attention as I looked over at the dining room from the kitchen door. A large pot of poinsettias wrapped in gold paper sat in the center of the table. "Oh. Those are nice. Who sent us flowers?"

"The card said 'Merry Christmas from Reginald Washington.' They were on the front porch this morning when I went out to get the paper."

"Oh, right. I saw Reggie unloading poinsettias when we bought the tree. That was nice of him. Why didn't he come in?" It was an unexpected gift but I was not really surprised that Reggie would show Mama how much he appreciated her help. I wondered if he might have thought about me, too, just a little.

"It was probably too early and he didn't want to wake us. I made cinnamon rolls and thought we could sit in the front room and open presents while we ate." Mama didn't wait for an answer but began piling rolls on a plate. Four gifts wrapped in holiday paper sat under the tree, three of them mine, and I opened each one before taking a bite of breakfast. I had given Mama a little gold bracelet with artificial rubies set in the middle, and when she unwrapped the slender box in which burgundy velvet held the bracelet securely, she seemed as pleased as any mother could be having received an unsolicited gift from her only child. Her needs were small but her gratitude was as colossal as her generosity. I took the shiny red and silver paper from a long dress box and lifted the lid. A navy blue linen coat lay in folds of white tissue paper, and below it was a white linen dress with red topstitching. It was the Vogue pattern she had been working on since summer, the one I assumed all along had been a dress for herself. I lifted the coat from the tissue and hugged it to my chest before reaching over to wrap my arms around my loving mother.

"Aren't you going to open the others?" she said with cloaked eagerness, still delighted with my euphoric display over my new clothes. As if any other gift could compare to her workmanship, I unwrapped what I knew to be books, two collections—one of Sandburg's poems and the other short stories by Christopher Isherwood. My mother the hobby seamstress led a creative life, but her real love was literature. Mama's literary genius tempered with modesty gave credence to her wisdom augmented by years of reading, especially the classics—the plays and poems and novels of literary giants. The prudent sagacity of Shakespeare, the passion of Romantic poets, and Nathaniel Hawthorne, Emerson and Thoreau, the men and women of the American Renaissance, but time and again she returned to the poems of life-has-loveliness-to-sell Sara Teasdale. They comprised her panoply of truths by which to live one's life in harmony. Their words fell into a kind of cadence in her everyday speech as if she were directing a play, hoping somehow that their shrewd sense of acumen and refinement, erudition acquired by the eminent, would indeed illuminate my path in life as well. We spent the rest of the day admiring our gifts and cooking Christmas dinner. When Mama called me into the kitchen to baste the turkey while she finished the crust for the apple pie, I was still in my coat and dress.

"What do you think? Pearls, or no?"

"Pearls. Definitely pearls. Hurry up and get out of those clothes and come help me with dinner." Although Mama intended to sound agitated, I knew she was secretly pleased that I didn't want to take off my new clothes that day, but I hung them in the closet and hoped I would be able to wear them soon. That Christmas would remain one of the happiest of days in my memories of her.

January arrived much too early. I hadn't been back in school very long before another upheaval toppled our tentatively peaceful neighborhood. The New Year brought in darkness as only the cloak of death can do one afternoon just as I was walking home from school. A Marine Corps vehicle was parked in front of the Bertrands' house, which looked official enough to make me keep a cautious distance. My first response was to knock on Jimmy's screened in porch door, but I had developed enough good sense by then, and an intuitive warning held me back. Mama arrived home not long after I did, which was unexpected since a faculty meeting was scheduled for that afternoon and the English department usually gathered afterwards. I was standing at the front door waiting for the news when she got out of the car and walked straight over to the Bertrand house. I threw open the door and followed her. I called out to her when I was two steps away, but she didn't answer. When Mrs. Bertrand opened the door, she hugged Mama and ushered both of us past the quiet and apprehensive living room and into the kitchen. Sarah Bertrand's bleary eyes revealed she had been crying for some time. She asked us to wait there for a moment, and as she pushed the door open, I saw two uniformed men sitting across from the couch where Mr. Bertrand was hunched over, his head in his hands. Mrs. Bertrand resumed her place near her husband. Although I knew something was wrong, I wasn't sure what I should do or say, the mystery of their presence causing more anxiety in me than the reality of the situation.

"Mama, what's going on? Why is the Marine Corps here?" I guess I already knew but I wanted to hear the words.

"Honey, it's Philip." Mama paused and put her arm around my shoulders. "Sarah called the school and asked if I would come. I told Mr. Reynolds and left my meeting early." Mama moved to the door as Mrs. Bertrand came into the kitchen. She looked like she needed propping up. "Sarah, what can I do?" I stood there in silence, invisible to adults who didn't want me to be part of the tableau of anguish that was unfolding. Mama put her arms around Mrs. Bertrand who wept unrestrained. I understood the sadness if not the depth of grief that comes with such a loss, but no matter how much I commanded tears, they never came.

As a matter of course, my mother didn't waste any time preparing food for the Bertrands. It was what neighbors did for each other, and assembling a ham and sweet potato supper was part of her state of mind that night. She went through the motions without thinking—baking, wrapping it in sheets of aluminum foil, and the two of us carting dinner over to a house filled with family members grieving over the inexplicable loss. Jimmy answered the door this time and invited us in. Mama and I went straight to the kitchen with her food offering, and Mrs. Bertrand began telling her about the circumstances surrounding Philip's death. I clung to the door that swung out into the dining room long enough to hear the words *attack on a key installation near Saigon*. She wasn't sure about the date of arrival at the airport in Carlton but the family had been told it would be a week. I slipped out at that point and found Judy sitting on the couch next to Jimmy. Mama wouldn't be leaving for an hour or more, so I took a chair near Jimmy and cleared my throat.

I was close enough to put my hand on Jimmy's, but what I really wanted to do was put my arms around him and comfort him. "I'm really sorry, Jimmy," I said as I covered his hand with mine. No one I ever knew had died and the awkward conversation that people have about death was mysterious, the right words to say murky and abstract. Jimmy mumbled thanks while Judy grabbed his hand from under mine and held it. She was good with tragedy and loss; her life seemed to be embroiled in it and so she responded to it with familiar banality. She was also sending me a message. Jimmy was hers and hers alone.

St. Anne's Catholic Church had been a source of solace for many in Carlton, its indomitable red brick exterior that seemed to protect its fragile old stained glass windows lending support, both ecclesiastical and emotional, for the weary of spirit. The Bertrands had been faithful members since I could remember, and each of their children had been christened and confirmed there. In time the three boys had received their first communion and were established as God's own. Philip alone of all the Bertrand siblings had served as an altar boy, in his parents' eyes a great source of pride and hope for his bright future as a model citizen of Carlton. No one had doubted that he would marry and settle down with his own children who would walk the path of rituals his own parents had trod. The funeral service seemed interminable, but after an hour it was over, all but the reception at the Bertrands' house. Mama made an apple spice cake for the reception.

The house was bulging with family from out of town and friends from various pockets of Carlton, the neighborhood, Mr. Bertrand's job, people associated with the church. Father Dubois was there and when it looked as though the house was teeming with humanity, he offered a blessing. Even the bereaved must eat, I discovered, but not because of hunger. Food has a way of connecting people and indeed mollifying the anguish of loss as if to assuage a little of the pain, and so people stood, balancing platefuls however they could manage. Judy nudged Jimmy and handed him her plate, clearly for a refill, but he didn't move. A new girl I didn't know was sitting across from them on the arm of Randy's chair as she leaned in to listen to Judy, adding her own quiet contributions now and then.

There are times when you are fully conscious of the fact that you shouldn't stick your toe in the water when the temperature dips below freezing. I was about to disregard consciousness. I found myself willing to join the conversation when Judy jumped up pulling Jimmy with her as she hurried to the dining room table laden with ample food of every sort, hot and cold. Ignoring the frosty reception, I looked at the new girl and introduced myself in an attempt to save face.

"Hi, I'm Lizzie Rowan. I live next door. Jimmy and I are in the same grade at school." I half expected Randy to introduce her, seeing that she was practically sitting in his lap, but he too got up and followed his brother to the table.

"Hi, I'm Cynthia, Randy's girlfriend," she giggled softly. That was the extent of our conversation, for a row had begun at the table between Randy and Mr. Bertrand, now escalating into a shouting match. All eyes turning toward the table, Randy was growling at his father with accusations aimed at Mama. My concern for her suddenly became relevant and I moved closer.

"Yeah, go on, tell me." The glint of Randy's angry eyes darted from his father to his brother to Mama like the abrupt discharge of an electric spark. "Why did Philip have to die when that nigger next door gets to live? He should have been the one lying in that box, not Phil." An utterance of *shut up* hissing through Jimmy's teeth accompanied a gentle shove toward the kitchen two feet away. Jimmy, in an attempt to prevent Randy from a dangerous revelation and perhaps even guide him toward conciliation, merely aggravated the growing discord in his brother's head. Randy pushed him so hard that Jimmy lost his balance and fell backwards in the direction of the guests standing around the table. Mama, who had been rearranging the dishes of food in an effort to provide the bewildered Mrs. Bertrand as much help as possible, fell across the side of the table and onto the floor, bringing with her bowls of potato salad and a strawberry congealed fruit salad. Jimmy looked horrified. When she gazed up from the floor stupefied at what had just occurred, she found herself surrounded by neighbors rushing over to help her up. Jimmy and his mother watched and then frantically tried to clean up the gooey, unsalvageable ruins. Randy flew over to Cynthia and grabbed her arm, yanking her like a rag doll to the door. In a rage he threw back the door dragging poor Cynthia staggering behind him. I watched them as they fled the scene, but as they approached his car, his rag doll fell on the sidewalk and skinned her knees. Instead of helping her up, Randy left her on the sidewalk and drove away. Recouping from the first mishap, Jimmy ran down the walk to pick her up and lead her back into the living room where he began to administer first aid. The Bertrands' house was soon empty and quiet as people began to leave the beleaguered sight. Mama, in her navy silk suit smudged with creamy salad and red Jell-O, led me home arm in arm, and, in line with the curative behavior expedient to recovery, we changed into our pajamas and drank tea in front of the cold fireplace.

Mama and Reggie were speaking in soft tones in the kitchen early the next morning. I clearly was not meant to be part of their conversation, but I didn't return to my room. I stood outside the door and listened.

"But Reggie, do you have relatives in that part of the state, people you could get settled with?" Mama was frowning.

"My uncle runs a tree farm south of Bossier City. We used to keep in touch," he replied, "but I haven't seen him in a while." My heart beat faster. Was Reggie leaving us again? The fact that Mama, who rarely showed her disappointment, could give up her stoicism for Reggie was a testimonial to her concern for him.

"I heard what happened last night. I'm really sorry, Mrs. Rowan."

"Oh, that. I'm fine. I don't let anything that young man does affect me, and you shouldn't either. He's just a lot of hot air, that Randy. Always has been. He was upset about Philip, and rightly so. He's harmless but then again it's best to stay out of his way." I was relieved that Mama still didn't know the details of graduation, but I wondered how Reggie had managed to find out about the debacle at the Bertrand's. "Reginald, please don't think we want you to go. I understand if this is something you have to do, but please know that you are always welcome here. I do hope your decision is not based on Randy's behavior toward me last night." He shook his head but he would never reveal to her what really happened to him that terrible night. He almost left it at that, but then he looked up at Mama and spoke in a tone that had changed from regret to resolve.

"I never did anything to him, Mrs. Rowan. Never." Reggie moved toward the back door and Mama followed.

"I know. I know you didn't." She watched him walk down the drive to his pickup before coming inside. I soon joined her in the kitchen as she began making breakfast.

"Morning. Can I help?"

"Morning, hon. Crack those four eggs into that bowl, please.

"So Reggie's gone back to his uncle's? I heard you talking."

"Yes. I think it's best for him right now. Tensions are higher than usual." She quickly changed the subject. "So, what do you have planned for today?"

"Oh, I don't know. Maybe I'll take a book into the garden and read. The sun's out and it's not that chilly. What about you?"

"I need to make a trip to the A&P. I didn't get a chance to go this week. Think you can hold down the fort while I'm gone?"

"Of course. What could possibly go wrong now? After yesterday....," I snarled. Breakfast over, Mama left and I grabbed my latest read, *Jamaica Inn*—I was into Du Maurier now, and headed out the back door. When I look back on that day in the garden, I still wonder why, of all the places to sit and read, I chose to climb the old oak tree that had once held a tree house, at least the floor of one. Jimmy and I never got around to finishing it and over time it fell apart. But four old boards were still nailed to the trunk, and if I climbed up to the first large branch, two more limbs fanned out and remnants of two pieces still nailed to the tree formed a platform, not an uncomfortable place to sit. There's something magical about being high up in a tree where the view is empowering. I climbed up, settled in and opened my book to the next chapter when I heard someone below me rummaging through the summer house. I leaned over the side and saw it was Reggie.

"Hey! I thought you were gone." He looked around as if he couldn't place the voice. "Up here. In the oak." A grin spread over his face as he walked toward me.

"What are you doing up there? Lookin' for squirrels? You better not fall. Might get hurt."

"Nah, not me. Aren't you supposed to be on the road now? Did you forget something?"

"Yeah. I was in a hurry. Left my jacket with my wallet in it on a chair in the shed."

"Oh, yeah. You don't want to get on the road without your wallet."

"You gonna be okay up there? Want some help down?'

"Are you kidding? I'm an expert tree climber from way back. Jimmy and I built this, well, what used to be a tree house right here when we were not even ten years old. Watch me." I started to put my foot on the first rung when my book slipped out of my hand. I tried to catch it, and when I reached for it, I twisted around and lurched forward, facing the tree. As I slid down the trunk, a broken, splintered branch protruding from the right side of the rungs like a jagged knife ripped open the inside of my thigh and I tumbled to the ground on my back. I was stunned but the pain was excruciating. All I managed to squeak out was, "Oh, my God!" over and over. Reggie was already at my side looking into the gaping hole in my leg. I looked up to see what he saw. "Oh, God! What are those white things?" And I fell back and screamed, "Oh, my God, it hurts so bad! Do something!"

"Looks like nerves. But don't look. I'm going inside your house to get some towels. Is your mother home? I didn't see her car." By then I couldn't answer him. I couldn't do anything but gasp and cry and think about the pain. Before long Reggie was wrapping towels around the wound to stop the bleeding. "We've got to get you to the hospital. Now!" And he picked me up and carried me all the way to his truck and put me in the front seat. "Put pressure on the towel if you can. It won't take us long to get to the emergency room." I don't recall much after that except I think Reggie told the nurse he was the gardener and he found me on the ground after I fell out the tree. She must have told him to sit in the waiting room because he didn't go into the room with me for the procedure. I wanted him with me, but someone, the doctor I guess, gave me a local anesthetic in my leg and cleaned the wound. I dared to glance at the bloody and torn skin and the white cordlike nerves that lay alongside the muscle as he closed the opening and stitched me back together. Mama peeked in just as the nurse was guiding me into the wheel chair. When she saw us, she rushed over to me.

"Dr. Perry, I'm Lizzie's mother. Thank you for taking such good care of my daughter. I was gone for only a short while to the grocery store when Reggie called me."

"Reggie? Did she come in with family? I don't think we met. Lizzie came in with the nurse."

"Reggie is our gardener." She glanced back at Reggie. "And friend. He's the one who wrapped her up and brought her in." And then Mama looked at me with tears in her eyes. "I was so worried. I came as fast as I could. Didn't even unpack the groceries. Just rushed over here. You scared me, hon. Thank God Reggie came back." Then she remembered why she was upset with me. "And Lizzie, what in the world possessed you to sit in that old tree house? Those old boards weren't safe!" I was too groggy to answer her.

When the nurse wheeled me out to the waiting room, Reggie was still there.

"Good. You've still got both legs. You can walk home." He smiled and I thought it might have been relief I saw on his face. "I'll follow you home. In case you need some help, Mrs. Rowan."

"Thank you, Reginald. I probably will need your help."

Mama drove us up the driveway and soon Reggie was carrying me to the porch as Mama opened the door.

"Follow me," Mama said as she walked down the hall to my bedroom. When Reggie saw where we were going, I could feel the hesitation in his arms and his pace, but he kept going. Mama pulled back the covers, and he deposited me into my bed. He started to cover me but stopped himself, realizing where he was.

But our eyes had met as he lay me down. "Thank you, Reggie," I whispered. "You did it again."

"Did what?" he said.

"Saved me. You keep doing that." He didn't say anything, just looked at me, and then quickly walked to the door as if he had invaded a sacred space.

He stopped at the threshold and turned around. "No more tree climbing for you, little girl," he said. Then he nodded his head and left. I heard Mama thank him again and close the door behind him. When she returned to my room, I was half asleep from the turmoil of the afternoon, mixed with pain pills, and I slept for the next three hours. I woke up and tried to turn over, but when I screamed in pain, Mama showed up at my door.

"Time for another pain pill, hon. Are you hungry?"

"No. No. No." I just wanted to sleep and make the pain go away, but she was soon standing over me with a glass of water and a pill in her palm.

When I woke up the next morning, I wanted to scream. But this time it wasn't just the pain in my thigh. Reggie had called me a little girl.

Consider carefully the decisions you make in planning a garden that can enrich the world in which you live. The unseen realm beneath the surface is teeming with life. Your little plot of land may be the only refuge for displaced wildlife, and the plants that grow there may be their only source of food and shelter.

The Art of Gardening by Emily Mayfield

CHAPTER 23

1970 | Time didn't wait for any of us to process the events of the previous year, and so not even the Bertrands were surprised when Randy and Cynthia announced they had eloped and would now be living as husband and wife. The family's disappointment that their son's intensely combative relationship had turned into a thing of permanence was soon mitigated when five months later a little boy was born, a child that might change Randy's life and turn it around to something positive and hopeful. I was now a senior in high school. We hadn't seen Reggie in a while. Mama said she thought he was still working with his uncle near Bossier, and one day in early May I received a card from Reggie, postmarked from Shreveport, with a dollar bill folded into a ring, for good luck as I graduated from high school he had written. It was so uncharacteristic of him that I spent the afternoon putting the ring on my finger and pulling it off, trying to figure him out once again, assuming there was nothing more to it than exactly what he had said, no other motive. Mama's plan was for me to go to nearby Louisiana College, but up until the day I actually left, my plans for higher education were entangled in an indefinite and unpredictable fate.

It was toward the end of another mundane week of my senior year, the impending graduation a week away and classes winding down, when I came home from school and found Reggie planting petunias near the big oak in the garden. He was temporarily back in Carlton working at the Green Thumb as a manager, agreeing to help Mama as a favor now and then. His uncle's farm had run into trouble, he was laid off for a while, and now he needed work. I congratulated him on his new position and wished him well, and he followed suit with the niceties of the moment, asking me how school was going and if I were ready to graduate in such a refined, adult like manner that it occurred to me, in his eyes, I was no longer that little girl. Nevertheless, I thanked him for the ring and he seemed embarrassed that I had brought it up, so I changed the subject. I told him I hadn't made up my mind about what I wanted to do, including going to college even though I had been accepted to three, thanks to Mama's diligent insistence in not only filling out the forms but putting them in the mail. He tried to reassure me, but his efforts availed in little change to my vapid attitude regarding my next step in life. In truth I didn't want to be convinced of anything at that moment. I told him I needed to go in and see my mother, whose growing weakness and nagging cough worried me. She hadn't felt well for weeks, but having just spied Reggie through the window of the back door, she seemed eager to talk to him and stepped outside to greet him. After catching up with the latest news of our lives, their conversation ended on the topic of trucks in town selling crabs. She had set her heart on making a shrimp and crab gumbo—had he noticed any on the edge of town? He told her no but he knew a good place to catch them and would be glad to do the job for her. Mama said she thought we still had an old crab net in the garden house that he could use as well as some string, and he could have that old meat in the freezer that she had intended to throw out. She added a sack lunch and a thermos of tea, and he offered to go the next morning, but then, he would have agreed to anything Mama asked of him. Reggie could come and get the supplies early in the morning before she went to school, she said. When he arrived the next day, it occurred to me in a deliriously joyful breakthrough idea of skipping school that I could slip unnoticed into the back of Reggie's truck under his tarp as a happy stowaway and avoid the drudgery of a wasted day of senior classes. Under the guise of staying back and finishing an assignment, I told Mama to go on without me, I would walk to school. Her only response was don't be late, and I brushed off the guilt I should have felt for lying to her.

The intended destination, a lovely Gulf inlet chock full of blue crabs, lay only an hour's drive away from Carlton. It didn't take long for my holiday bubble to burst in the hot, suffocating, never ending drive to the coast. The strong fumes of gasoline and the shock of road after road of potholes that hadn't been repaired for years made for a weary, bone shattering journey. I reminded myself to speak to Reggie about his truck's shocks later, but for now the truck slowed and I heard the crunching sound of turning onto shells covering the water's edge. Reggie got out and began to unload the supplies from the back when I thrust my legs out from under my secret hideaway to stretch. Suddenly Reggie threw back the tarp and looked at me aghast.

"Surprise!" I laughed meekly as I sat up and breathed in fresh air, not a cloud overhead, just blue sky and a cool breeze. "Man, was it hot under there." I grabbed the side of the truck and stood up.

"Oh, no, get back under that tarp. I'm taking you home. What do you think you're doing, Lizzie? "

"What do you mean? No way I'm getting back under that hot thing! You want me to suffocate?" Reggie lowered his jaw and folded his arms across his chest, resolute. "Aw, Reggie. C'mon. Please let me stay. I haven't been crabbing in years and I really wanted to. Please, Reggie," I begged, moving closer toward him.

"You should be in school."

"I'm not a child, Reggie. Besides, graduation is a week away. We're not doing anything important. And if you take me home now, you'll miss the best time to catch crabs. For Mama, remember?" I was sure I was gaining on him.

Reggie just shook his head, but his eyes were blazing. "Lizzie," he sighed. "Lizzie, what are people going to say—a white girl and a black boy out by themselves on the water all day? Are you trying to get me lynched?" It was the first time Reggie ever said the words that defined who we were. No laws, no actions authorized by the federal government played a role in a boy and a girl enjoying a sunny day together, unless one was black and the other was white, and even then it was a stern but unwritten law the people of Carlton took for granted. Reggie looked at me, really looked at me. The reality of his words was written all over my face and he knew I finally got it. "Look," he conceded reluctantly. "We're already here. I can't believe I'm doing this. You can stay but if someone comes along, I mean anyone, and I tell you to get out of sight, you'll do it—fast. Do you understand?" I nodded. "Do you understand?" Reggie repeated his dictum more forcefully this time. I answered yes, that I did, but I wasn't worried. It was early morning and we hadn't seen, or heard in my case, many cars since we left the house. "Grab that ice chest and hand it to me." He barked out the orders as if it restored his control of the situation. Reggie glanced nervously over at the road every five minutes while he measured out four lines and attached the turkey necks and other odd pieces of meat Mama had given him, staking each line close to the water's edge. He instructed me to throw the lines in and then we waited. I stood between the first two, and when I saw the string become taut, I reached for it and began to pull it in slowly. A large blue crab had taken the bait.

"Lizzie, get under the bridge." I had already forgotten his warning, and it took me a moment to look up. A car was approaching in the distance, over a mile away. I looked back at the crab pulling the line further away from me, and I held my grip.

"Okay. Wait a minute. I've almost got him. He's a big one, too. If I let go, he'll get away."

Reggie raised his voice at me. "Now, Lizzie!" He dropped his line and lunged toward me like he was going to shove me under the bridge, but he stopped just short of touching me. I dropped the line and scrambled toward the road, hiding as best I could behind a pier near the foot of the bridge. I was standing in shallow water, making myself invisible behind the concrete post when the patrol car pulled up and an officer got out. I was afraid to look but I could hear them clearly.

"Mornin'."

"Mo'nin', officer."

"You must be catching a passel with all them lines."

"Naw, not yet, suh. No bites yet. Still early though." Reggie's voice was different, not just calm, and more than polite. It was colored talk—humble even, as if he knew how it must go. Concealed by concrete, trapped under a bridge, I felt lightheaded and my heart was pounding, more guilt heavy on my chest, piling up with every decision I seemed to make regarding Reggie.

"Seen many cars pass? Anybody on foot? Just got an APB for a murder suspect possibly in this area."

"No, suh. You the fust one I seen all mo'nin', suh."

"All right then, boy. You keep your eyes peeled."

"Yes, suh," he said, tipping his cap to the officer. He didn't leave right away. I peeked over the edge of the pier holding up the end of the bridge as the officer spoke to Reggie, his back to me. When he turned around, I quietly leaned as far back under the bridge as possible and would have crawled inside had the space between pier and span been large enough. I heard his footsteps crunching shells as he moved in my direction. My heart was racing and I felt any minute it would leap out of my chest. I was paralyzed. Had he suspected someone was hiding under the bridge? I didn't move even after I heard what I thought was the patrol car's engine start. It must have disappeared down the road because Reggie came over to my hideout and stood there. When I finally opened my eyes, I wondered how long he had been staring at me.

"You can come out now." He was himself again with relief in his eyes, but I was still numb, not only from our close call but also from watching Reggie transform himself into a person I didn't recognize. This Negro man had humbled himself in speech and body language before an officer of the law. Was it fear, or careful adherence to his assigned abject status that made him subjugate himself? The weight of the pain he must have felt bore down on my already depleted heart and I wanted to cry. He saw it in my face, my quivering lips and spoke, "He was just looking for someone. No need to get upset. Just another day in the life of a black man." I wiped my eyes and walked back to the crab lines. Half an hour later, Reggie was himself again. Capturing a runaway crab broke the silence between us, and we spent the rest of the day out on the water's edge laughing and filling up Mama's ice chest with crabs. I was starving and told him so, but Reggie just smiled and walked back to the truck to get the surreptitious tarp for us to spread on the ground picnic style. He shared the sandwiches Mama had made for him and a thermos of ice tea, the lunch I had neglected to think about that morning, or maybe I assumed Reggie would offer part of his. Spending time on the water made me hungry, and I was grateful for his generosity, most of all for the afternoon we would be sharing. I sat down and took off my wet sneakers so they could dry out in the sun. Reggie poured the tea into the cap for me and he drank from the thermos, all the while watching the crab lines just inches away from us. I could feel his eyes on my thigh as I sat cross-legged on the tarp.

"Are you looking at my scar, Reggie? Yes, it's still there, probably always will be. It wouldn't be there if I hadn't bragged about my tree climbing skills with a book in my hand. I owe you. Again." Reggie didn't say anything, just kept looking at my thigh. "What's wrong? Why are you still looking at my legs? You about to make a pass at me, Reginald Washington?" I teased. A smile spread across his face and I thought he was going to hang his head in embarrassment but he didn't. He grabbed my shoulders and pulled me toward him. I was closer to his face than I had ever been, but I didn't wait to see what he would do next. If I had learned anything from Judy and Jimmy, it was what to do with your mouth when you wanted to kiss a boy, and when I did, Reggie kissed me back. He gently leaned me to the ground across the tarp and kissed me again and again. When I sat up and pulled my tee shirt off, Reggie's eyes opened wide. He quickly grabbed my shirt, handed it to me and stood up.

"Girl, put your clothes back on. We're already on thin ice, you know." He remained standing until I put my shirt back on.

"You can sit down now. I'm fully covered. And you can stop worrying." He sat down, but an awkward silence followed until he brought up graduation and my plans for after, completely ignoring the passionate kiss between us. Then came the curveball.

"Will your father be coming to your graduation?" No one had ever mentioned my father and I certainly wasn't going to speculate on that topic if I could help it.

"Nope," was my answer and I assumed Reggie would leave it at that.

"Why not?" He wasn't going to let it go.

"I have no idea where he is. Mama spoke to him on the phone, I think, thirteen years or so ago, when he called from New Zealand, but he could be anywhere by now. He could be dead for all I know."

"So I guess you didn't really get to know him."

"I never missed him. Didn't know what it was like to have a father."

"I saw him once."

"Saw who?"

"Your father. I saw him once at your house. Not the house you live in now but another one."

"What do you mean you saw my father? How could you? When was this? Where was I?"

"My mama cleaned houses. She worked for your parents." I'm sure my mouth dropped wide open with that revelation, but I was speechless. "It was a long time ago. You were just a toddler. You threw a ball at me." This was too much. I felt like I had walked through the portal of another dimension in time. Perhaps I was dreaming. Or maybe Reggie was making this up to get back at me for encroaching on his peaceful day out on the water. "You couldn't have been more than two, maybe three. I was in the second grade and it was summer. My aunt couldn't keep me so Mama brought me to work with her. Something happened that day, not sure what, but that was the last day my mama worked there. Next week she was cleaning for somebody else. A lady from your church, I think, and she worked there for years. Up until she moved to California."

"And why have you never mentioned this before?" I spewed at him, furious that he'd held on to this information without telling me.

"Never the right time. Besides, I didn't think it was important."

"What? There is never a *right* time to share information like this!"

"Well, we never talked like this before, did we. I mean about personal stuff."

"So that means Mama knew you already. The day you stepped into her classroom."

"Well, not really. She only knew Mama had two children. That's all." I was starting to calm down but the questions were forming one after the other in my head. Mama would hear about this when I got home.

"It's odd that Mama never mentioned telling me your mother worked for us."

"I think whatever happened that day must have been serious. Obviously your mama didn't want to talk about it, and that's okay. Everyone's entitled to their privacy. Leave it alone, Lizzie. Let the past be."

"Right. Easier said than done. So, what about you? Where's your father? You've never mentioned him."

"Oh, I've got one, all right. He's been in prison for the last eight years."

"In prison? What'd he do?" I asked.

"Nothin," Reggie answered without explaining.

"Well, he must have done something." The minute the words came out, I knew I had crossed a line and I was starting to feel ashamed, but it was too late.

"Why? Why must he have done something?" he looked straight at me and asked with a tone I didn't recognize. Was Reggie angry with me and my blunder? I couldn't stop myself.

"Because people don't go to prison for nothing?" My words overflowed with the authoritative dogma I had imbibed for eighteen years. You received the consequences for what you did wrong, period. As sure of myself as that sounded, I was not actually convinced of the veracity of that lie. It had simply become a habit, someone else's truth, not the one I was now living and suddenly I wanted out of this conversation.

"Well, he did." Reggie got up to inspect a line as if to say *subject closed*. He had become an expert at cutting the lines of conversation that wouldn't precipitate his preferred resolution. He tugged on the crab line and when it became taut, he gently pulled in a crab coming to the surface and swimming under again.

"Grab the net! I can get this one but I need your help. This one's big, and he thinks he can outsmart us." Reggie pulled the crab close enough for me to slip the net under him. It took several attempts, but when the crab was finally in the net, Reggie grabbed the pole over my hands and together we scooped him up and dropped the crab into the ice chest.

"We've got a dozen," I calculated. "Is that enough? Can we go now?"

"I thought you wanted to come. You're not getting tired already, are you?" Reggie laughed.

"No, I'm not getting tired," I retorted. "I just didn't know how many crabs Mama wanted, that's all." My defense was shabby but I found myself needing to justify myself to him.

"Well, it's not even two o'clock. My plan was to stay until at least four. Think you can handle that?" I said I did but the truth was, the sun was beginning to beat down on us and I was tired. I'd pass out before I'd admit it, though. Reggie walked over to the truck and came back with a cap that said

Jake's Bait Shop on the front. "Here. Wear this. It'll help keep the sun off that pasty white face of yours," he laughed. I shoved him in mock rebellion of his playful insult, but as he put the cap on my head, his hand brushed my cheek. I smiled and thanked him and wore the cap for the rest of the day, even after the sun went down, thinking all the while of his hand on my face. He had also retrieved his transistor radio from the cab of the truck.

"You have a radio!" I squealed. "Why didn't you tell me hours ago? Find a good station fast!" Reggie obliged with a smile, knowing he had immediately improved my faltering attitude. James Brown was moaning a bluesy tune when Reggie quickly found the station, and he set the little transistor radio on the tarp while we returned to crabbing.

Reggie and I caught three dozen crabs, a productive day, but I was also pleased with myself that I now knew even more about him. Sunshine and water free the spirit, and I told Reggie my fears and anxieties and he listened. He didn't share as much about himself, but he was willing to answer the few questions I had. Just spending time with him was an education in itself. Hours later when the sun was going down, Reggie decided we needed to pack up and head home. He started to pick up the ice chest first when "Nights in White Satin" came on. It was my favorite song, and in a move of the great unexpected, Reggie walked over to me with his outstretched arm as if asking me to dance. Without hesitation I took his warm hand in mine. My heart beating fast, he drew me closer to him, bent slightly to wrap his arm around my waist, and began a slow dance on the tarp-covered shells. Halfway through the song, I lay my head on his chest and his arm drew me even closer. When the song ended I wanted us to return to the comfortable old Reggie and Lizzie, as if the dance had only been a dream, but he didn't move. He kissed the top of my head and remained there for several seconds before letting me go. I followed him to the truck where he placed the net and lunch supplies behind the ice chest, securing them in place with a strap before picking up the tarp to cover them.

"Okay, that's done. We better go." The back of the truck open, he waited for me to climb in, but I moved closer to him instead. When he turned around, our faces were inches apart and he quickly stepped back. "Everything okay? Ready to go?"

"Reggie," I murmured, my voice almost squeaking. "I had a really good time today. Please don't make me ride back under that awful tarp."

"I don't know, Lizzie. What if someone sees us? What then?"

"Reggie, I...." I couldn't finish my sentence. I threw my arms around him in the fading light and buried my face in his now familiar chest. For a minute he didn't move, but I knew he wouldn't push me away, and slowly, softly I felt his hands on my back once again, this time with the tentative faltering of a man waking from a dream in the uncertainty of what was now happening. It must have been only a minute or two, but it was a pivotal moment. Pent up feelings suddenly became too much for him and he dropped his hands.

"We should go." I wanted this day to last forever, and Reggie, caught between reality and desire, led me to the door of the truck and opened it for me to get in. I sat on the front seat and rode home quietly with no thought of what might come next. The open window blew my hair about, but I put the cap back on and replayed the events of the day in my mind. Reggie looked at me and smiled softly but no words passed between us.

The sinking sun turned the horizon pink and orange along the low sea level roads. It was six o'clock when we drove up to the house. Mama was standing on the porch when Reggie pulled his truck in to the drive. As we hauled the ice chest up to the sidewalk, she stared straight at me, and it wasn't a happy welcome home. I knew I was in trouble.

"I went by your economics class this afternoon to tell you I had a meeting and wouldn't be home until late, but your teacher said you weren't in class today. I'm not used to being made a fool of, Elizabeth. You can imagine how I felt. And Reginald, you let her talk you into this little act of deceit. I'm disappointed with you both." Reggie was quiet and I could see the hurt in his eyes.

"Mama, come on. No one was trying to deceive you and, believe me, nobody planned it, least of all Reggie. I just wanted to go crabbing and I knew you both would say no, so I hid under the tarp in his truck. I'm sorry, but I'm a senior. I'm sick of school and I needed a break! It's really no big deal. We got your crabs, didn't we?"

Mama wasn't placated by my half-hearted apology or my lame speech of justification. She turned around and slammed the door shut while we picked up the ice chest and carried it around to the back. Reggie hung his head and said nothing, and then he went right up to the door and knocked.

"Just go in, Reggie. I'm right behind you." By the time he opened the door, Mama was in the kitchen, and he began telling her the whole story. When he got to the part about finding me under the tarp, sweaty and gasping for air, she forgot about being mad, almost laughed a couple of times, and invited him to stay for supper. Only in the necessity of making peace did he accept, the one and only time he sat at the table with us for a meal. His recounting of the day, however, did not include the patrol car and the APB.

A little after ten p.m. and Reggie had gone home, the phone rang, followed soon after by Mrs. Bertrand at the front door, Mama standing in her housecoat and slippers. I could hear the high-pitched urgency in her voice and then the soul wrenching sobs as Mama escorted her to the kitchen and began making coffee. Randy's wife Cynthia had been found beaten to death, bludgeoned with a heavy instrument. I stood on the other side of the kitchen door in my bare feet listening to the story. Timid, unassuming Cynthia who allowed the man she trusted to abuse her had paid the ultimate price for love that would never be forthcoming. The baby, spattered with his mother's blood, lay unharmed on the bed and Randy was a person of interest.

It is important to know what level of infestation can be tolerated in your garden. The aim of the gardener is to keep pests at an approved and manageable level.

The Art of Gardening by Emily Mayfield

CHAPTER 24

1970 | In spite of the hysteria of the previous night's news that left us stunned, I woke up Saturday with no expectations other than my usual but slightly anesthetizing routine—sleep in, trudge to the kitchen for a bowl of cold cereal and milk, watch cartoons—a mindless antithesis to the previous days-long tempest of studying for exams and sitting in the hot sun near the Gulf. Yet unbeknownst to the inhabitants of sleepy little Carlton, all hell was about to break loose. On the other side of town in an apartment near the junior college, a brutal murder had taken place only twenty-four hours before, and we knew the victim and alleged perpetrator. I stuffed milky Cheerios into my mouth, and in my mind, the kiss on the water the day before was still on my lips. More details of the ghastly murder, I thought, would emerge later that evening on the five o'clock news.

Wiley Coyote was speeding away when a knock at the front door produced my mother's friend Officer Corley. Standing like a sentinel in the blinding light of the morning, he announced in an authoritative tone that he would need to look in the summer house in our back yard for anything that might be related to the murder of Cynthia Bertrand. After interviewing the members of the family next door, he had reason to believe he might find evidence. Mama stood mutely perplexed for a moment before leading the officer out back. Her petite form barely filled the entrance to the little screened-in house where she believed nothing more sinister than garden supplies would be found. Stuffed between bags of cow manure, however, was a man's blood streaked shirt as if waiting to be discovered.

"Don't you have a yard boy who uses this shed?" Officer Corley found the shirt with little effort and then looked through the screen at Reggie, the man who at that very moment was on his knees weeding her flower beds. Reginald Washington had worked in our yard every week for the last three, almost four years off and on, she explained. What she didn't say, however, was that she had allowed him to make it his dominion, and oddly enough I had become the guest, perhaps even an intruder at times. He had simply kept to himself, at least when I wasn't bothering him in my veiled if not hermetic fascination with him. Suddenly he was the center of attention, all eyes on Mrs. Rowan's gardener.

"Reggie's been with us for several years now without one incident. I trust him implicitly." I peered out the back door so I could hear, the fearful truth not yet registering. Officer Corley walked out the summer house and into the garden. Mama's gasp was audible when suddenly he began leading Reggie to his patrol car. Reggie, subdued in his self-annihilating compliance and with no resistance, walked ahead of him. Mama stepped closer to him. "Jim, is this really necessary? There must be some mistake. Reginald's a good boy. He wouldn't do this. I'm telling you—this is a mistake."

"Louise, I'm taking him in for questioning, that's all."

Officer Corley walked Reggie around to the front and put him in the patrol car. Mama followed them and when he had driven away she walked back to the porch where I was waiting.

"Mama, there's no way Reggie could have done this."

"I know Reggie didn't do this. I know he didn't." Her voice, trembling, betrayed her fear. "I don't know what Jim Corley thinks he's doing, but he's way off base with this."

"Mama, wait a minute. We can help. Where was Reggie yesterday—all day—and who was with him?"

When the five o'clock news came on, Mama and I sat down in front of the television to see what news was being shared with the public. I caught only a few words—blood spattered walls, baby crying—no doubt drowning out the screams of his mother as her assailant beat the life out of his victim. They said the baby lying on the bed covered with his mother's blood had not been harmed. According to the report, the husband had been away in a nearby city trying repeatedly, he stated, to call his wife. The same familiar story confirmed the account that Mrs. Bertrand had related to us that morning. We knew Randy. We had a history with him, the middle son of our next door neighbors who had watched us grow up, yet the minute the reporter said his name, I had no doubt that Randy Bertrand was guilty. But once again, there was Reginald Washington bowing to a price he shouldn't pay.

It was going to be a long night, tumbling into the darkness of every event and circumstance surrounding Reggie, from the first day we met to the night I betrayed him and every moment after. Unable to sleep, Mama and I sat in the kitchen drinking tea while she related the conversation she had earlier that morning. Sarah Bertrand poured out the story as she knew it for over an hour, crying and wringing her handkerchief every time she thought of not only the loss of her daughter-in-law but, as she woefully added, the final supreme disappointment of a son who had so little value for life. The shame and disgrace was unbearable. Randy's neighbors in the adjacent apartment heard the baby screaming for hours and finally tried knocking on the door. One of them pushed open the unlocked door, went inside, and, upon seeing the bloody scene, called the police. Randy claimed he had been in Lafayette, a two hour drive away, picking up shrimp from the friend of a friend who operated a boat on the coast, but the time of his whereabouts was unclear. He told the police he had tried calling his wife several times from a nearby bait shop, and when she didn't answer, he drove home. At best, it was a shaky alibi, but Randy, who was taken in for questioning, was released later that day. His calls had checked out.

According to the coroner's office, the crime had occurred on Friday mid-morning, but, when the truth came out weeks later, Jimmy had already found his Mickey Mantle that afternoon. Once again dried blood covered the entire wood surface of the bat, wrapped in Randy's bloody shirt in a cupboard in the garage. The fact that it had been recently padlocked was enough to make him pry it open with one thought in mind. Randy had taken his bat again as repayment for any number of infractions, the most recent, Jimmy's refusal to babysit, he reasoned. When Jimmy and I talked later, he said he was beaming at his own cleverness, outsmarting his older brother, until he put the horror of it all together. The slowly grasped acknowledgement of dried blood on the bat and clothes became clear to him. *Cynthia.* Brotherly aggravation or not, he would never betray his family, and the only thing to do was to make everyone believe that someone else had committed the crime. Mrs. Rowan's yard boy could be disposed of, couldn't he? Randy, inconsolably angry and bad-tempered and vicious at times, was after all Jimmy's brother, his own flesh and blood. How could he turn his own brother over to the cops? Jimmy wasn't giving up his bat again, but the blood soaked shirt could easily be relocated, and in the middle of the night, Jimmy had done just that and he kept this secret to himself. In the end when all the facts coalesced in my head, a stark realization emerged. Randy had used his brother's bat again, and it was because I had not spoken up the first time.

Good cultural practice—soil preparation, weeding, and watering in the garden may not be sufficient to keep persistent pests away. Defensive action must be administered if susceptible plants are to survive.

The Art of Gardening by Emily Mayfield

CHAPTER 25

1970 | Before we left the house, Mama called Officer Corley, who agreed to meet us at the front door of the station. She and the officer had dated when I was in the fourth grade, when he represented the police department at the high school and Mama served on the committee for career day. It fizzled out after a while and that was that, but they remained friends, Mama believing a friendly relationship with a member of law enforcement was better than no relationship. I was beginning to see her point.

We sat on a bench for over an hour before an officer took us through a maze of hallways to a small room where we waited again. When Officer Corley walked in, Mama rose from her seat to greet him, as a friend might do without even thinking, but the circumstances were clearly not amicable. Instead he made no eye contact with either of us as he told her to sit down on the bench in the hall while he talked to me first. He escorted me into an interrogation room and motioned for me to sit down.

"Can I get you some water," he said.

Unfamiliar with hospitality norms at a police station, I simply shook my head no. He then opened a folder, clicked his pen, and began to write, what I couldn't imagine since I had uttered nothing. His slow interminable pace culminated in asking me where I had been on Friday morning and why, every detail. I related that unforgettable day as I relived it in my head from the moment I hid under the tarp and the patrol car stopped to question Reggie to Mama standing on the porch with her arms folded across her chest as we carried the ice chest of crabs into the kitchen.

"Why were you hiding under the tarp in Reginald Washington's truck?" he asked. I hesitated, looking at his face for clues to why he would ask a question with such an obvious answer.

"I...I wasn't supposed to be there."

"And why would that be?"

Explaining to a white police officer why a white girl was secretly escaping for a rendezvous on the Gulf with a black boy was painful, and I was angry that he made me explain it. "I guess because I was skipping school to go crabbing with him." I knew what he wanted me to admit but I tried to sidestep it. "It was so close to graduation and I guess I had a bad case of senioritis. I just wanted to have some fun and...." I stopped myself as I slid into the land of emotional excuses and said no more.

"Lizzie," he sighed and put his pen down. "What were you thinking, getting in the back of a truck with a colored boy?" The look of disapproval removed him from being the investigating officer to Mama's good friend who couldn't understand what I might see in a black boy. "He didn't take advantage of you, did he?" I didn't answer him but shot him a glance that said *Don't even ask! Of course not!* For all Reggie had once been and was even now, Officer Corley saw him only as a colored boy of so low a caliber that merely being in his presence might cast a stain on my character. He didn't press me on it but shook his head and continued with other questions, like what time did we leave and what time did we return, did we see anybody out there, did anyone see us together? I didn't want to mention the officer who drove up that day around the bridge where Reggie stood, but I blurted it out anyway, anything to help Reggie. "Actually, there was an officer who drove his car around the bridge and onto the shells where we were crabbing, but I didn't get a good look at him."

"Why not?"

It was then that I realized I was digging another hole for myself, or maybe just digging the one I was already in deeper. "Reggie thought....I thought that we might get in trouble if the officer saw us together. I hid under the bridge when he came." I lowered my head, feeling a shame I knew was wrong. But how could being with someone you cared about be wrong? I looked up quickly, determined not to provoke Officer Corley, and I added, "After all, I was skipping school that day."

"And you don't remember anything about him? Not one thing? This officer could be a potential witness."

"All I remember is he had a khaki uniform and brown hair. And he was short and fat. I think. Anyway he was shorter than Reggie. That's all I could see from where I was." He didn't say anything else but glanced up at me quickly as he gathered his materials together. He then handed me a blank sheet of paper and asked me to write in my own words everything I had told him, adding, "Sign it when you're done. And make sure I can read your name clearly." Officer Corley's chair screeched as he pushed back and got up to leave. "I'll be back. Just sit here a minute when you're done." Half an hour later he returned and looked over my statement. "You can go sit with your mother now, and then I'll need to speak with her."

I turned around and stopped in the middle of the hallway. "What about Reggie? When will he be able to leave? He's innocent, you know. He shouldn't be here." I could hear the emotion rising again.

"All this takes time, Lizzie. I can't answer that. We'll need to look into it further and talk to any other possible witnesses. That's all I can tell you. It just takes time." As we approached the hallway, I saw Mama still sitting on the bench reading a magazine. "Can I get you a soft drink?" he said.

"No, I don't think so, thank you anyway." How could I enjoy a Coca Cola or a Barq's when Reggie was still a suspect? I sat down next to Mama who took my hand and looked at me with sorrow in her eyes. She didn't say anything, just squeezed my hand, and Officer Corley took my statement to the back. We didn't sit there long. Another officer came around and took Mama down the hall. I put my head down and let the tears drop into my lap.

It was after dark when we left the police station to return home, unsure what would happen to Reggie. I wondered when he would be released, assuming in light of our testimony that he would be. As it turned out, after only a few hours he was freed from one more injustice he had to endure.

"Jim—Officer Corley, wasn't too happy that you skipped school to spend the day with Reggie," Mama sighed as we got in the car.

"Is that what he told you?" I could feel my frustration turning into anger now. "He asked me what I could have been thinking when I got in the truck with a colored boy. I mean, he didn't dwell on it, but I knew he was disappointed in me."

"Yes, I know. He asked me how I could have let this happen—you and a colored boy. Together. Having fun."

"Mama, Reggie isn't just a colored boy." Tears would come any minute now, and the semblance of courage that I had assumed earlier was dissipating quickly. "He's a good friend, maybe the best I've ever had. I feel so lost in this town. Is the color of his skin all that matters?" I was wailing now. "I can't help how I feel about him. I can't…." And the floodgates opened. My head and heart hurt with a sadness of hope lost, so much that I wrapped my arms around myself and put my head in my lap. Mama reached out and put her hand on me as she drove home, but she didn't say anything until she pulled into our driveway and turned off the engine. When she didn't move, I sat up.

"Lizzie, honey, there's something you need to understand. Ever since your father left, you and I have lived in two worlds. We have one foot in a community of traditional white folks who hold on to the past and everything familiar and comfortable in it. And there's much to be said about the good in it. But we also stepped into a sometimes darker place where only foolish or courageous people live outside the boundaries of what is expected. We cross the line every day. I'm raising a daughter without a husband, and we have a Negro man who is often at our house, not only as a gardener but as our friend. It's a field day for misunderstandings. One day things will be different, but for now it'll help if you just try to accept the reality of our situation and make peace with it."

"But we didn't choose that life," I sobbed. "It just happened. Is that how you've coped all these years?"

"Oh, honey, our life hasn't been so bad has it? I mean, other than the odd visit from your grandparents, we've done all right, haven't we?"

"You have." Now was as good a time as any to bring up Reggie's mother. "Mama, Reggie said you knew his mother a long time ago, when you and Daddy were still together. Why didn't you tell me?"

"It was a long time ago. Too much water under that bridge to revisit it."

"Reggie said he saw me when I was just a baby but he didn't see you. Where were you? Was I alone with Daddy?"

Mama sighed, realizing I was searching for answers she had been holding close to her without sharing. "Your father was taking care of you while I was in Alabama. Your grandfather was in the hospital following an appendectomy and I went to be with him while your grandmother tended the store."

"Oh. So why did you let his mother go? Was she not a good house-keeper? What happened?" Mama looked defeated at that moment, but I had to know.

"Liz, honey, there are some things that are better left unsaid. We can't change the past. We can only move on and be better than we were, live better than we've lived."

"No, Mama. Tell me exactly what happened. I'm old enough to understand. I'm not a child anymore." Mama exhaled a long deep breath and looked up at me. She put her hands on the steering wheel as if holding on to something made what she had to say easier.

"When I returned from Mobile, I saw Mrs. Washington—Bessie, in the A&P. I told her how sorry I was to lose her and hoped nothing had happened to make her leave. I asked her if she would reconsider coming to work for us. She seemed agitated, like she had something to tell me. Toward the end of the week before I was to return to Carlton, she said, she had let herself in as usual to clean the house, but your father must have forgotten she was coming because she said he....he had a....a friend with him."

"A friend? Are you trying to tell me he was with another woman, Mama? Is that what you're trying to say? What does that have to do with Reggie's mama?"

"He let her go that instant. Told her never to come back again."

"And you stayed with him for three more years?"

"Who told you that?"

"Well, I can count. Reggie said he was seven. I must have been two, and Daddy left when I was five. How could you forgive him for that? Did he stop seeing that woman? Mama, you must have felt terrible. How could he do that to you?" I wanted to cry but I was glad he was gone, for my sake as well as Mama's.

"Oh, honey. You just do what you have to do to keep your family together. He didn't want to be married, not to me, not to anyone. He wanted a life of adventure and I suppose he felt tied down. That was so long ago. Don't waste any more time thinking about it. I've moved on and you need to do the same."

"Were you surprised when you saw Reggie in your classroom?"

"I didn't know who he was at first. I looked at his records and found out that his mother was Bessie Washington. I later told Reginald I knew his mother, but that was the extent of our conversation about her. This is the first time I've heard that he was with her that day. But enough." Mama opened the car door and got out. Without looking back, she said, "Come on in and help me get dinner started." I followed her up the walk and that was the end of it.

Neither of us slept well that night, maybe because we gouged ourselves on ice cream, but in the early hours of the morning, just past midnight, a large rock crashed through the front window, sending Mama first to the living room and then to my room.

"Lizzie, Lizzie, honey! Get up! Quick, Liz! Our front yard's on fire."

Drugged with fatigue, I managed to get out the words, "What? Did you call the Fire Department?" Fire, I reasoned, simply meant fire and nothing more sinister than that.

"Yes, get dressed and come with me." I pulled on a tee shirt and some shorts and met Mama standing at the open front door. We gazed at each other as our thoughts aligned.

"Mama, I think you'd better call the police, too." The quivering in my voice belied my panic. As if the plight of fire and the danger to life and limb weren't intimidating enough, the juncture of a fiery cross towering over our yard proclaimed a corrosive impasse. We had been marked, singled out as traitors with the promise of retribution to follow. The flames leapt higher and higher until I thought they were going to surge toward the oak just feet away, its branches brushing the roof of our house, and set all of our worldly possessions ablaze. Appearing taller and more engulfing than they probably were, they emitted intermittent waves of heat, yet it was the wall of flame separating us from the street, apocalyptic in its covenant of total destruction that terrified me more. We were told later that the inferno was only three feet tall, but its twitching fingers of flame reaching upward implied otherwise and magnified the anxiety as only fear of the unknown can deliver. While Mama called the police from the kitchen, I moved out to the porch to see our neighbors, the Caldwells, Abbotts, and Bertrands, and others I didn't know well from down the street making their way over to gawk at the spectacle of a cross burning, a sight no one ever expected to see in the front yard of a highly respected white teacher in Carlton. Multiple sounds of sirens wailed as they proceeded in slow motion down the street, howling louder and louder as the vehicles approached our house. Flashing lights amidst the smoke that hung on the humid night air, a fire that threatened our home, and curious neighbors in their robes and night clothes who had risen out of their sleep to watch created a panorama of surreal dimension.

Calls made, Mama joined me and put an arm around my shoulder as if to say we could get through the nightmare together. Another siren pierced the night air while the firemen extinguished the cross of flames and surrounding grass and spoke to Mr. Caldwell and Mr. Bertrand. Our kind neighbors had offered to drag the logs, heavy with ash and water, out of sight, but Mr. Bertrand told Mama that a fire inspector would be along in a few days to collect them as evidence, so they left the logs lying where they were. I went inside. I could see Mama talking to a police officer and then she turned and walked back down the long sidewalk to our front door, past the appalling debris of singed grass and blackened wood, odious tokens of the shame cast on our home and its inhabitants. The officer assured her a police car would be patrolling our street for the next few weeks. Mrs. Bertrand handed Mama a cup of coffee and soon everyone disappeared into the safety of their own homes as quickly as they had emerged only half an hour before. In the early morning light, I surveyed the damage from the front window. The lawn was now a barren wasteland, my new catchwords that could send me to some forsaken place in my mind where youthful energy was quickly fading.

The police did patrol the neighborhood that week, but neither of us felt safe. The next afternoon I was sitting in the swing when Jimmy came into our yard. They had seen the charred cross and the blackened grass stretching across most of the yard, and if there had been any doubt as to the reason, they weren't going to talk about it. Certainly the word had spread all over town about the Rowans' cross burning. Jimmy had brought an axe to chop it up until I stopped him, "No, Jimmy—it's evidence and it's going to be taken away soon." He didn't say anything, just stared back at me as if frozen. "That's what the fireman said last night, anyway." I looked away and put my head down, closing my eyes to control the shaking that had begun to rattle my body, rocking back and forth in the swing. I felt his gentle hand stroking the top of my head and the tears came. When I looked up again, he was gone and I wiped my eyes and stood up to go inside. After dinner, sleep deprivation diminishing my chances of staying awake much longer, Mama came into my room and sat down on my bed. I was dozing off and on through the latest book she had given me, but she wanted a kind of mother-daughter debriefing of our hellish night before. All I wanted was to extricate myself from the entire episode, but I sat up and gave her my full attention.

"Well, at least there's the graduation party at the Heberts' house this Saturday—that should be a welcomed diversion. Do you need something new to wear, hon?" If only she hadn't brought it up. I took a deep breath. Did she really think I was in the mood for a party?

"I'm not going," I answered.

"What do you mean you're not going? Why not?" Once again Mama was projecting herself onto me, always resigned to whatever life handed her and expecting me to follow her example, but this time I rebelled.

"I just don't want to. I'm tired and I want to be left alone."

"That's nonsense. Come on. Let's look in your closet and see what you have to wear. Maybe I can get out my machine and whip up a new shift. I have a cute belt you can wear with it."

"Mama, stop." She was still going through my closet with an uncanny revival of enthusiasm. "Mama, listen to me. I was uninvited today." She stopped without turning around. Instead she held on to the hangers in the closet and was quiet before closing the door and sitting down again. It was as if she already knew this could happen, and yet she didn't want to face the injustice of it all.

"Oh, Lizzie, are you sure? How do you know?" Her voice overflowed with the disappointment that anyone could reject her daughter.

"I sat with some girls at lunch, and Sharon Hebert told me it would be best for everyone if I didn't come to her party. She said my being there might make people feel uncomfortable. Apparently word had spread that I skipped school to spend a day crabbing with Reggie. I guess the cross burning sealed my fate. People are afraid to be around me." I let out a deep breath. "It's fine, Mama. I wasn't really interested in going in the first place. I mean, who wants to play croquet in a dress for three hours?" My excuse sounded like something I would say, but in truth, my feelings were shattered. No matter what justification I leaned on, I never understood until much later why my classmates, most of whom I had known since first grade, had done this to me. After years of disillusionment about relationships, I began to redefine loyalty. It was, I had discovered with heart-rending effect, a gift that only saint-like people possessed—and knew the gift they had, people with hearts big enough to accommodate defeat with a kind of selfless selfishness. Loyalty was a rare and precious union of opposites that, after all was said and done, engendered unfettered love. I've yet to know more than a handful of these saints, but sadly at the time I didn't fully appreciate or understand their sacrifices.

"That's just plain cruel. I'm really sorry, honey. Did anyone else say something?" Mama wasn't taking the news well and I wasn't keen on finishing the story, but now wasn't the time for soft soaping it. More and more, pretense was no longer working for me as a modus operandi.

"You might as well know. You'll find out soon enough."

Someone had scribbled in huge red marker across the face of my locker words that seared. I saw them long before I got to my locker late that afternoon, loathsome words that glared no less fearfully than the fiery cross raised on our lawn. The hall was clear by then and I stood alone in front of the abomination and cried. No one could hear me in the hollowness that surrounded me and I let the tears flow. Who else had seen this?

Before heading home, I tried to wipe it off with wet paper towels from the bathroom, but my efforts left only a huge red smudge. The janitor must have taken care of it on his evening rounds because it was gone by morning.

Mama didn't need to ask what it said. Somehow saying the words didn't make me feel vindicated and I was quiet. I never told her. She put her hand on mine and began to cry. I rarely saw her do this—her resignation toward disappointment never ceased to replace any serious residual lamenting over disappointments that fell her way. Finally she took my hand

and kissed it, then left the room. I put a bookmark in my book, pulled the covers back and tried to sleep, but all I could think of was Reggie. All along I had felt sorry for myself when he was the one who had to carry the burden for all of us. It was because Reginald Washington, a clever, handsome, kind Negro boy—no, Reggie was a man now, had the sober misfortune of being put in the company of a white girl. Through no fault of his own, we had been visited upon by cowards who tried to pin a murder on him. We had found a cross burning on our lawn and a society had excluded me from their company. Crying myself to sleep was becoming a habit, yet buckets of tears weren't going to wash away the stain I was to wear until I left.

Summer was the reprieve I needed. Graduation had been a quick affair, minus the usual celebration, and Mama and I had driven to the coast for a quiet seafood buffet. The whole thing was over without fanfare. Cynthia's funeral had taken place a week after her death and the Bertrands stayed at home as much as possible, away from prying eyes and ears. Mama and I attended but there was no reception to celebrate a life. Sadness hung over the house and got heavier and heavier as the weeks passed. I went to work for the Kelly Girl Company as a temp secretary for an oil company. Lucky for me, the job lasted two months and could have gone on longer had I not needed to leave to get settled in the dorm and registered for classes. At the last minute I enrolled in a degree program at Faraday College, a small educational institution two and a half hours north of Carlton with an interesting history dating back to the early 1800s. Most of my graduating class went straight to the work force or to the junior college nearby, and an elite few went off to LSU. Reggie had been gone for almost three months. Released without enough evidence and with two alibis, Reggie took off for his uncle's farm outside of Bossier City without saying goodbye. Talk of him petered out to a casual mention until we stopped altogether. Hopefulness turned into waiting patiently and then to moving on with life. I was packing for college and trying to focus on the future. One afternoon, Jimmy, who had been accepted to LSU and would be leaving soon to meet his roommates and set up his dorm room, walked over to the garden where I was feeding the fish and stood in front of me with his hands in his pockets, looking like the old Jimmy I had always known.

"Hey, Lizzie. Mind if I join you?" he said.

"Hey. 'Course not. What's up? I was hoping to say goodbye. When are you leaving for Baton Rouge?" I handed him some bread for the fish.

"Not until Sunday. I haven't even started packing yet. You?"

"Yeah, I'm packed, almost finished anyway." We didn't say much, typical of most of our conversations, until he tossed the rest of the crumbs into the water and looked at me.

"I'm glad I'm leaving. I can't wait to get away from here," he said, staring back at the ground and drawing in the dirt with a stick.

"Well, I'll miss you, too!" He didn't respond to my attempt at humor but continued scraping a line in the dirt. "That bad, huh? Listen, I'm really sorry about Cynthia. Things must be awful at your house."

"You have no idea," he said, and when he looked up, his eyes were glistening.

"Oh, Jimmy, I'm so sorry. I wish I could do something." I put my hand on his arm and he let me leave it there. I squeezed his hand in a show of sympathy and he started to walk away. He stopped a few feet from the swing with his head hanging down, bent over with his hands on his knees. I ran over to him, thinking he might be sick. He was shaking and crying as I had never seen him. "Hey, listen, do you want to come in and talk?" But he didn't answer. He slowly stood up limp, and I put my arms around him. He cried even harder. "Come over here and let's sit on the back steps." We managed to walk to the back door before he collapsed on the steps. He put his head in his hands and spoke.

"I'm going to hell, Lizzie. I've done a really bad thing, and I'm going to hell."

"Jimmy, what are you talking about? You're one of the nicest people I know. Stop saying things like that. You're a good Catholic boy and you've just been through too much, more than your share of what a family should have to endure. Things are going to settle down, especially when you get to LSU and start classes."

Jimmy looked at me as if I couldn't possibly know what I was talking about. "Oh, the things you don't know about me and my family."

"Are you forgetting that we've been neighbors a long time, how many years? Thirteen at least? Our mothers are best friends. You and I grew up together. What more is there?"

"How about my fuckin' monster brother....who I've protected."

"What do you mean, protected? You've always done just the opposite."

"Yeah. Well, not this time. And I'm going to hell for what I've done."

"Jimmy, stop that! What have you done that's so bad?"

And then he started crying again, so hard I could barely make out what he was saying. "It was me, Lizzie. I'm the one who put the bloody shirt in the summer house." Jimmy hung his head and cried, swallowing air and spitting out blubbering sobs. I was dumbfounded that good, kind Jimmy was willing to send Reggie to the electric chair for murder, knowing he was innocent. I sat there stupefied, then so angry that I had no words of comfort to offer him. When he finally calmed down, he got up and began walking toward his house. "I'm going to hell for what I did."

"Hold on a minute! You would let an innocent man die for what your brother did?" I was furious. "Reggie might have been released, but what about his good name? You are not going to do this to him, do you hear me?" I was yelling now. "You have to tell someone, Jimmy. Not just for Reggie but for yourself. You have to tell. Reggie's innocent and you have to tell the truth. We cannot stand by and watch him take on the guilt of your hateful, evil brother. I won't let it happen. If you don't tell someone, I will."

"I know." He was broken, but did he recognize what had to be done?

"When, Jimmy? When are you going to tell the truth?"

"Now, Lizzie!" he yelled back, and then he calmly repeated himself. "Right now. I'll go in and find my mother," and he opened the screen door to his sleeping porch. Jimmy turned and looked at me, "I'm so sorry, Lizzie." His voice was quivering and he gazed at me before closing the door.

Without fanfare, Sarah Bertrand announced the next Saturday morning in our kitchen that Jimmy and Judy had eloped. They had already found an apartment in Baton Rouge and Mr. Bertrand was in the process of moving them in. I would never understand how Jimmy could confess his part in his brother's crime, but he couldn't tell me he was about to get married.

Mama drove me up to Faraday on the weekend before classes were to begin, her excitement feeble, almost contrived. I had decided long before that day with little enthusiasm to major in history instead of English, with journalism still undecided, but Mama seemed oddly dispassionate to the point of apathetic. She had waited for this moment when I would go to college, had spent her life preparing me for it. Yet from my side of the car, when I looked over at her face, it was empty and unassuming as if we were simply making another trip to the A & P. It finally occurred to me that the burdensome events of spring and summer finally weighed her down, and the load had begun to alter everything about her. We didn't speak for the first hour and a half, sharing only the snacks she had packed, words of encouragement and advice noticeably absent. All along I had thought only of myself and the distress I had suffered, not once seriously weighing the effects taking a toll on her. I retreated to the solace of thinking about my new major, a choice initially made without enthusiasm. A typical heartfelt interest in anything hadn't played a part in the decision of what I would study, and, as almost every other decision I made that summer, I relied heavily on an avoidance of the familiar, whatever reminded me of anything remotely connected to Reggie or Carlton. And yet, when I later sat in a history lecture on campus for the next two years, my mind drifted to Reggie—slaves who were forced to move west with their owners, the Civil War, Martin Luther King's assassination, the Kennedy assassinations, the Civil Rights Act, Bloody Sunday. Everything of interest in the history of our country I absorbed because of him. No, not at first, rather I had offered him an undignified denial of his history that Reggie understood as my arrogance, even though I knew him to be capable of telling only the truth.

Mama helped me move into the dorm and we met my roommate, a girl from Shreveport majoring in home economics who had already moved in the day before and was scurrying off to meet friends from her home town. We sat down on my bed in awkward silence until I said I would unpack later and suggested we find a little café in town for a quick lunch. Mama was anxious to get back before dark so we said goodbye. She would call me later on the dorm's community phone.

The first semester of college crept by like one of Reggie's green caterpillars looking for a place to curl up, slowly moving me forward with a nevertheless warrior like spirit determined to reach my predestination. Christmas break was my target goal. Despite making friends with the girls on my floor in the dorm, who invariably had attempted to organize their schedules around the weekly TV soaps in the community lounge, I was homesick for Mama. In one of her weekly letters I learned that soon after Jimmy's tearful confession, Randy had been charged with the death of his wife, a crime of passion. A year later he would be sentenced to eleven years for voluntary manslaughter. Reggie, after saying goodbye to Mama, had left for his uncle's farm in north Louisiana where he hoped to find work. Everyone was talking about the possible outcome of the murder investigation with a range of opinions from gross injustice to fear of leniency. Sarah Bertrand had confided to Mama that Jimmy finally came clean and confessed to pinning the blame on Reggie. He acknowledged to his mother and later to the police his stunt with not only the shirt but also his bat. More startling news, I would be returning to a neighborhood without the Bertrands. After living there so many years, the family had left Carlton, informing only a few close friends. Randy's trial and potential incarceration after losing a son in Viet Nam were frankly too much to cope with. The family abandoned the life they knew and moved to Alexandria to be close to Mrs. Bertrand's brother and his family. Cynthia's mother lived an hour away and, after the initial shock and anger toward Randy, even Randy's family, she agreed to let them see their grandson often. Mama would no doubt feel the loss keenly. Sarah Bertrand's neighborly visits ranged from the proverbial borrowed sticks of margarine and cups of sugar to moments of gossip and, lately, distress and even tragedy, and her absence would leave a gap not only in Mama's weekly routine but especially in her need for the comfort and solace of friendship. She had come to expect that sort of community from the women who lived on our street, but most of all, from Sarah Bertrand.

Christmas break finally arrived. I found it odd that she had put up the tree without decorating it, but she was baking Christmas sugar cookies by the time my ride, a boy from school that I had been seeing lately, pulled into the driveway. I invited him in, but he was anxious to get home himself and said he'd call me later. Mama was in the kitchen taking a tray of cookies out the oven when I came in. As always, her cheerful welcome energized me after the long drive. I picked up a shiny red ball from the box near the tree and hooked it to a branch.

"Well, you're just in time. Cup of tea? I have some spice tea one of my students gave me for Christmas. Danny isn't coming in?"

"No, he wanted to get home and go to the range with his brother. And yes, actually, I need something. Tea sounds good. That long, boring drive makes me sleepy." I took off my coat and threw it on a chair, a habit of living in a dorm, as Mama's warning glance made me pick it up again and take it to my room. My old bed was inviting but I knew she would expect me to help decorate the batch that had cooled while we drank our tea and caught up. Christmas this year would consist of just the two of us, a quiet one that I looked forward to sharing with her. In her last letter Mama had asked me what I wanted for Christmas, and without hesitation, I replied some new clothes or a warm robe—the old heating system in my room, a capricious radiator that worked erratically and even noisily at times, left me freezing in the morning—and some slippers, too, if it wouldn't be too much trouble. On Christmas morning when we opened our gifts to each other, I had given Mama what I wanted—a red plush robe and slippers to match, and she had given me books and a camera, a little Kodak flash camera with a strap attached to put around my neck, and four rolls of film. I hid my disappointment and silently worried about braving that ice cold dorm room that I now occupied alone in my thin cotton robe. My roommate had quit in the middle of our first semester and moved out one weekend, but I soon began to see this camera in a different light, a new source of creativity, a welcomed endeavor for a loner. Besides taking pictures of each other in front of the Christmas tree, however, it remained in its box for several weeks. One evening before I was to make the long drive back to school, we sat in front of the blazing fireplace drinking cocoa as she listened to more details of college life. As if she had suddenly remembered some news she was excited to share, Mama perked up and announced she had been working on a new dress for me and would show me her masterpiece that afternoon. No amount of quizzing and persuasion, however, would appease my curiosity. Finally I broached the subject of Reggie.

"Any word from him?" I inquired as if the idea were incidental.

"Yes, as a matter of fact. Let me see where I put it." Mama got up and walked over to her roll top desk. "He sent us a Christmas card. Yes, here it is." It was lying on top of a number of other cards she had received, out of its envelope, and, holding it up to show me a lovely snow covered tree filled with an array of cardinals, blue jays, and sparrows, she opened the card and read aloud, "Merry Christmas to Mrs. Rowan and Lizzie. I'm still at my uncle's farm working as a landscaper with my cousin. Hope you have a good holiday. Reginald Washington."

"A landscaper, huh? Good for him. I guess you're missing his help in the garden now. How are you managing Reggie's garden masterpiece?" I laughed. Mama didn't laugh, however, and said she wasn't giving it much thought now that it was winter. I suspected she was concerned about taking too much on herself. "How are the fish?"

"Oh, don't worry. I'm still feeding the fish and birds every day. I miss him terribly, but I'll cross that bridge in spring. I have a few months to decide." And that was the end of our discussion about Reginald Washington. Although I thought about him off and on, I never brought up his name or the garden again that Christmas.

Gardens as places of beauty and retreat should have focal points to give a sense of purpose. A tree can function in this way to draw attention to a particular spot in the garden and may even serve as a centerpiece of the entire display, adding life to the land and its inhabitants.

The Art of Gardening by Emily Mayfield

CHAPTER 26

1972 | It was raining hard when I packed up my car—a used Oldsmobile Mama took off the Abbotts' hands after Christmas, and drove home from college. The difficulty of bad roads in early spring weather aggravated the concern for my mother. Almost halfway through my degree course at the end of March, I received a letter from her complaining one too many times about a cough she couldn't clear up. I packed a bag on Friday after my last class and hit the road to Carlton, a treacherous drive away in bad weather on two lane roads winding through the Kisatchie National Forest. Daunted by years of hauling my gear to the third floor in the dorm every semester, I used the excuse that I had become acclimated to a comfortable routine, and several months would pass before I would tackle that road and return home for a weekend. The moment I arrived I looked at her thin face and arms and realized Mama's health had been rapidly deteriorating, a condition she had kept from me. We were sitting in the kitchen with a cup of tea as she explained the disease that would now require constant medical attention. I heard a knock at the door and got up to answer it. Reggie, whom I had not seen in two years, was standing there.

"Good Lord, I can't believe it. Hello, stranger!" Warm memories of a closeness once encountered with him kicked in and I leaned in to him to hug him. Reggie stood there surprised and I quickly backed away and invited him in. "What brings you to town? Come in. Come in." Reggie, unaccustomed to entering through the front door, nevertheless walked in, took off his coat and made himself at home as if he had always done it. He was in Carlton for the wedding of a friend he had known since childhood and didn't want to leave without stopping by for a visit long overdue. I was surprised to hear about this hitherto unknown friend—yet another clue to the reality of two years absence that was alien to me, but we spoke quietly as I let him know the more prevailing information about just how sick I thought Mama was. He asked if he could see her. I led him into the kitchen where she perked up the minute she saw him. She tried to get up too quickly and held on to the chair, but Mama was elated to see him and immediately welcomed Reggie to her table for the coffee we now began brewing. He would never be her yard boy again, instead, the welcomed guest he had long ago come to be. The three of us sat in the kitchen, the way I dared to imagine it might be again, the carefree buoyancy of good friends passing the time with ease. I let them talk while I absorbed all his news. He had been working in north Louisiana with his uncle whose tree farm and garden were now prospering. He told us stories of working the soil and going to market, of good deals and of men who tried to cheat them. He made Mama laugh and forget the illness that would in the end take her mind as well as her body.

"Oh, my goodness, Reginald Washington. You have been busy and clever, too. We've missed you."

"Well, I've missed you, too, Mrs. Rowan. How's the pond doing? Lost any more fish? They live a long time, some of them for ten years."

"All there as far as I know. After you covered the top, I don't believe we've lost a one yet. Good thing you and Lizzie held a stakeout and found out it was Mama Raccoon teaching her babies to fish," she said, a friendly smirk at her revelation.

"I suspected you knew," I blushed. She didn't answer and Reggie flashed his big toothy grin at her.

"I brought you a tree from my uncle's farm. It's a sapling but I think it'll grow fast. A river birch."

"A birch? You brought me a birch? Thank you, Reginald. You remembered." Mama looked at Reggie and smiled.

"Remembered what?" I asked, feeling left out of the sudden collusion between them.

"A birch tree brings good luck," Mama answered audibly drawing breath in as she leaned into the chair.

"Oh, really? How so?" I pushed back and Reggie took over. I poured three cups of coffee and put milk and sugar on the table.

"Celtic symbol of hope and promise. It was that story we read, Grainne and Diarmuid, if I remember correctly."

"Right you are, Reginald. I should have known you'd remember," Mama said.

Reggie must have recognized that explanation was lost on me and added, "Mrs. Rowan's senior English class." He grinned proudly, still looking at Mama.

"Who?" I asked, still puzzled.

"Grainne and Diarmuid," Mama mused.

"An old story of forbidden love—two people who ran away to be together—in Celtic Ireland, a long time ago." Clearly uncomfortable with that brief explanation, Reggie turned to Mama. "I can put it in the ground for you today if that's all right." It was clear the roles had switched. Reggie's soothing voice was full of a love that said *lean on me now*, but in truth, we both had leaned on him for years.

When she spoke again, her words were regulated but unrestrained. "You know, Reginald, the day you came to work in this yard was the day everything changed." She paused to catch her breath, but he waited to speak. "You didn't just rescue that old weed patch. I think you know that. You brought garden alchemy to us, that's what you did. The Good Gardener of Life." Mama's voice was giving out, but she continued. "The very one, my dear boy, the bearer of good things to come. Thank you for my lovely tree." Mama closed her eyes for a moment. "Thank you, Reginald, for everything. And now, I'm feeling rather tired. So good of you to come." She slowly got up, patted and squeezed his hand, and Reggie rose to assist her. Mama then turned around and, taking my arm, walked out the kitchen and down the hall, suddenly pushing me away as if to say, *stay, stay with him.* I helped her to the bed and returned to Reggie. "Let's go outside." Before we could get to the back door, I felt a great cry of despair rising up from deep within, and by the time I made it to the swing, my chest was heaving and I was gasping for air.

"I'm sorry, Lizzie. She's more than sick, isn't she. She's...." He couldn't say the word. When I was calm again, I spoke to him.

"I thought it was just a cold, but when I got home and saw her, I couldn't believe how altered she was. I don't know how to live without her, Reggie. I never even considered that I would be required to live without her."

"Medicine has come a long way." His voice was unconvincing and not even he felt comfort in those words. Two years had passed and, although Reggie was always a thought away, my life at college had gone on without him. Now when I wanted him to hold me and tell me the gentle deception I longed to hear, he stepped away and leaned against the swing set pole. Maybe he was afraid that he might need my support as well. Reggie admitted that Mama saved his life, grateful she had rescued him that day from a mound of broken pickle bottles. Throughout his time with us, I laughed to think she might have taken him on for my sake. Reggie changed his tone and I realized then that he was reacting to her condition with his own brand of anger.

"She's too good for this world."

"What do you mean?" I sensed his vexation rising.

"I'm not sure people really ever appreciated her, for what she's done for everyone."

"You mean me, don't you, Reggie." He looked at me, wide-eyed.

"I didn't say that. Don't put words in my mouth."

"You didn't say that exactly, but that's what you meant. I love my mother, Reggie, even when she sometimes favored you over me. I've never stopped loving her." I sensed an unrestrained anger in myself that seemed to rise out of…. where? Wasn't I happy to see him?

"Come on, Liz. You're upset now and you have a right to be."

"You're damn right I'm upset! She's my mother, Reggie. Not yours." There. I had said it and I wanted to shrivel up and disappear but I had to get it out. "Look, Reggie, just stop with your reasoning and let me feel what I feel."

"I'm sorry. You're right. Expressing my feelings isn't a luxury I've been able to enjoy. But your mother? Come on, Lizzie. This isn't a competition. Never was. Don't do this." He moved closer to me. "It isn't the time for beating both of us up for what you think might have happened. Leave it." And then as if he remembered an old wound, something in him changed. I could see it in his eyes. "You think I've loved the way my life turned out? I wish to God things had been different. I tried hard enough." Neither of us needed to speak of events so long ago, and we stood in silence giving in to the awkwardness of the moment. There didn't seem to be any point in rehashing what we wanted left behind.

"So you're going to a wedding this evening?"

"Yeah. A friend I've known since elementary school—he and his girlfriend of six years are finally tying the knot."

"Will you be in town long?"

"No, Janelle and I are leaving in the morning." Without realizing he had just dropped a bombshell on me, he continued, "I've got to get back and help my uncle with a big order." This was the first time since I had known Reggie that he had ever mentioned a girl, and I admit I was taken aback.

"Janelle?" Slightly flustered at my surprise, he paused as if he didn't know how to respond.

"My date for the wedding," he said softly, almost inaudibly. And then he continued nervously, acknowledging the unexpected reaction from me. "She's just a friend. From Bossier."

"Oh." I was struggling to say the right thing, but more than that, I was astounded at having to confront these new emotions from simply hearing this girl's name. What did she mean to him? Was he interested in a relationship with this girl? It had never occurred to me that he might have feelings for someone, and especially that I would find myself jealous. How could I have been so selfish to think Reggie didn't need love in his life? I wanted to run but I knew I had to be civil, and I replied with inane cordiality. "Right. It's good you don't have to make the long trip back alone. Well, have fun tonight. Good to see you again." I headed for the back door of the house.

"Lizzie, wait…." My behavior was transparent and now he wanted us to deal with it. He grabbed my arm. "Lizzie, hold on. You've been a good friend to me. You know that, don't you? God knows what I would have done without you. And your mother. I was in a bad place and I will always appreciate what you did for me. Even though you were annoying as hell sometimes," and he laughed to soften the blow. "But we were always friends. I hope we still can be."

"Of course," I said as I released myself from him. "But, you know, it was really the other way around. You saved my life and I'm grateful for that." We were finally saying the words we had needed to say for a long time. I walked him to the front of the house where he got in his truck and left. The next morning I went to the back door in my robe and saw that he had planted Mama's birch outside her bedroom window and was already gone. No doubt with Janelle.

I didn't return to school that semester. As strong-willed as she was, it was clear that Mama couldn't function on her own and I was determined to stay with her. My professors understood and although I made arrangements to send my final papers, they gave me Incompletes in all my subjects with the assurance that I would return and take my finals.

Mama was a feisty patient, and I made her laugh even though I had never been good at making jokes. I could never get the punch line right, but she laughed anyway at my bungling attempt at humor. We drank tea in the evenings when nothing else seemed appetizing to her, and I read aloud until she fell asleep. Her strength was palpable, maybe because I was there for her night and day, but it was temporary and we soon began weekly trips to the hospital for treatment. Of all the good that came from those five months, it was surely the new bond between us, one that I did not know could be any more steadfast. I grew to love her in ways that didn't seem possible. Time and experience, the great teachers of humanity, sharpen our endurance and tutor us in the painful art of dying, profound and elusive and relentless. Those last few months with my mother showed me a glimpse of an unfathomable love, not only for my mother but also for myself.

Mama died at the end of July. Five months with her had catechized me in the intricacies of preparing for the end of her life, and I was able to walk mindlessly through the phone calls and decisions. I learned more about funerary caskets and burial plots than I wanted to know, but the ladies at the church took care of everything else with kindness and generosity. The strange busyness of the time kept my mind from concentrating on the loss, and it wasn't until I finally sat down with a cup of tea to rest that it dawned on me. It was the last time I would be with the one who meant everything to me.

Understanding the environment in which you live is key to success as a gardener. Work with the climate and the growing conditions you have. Accept the evidence that the life-death-rebirth cycle reigns over your garden.

The Art of Gardening by Emily Mayfield

CHAPTER 27

1972 | Mama's request of a closed casket with only a graveside service led incongruously to a packed funeral home, a public expression of appreciation for a woman whose purity of spirit made her beloved. So many potted plants and flowers were delivered that florists began arranging them on the sides of the large room, and before the director opened the door to reception, he allowed my grandparents who had arrived the day before from Mobile to accompany me to the viewing before final good-byes. My grandfather wiped away tears with a handkerchief he pulled from his pocket, but Grandmother's silence was opaque although she dabbed at her eyes stoically before taking me by the arm and leading me out. Suddenly she spoke clearly with the voice of duress. It startled me.

"Let's not dally, dear. She's gone to a better place. Jacob, we need to go.

"You're not going out to the cemetery? For the graveside service?" I asked.

"I'm afraid we need to get on the road now while it's still daylight. Your grandfather doesn't see well at night and he needs to open the store in the morning." Couldn't it wait one more day, I thought. But I didn't say the words. I didn't want them around any longer than necessary. Her overt exasperation further demonstrated that my grandmother was indeed a cold woman, if nothing else, and it made me sad to think of Mama having been raised without the same love and compassion she herself had so freely given others. I attributed my grandmother's glacial demeanor to her own way of coping with whatever life had handed her, the details of which were sadly unknown. My grandparents were strangers to me, and apparently to my mother, so I didn't expect to see much of them again after they left. Tumbling face down through endless conversations of condolences interspersed with the occasional lighthearted story about Mama, I watched the crowd grow thin until it was time to pack up the platters of food that I would take back to the house. The minister's brief words at the graveside were equally cold, a mélange of scripture and generic phrases about life after death, no words that could possibly describe the tower of strength and love that had filled the lives of everyone she knew.

Darkness settled into the palpable sadness of the yellow house, and yet it was with the promise of relief that I retreated into its quiet and empty austerity. I sat in Mama's rocker near the fireplace in the dark and closed my eyes, trying to remember our days together. The sweet sigh as she settled into her chair, the sting of disappointment long obscured by daily obligations. The fatal cigarette in one hand and a cup of coffee in the other, her gaze drifted up to the mantle where her grandfather's book of poetry never stirred.

"I'm home, Mama."

"Pan of brownies on the side. How was play practice?"

"Good. Reggie's teaching me the art of props....and I do mean art. I thought it would be a piece of cake, but it's not easy remembering where everything goes. It's hard to see in the dark. He's nice about it, though."

"Yes, that sounds like Reginald. Salmon okay for dinner, hon?"

It was a little after nine when the door bell rang. There stood Reggie looking forlorn. He seemed taller than I remembered and he was sporting a pointy little beard on his chin.

"Hi. Sorry I missed the funeral. Thanks for letting me know." He paused and I waited for more. "I couldn't leave work at the last minute, and the drive took longer than I thought. I'm really sorry, Lizzie. I got here as soon as I could." We shared a warm if not obligatory embrace, but this time he initiated it. I looked at his face up close as he released me. He had grown a moustache and goatee. I never imagined Reggie with facial hair. It made him look older.

"Come on in. I'm glad you're here." I turned around and walked to the kitchen, knowing he would follow me. Reginald Washington had showed up after all. Part of me knew he would after our last encounter, but another part of me didn't know what to expect. Reggie's auspicious timing months before had resulted in the planting of the birch of hope and promise, the irony of which still puzzled me. What hope? Mama's illness had progressed so rapidly that no amount of Celtic mythology could have saved her. Reggie had left Carlton under brutal circumstances that would have prevented any sane person from making a home in Carlton ever again, but he had his reasons for returning. My mother had saved his life not once, when she rescued him from the A&P, but every day of his life that he worked in her garden, his respite from the menacing restraints with which he had been unfairly burdened.

"Coffee?"

"Uh, sure, if you're going to have some."

"Why not. Have a seat."

As familiar as the day he had brought in the baby squirrel, Reggie walked across the kitchen and pulled out a chair near the window. I got the bag of ground dark roast from the canister and put a pot of water on the stove. A drip pot was the one I had seen Mama use since I was little, and I began taking it apart to assemble the coffee. We each waited for the other to speak. "Milk?" When he didn't answer, I looked over at him. He was unraveling. His lips slightly parted and quivering, his eyes became black glistening lakes ready to overflow their banks. I didn't have any words for him, but without feeling my body I somehow transported myself in his direction and put my hand on his shoulder.

"Reggie," I whispered. But the words wouldn't come and the more I struggled, the more I couldn't speak. And then he put his hand on mine, opening the door to my own cavernous well of sorrow. I tightened my grip on his shoulder to steady myself. Reggie stood up and wrapped his arms around me, sharing years of shame and guilt and sadness in that one moment of time. Despite my own wailing, I could not remember when I had heard a grown man weep so audibly, and his tears became the catalyst for my own grief resurfacing. We were both silent for a minute before I disconnected myself to the more mundane task of checking on the coffee. When I poured him a cup, he sat down again and began to talk about her, story after story of his gratitude. I looked at the clock. After almost two hours had passed recalling moments with Mama, I could barely keep my eyes open.

"Where are you staying?"

"At the Holiday Inn near the highway."

"Oh. Is Janelle with you?"

"Janelle? No." He must have read the apprehension in my face. "Look, Lizzie. Janelle was just a friend. I've never seen her as anything more. In fact, I hardly ever see her at all. She works….." He looked at the floor, aware that any attempt at explanation might sound like an excuse.

"It's okay, Reggie. You don't owe me any explanations. I just thought you'd be married by now."

"Married? You know me better than that," he answered as if my suggestion were unthinkable.

"I'm not so sure about that. Why not? You're a nice enough guy and you're good looking and you're a hard worker and really smart. Who wouldn't want to be with you?" I could tell I had overshot my bounds because he looked embarrassed. It didn't take long for him to recover and be the responsible adult again.

"I have standards, Lizzie."

"Oh, you mean, you haven't met anyone good enough yet?" I laughed at the lighthearted insult I was tossing him, but he obviously didn't see the humor in it.

"Standards for *myself*. I don't have an education, I don't have a career. I don't have what I think I should have before I can even begin to think about offering myself to a woman. To ask a woman to consider a partnership with a man whose life isn't the success it should be? A man who hasn't finished taking care of his own life? I can't. I won't do it." I couldn't think of anything to say to him. He was so much more than he gave himself credit for being, and yet I knew he believed in every word he said. And then I remembered. I had fallen in love with Reggie's so-called standards the day I began working on props under him for the high school play. To this day I have never known a man who knew exactly who he was the way Reggie did.

"Well, Reggie, there's a very lucky girl somewhere out there," I said and stood up to say goodbye. He smiled but didn't answer. "It was nice of you to come by. Thanks. Mama loved you, you know." I spoke to Reggie as if he were merely one more visitor at the funeral home and not the man who had held me to him, joined by confluent sorrow.

"Yes. She was a kind and decent woman, the very best." He moved toward the door to leave, but suddenly turned around as if he wanted to say something to me. Our eyes locked and in that instant, years of memories colliding, connecting, coalescing assembled a montage of us, permanent and somehow full of comfort, and then he was gone.

Early the next morning I went outside to fetch the paper. It had rained hard during the night, the air still heavy with moisture, and several branches were strewn across the grass. As I approached the street to retrieve the paper at the edge of the sidewalk, I noticed a truck parked in front of the vacant house next door. The Bertrands had been our neighbors for many years, but when Randy was found guilty of murdering his wife, the family—Jimmy and his parents, couldn't bear the thought of the stares and whispers, even from their friends and neighbors. In the middle of the night, they packed up their belongings, enlisted a moving company to transport what remained, and moved to Alexandria to be close to family. I thought I saw someone in the truck, so I stood there, opening up the newspaper, and pretended to read. No one stirred. My curiosity unassuaged, I continued down the sidewalk to get a better look. Had one of the Bertrands returned? The truck looked empty, so I headed back to the house when I heard my name coming from the direction of the street. There was Reggie stepping out of the truck and walking toward me.

"Reggie? What...I thought.... I wasn't sure."

"It's my uncle's," he said, pointing to the truck. "Borrowed it to come down here. I couldn't leave last night. I wanted to but then I just sat in the truck during the storm until I fell asleep. By the time I woke up, it was too late to check in to the motel. No point."

"Come in and have some breakfast." There would be no more talk about his night on the street in light of the implicit understanding between us.

There's something about breakfast—fried, scrambled, boiled, baked or toasted, that dispatches a happy form of oblivion to those who indulge in this sensory packed experience, short-lived as it may be. Much like Lotus Eaters, neither of us thought of the anguish and discomfort of the past twenty-four hours. When Reggie had devoured everything I put in front of him, he asked to see the garden. We left the vestiges of the meal on the table and he followed me through the utility room to the back porch, down the wooden steps and across the deck, sidestepping a neglected board that had become loose. The flower beds were full of weeds and the lawn hadn't been mowed in weeks. Reggie just stood there gazing out over the skeletal remains of rose bushes, thin and brown and abandoned. I walked on ahead of him to the pond, past her althea trees that seemed to thrive despite their neglect and picked a white blossom. Reggie followed.

"What will happen to the fish? Maybe The Green Thumb will take them back."

"I don't know. I've fed them, but that's about it."

"I should have been here for her."

"No, Reggie, don't start that. It doesn't help. Actually, if anyone should feel ashamed, it should be…." and I stopped myself before I went so far that I couldn't recover. I gently swept the blossom over my cheek, and as if waking up memories, I recalled Mama placing an althea blossom in my ponytail. I was fourteen and Reginald Washington had only just begun his long journey. The tightness in my chest returned, and then one by one the tears. I didn't think of Reggie until I saw his feet planted in front of mine. Suddenly his arms circled my body and held me while, between sobs, I spoke of his graduation night, the interfusing mosaic of the guilt, repulsion and fear, the day when Mama hired him to work in the garden, when we planted roses and I wanted him to kiss me. All he could say was, *I know, I know, I know.* Yet it was the culminating moment when past and present met head on. Without warning, he turned my face toward his and kissed me, not two lips brushing mine but a kiss that bespoke the passion of despair and longing and waiting. With tongues touching and flesh and bone melding as one, I wanted the long-postponed kiss to last forever. I could feel his arms, his body, strong and muscled from the work he did, drawing me in to him with the physical closeness I had coveted. I was feverish with desperate desire and I held on tight. Reggie slowly pulled away, then leaned forward, took my head in his hands and rested his lips on my forehead. We remained there in the comfort of each other's arms for several minutes more until he whispered, "I should go." *No, no, not yet.* I wasn't ready to let him go, but he released me and walked around the house across the grassy drive without looking back.

I finished college a year and a half later with my degree in history, never forgetting Reggie's ancestral stories regarding the Civil War that led me to tackle something about which I knew far too little. On the drive home, I didn't care what I did with the degree and I certainly wasn't ready to find out. Reggie was gone now, and escaping pain and loss was all I cared about. I hung out around the house, looking for any mind-numbing job, knowing all along that I was plotting my eventual deliverance. By November I had taken care of business, including selling the house. I packed the car to leave and walked around to the back to say goodbye. It was early December and the back garden looked bleak. The birch Reggie had planted for Mama, a piece of the garden that was intended to bring healing to all of us, was losing its leaves to the cycle of autumnal death. Behind the summer house where Reggie and I so long ago planted milkweed, a monarch was hanging from a chrysalis—just emerged and filling out her wings. Because the previous night's sudden freeze had iced over any remaining flowers in the garden, its fate would be an untimely end. I hurried back to my car as if walking away from misery would make it disappear.

Deadheading flowers, the process of snapping off dead blooms
in spring and summer, will encourage more flowers
to bloom in altogether healthier foliage.

The Art of Gardening by Emily Mayfield

CHAPTER 28

1977 | Galveston was subject to a condition commonly known as island
mentality with ensuing generations of sleepy, perambulatory denizens who
moved through life with a kind of productive inertia. Not that such a view
of life was harmful. Not at all. I found it to be a groove I could easily fall into
with my current fickle state of impermanence. For the first few months that
I'd been skulking around Mimi's, I had developed only a professional if not
somewhat distant relationship with the owner. She would frequently wan-
der into the store hours after I had opened up and, being a good natured
sort, never seemed overly concerned about anything. Mimi paid me on
time without fail, which I appreciated, and she entrusted me with running
the operation without cheating her. If ever there was an emergency and I
had to leave the shop, which was seldom, I locked the door and put up a
sign indicating when I would return. As time went on my friendship with
Mary became spontaneous, almost involuntary, and through numerous
family gatherings, my connection to Mimi and her family grew stronger,
too. I began to see them as my own family. When warm island breezes

eventually returned announcing summer had indeed arrived, I decided to venture out and take advantage of the island's prospects for exploring. The north side of the island gave refuge to shrimp boats and larger vessels that came in to port, and a small family owned tour boat transported visitors around the north shore to look at and take pictures of the native wildlife, mainly birds and dolphins that would swim together alongside the boat. Janie had just finished fifth grade and began helping her mother in the shop two days a week when school ended, which allowed me a bit of relief. On my day off I decided to pack up a lunch, take Mama's camera out of its box, and head over to the port where I might find this tour boat. I called Anne Marie, sure she would jump at the chance of a new adventure. No answer. I called several times until I finally gave up, assuming that she had made other plans.

Fresh salt air, I found, altered my brain waves soon after I began running or cycling along the beachfront. Athletics never interested me in school, especially after the swimming teacher said I had absolutely no future in the only sport I liked, but running mindfully along the sand with blue skies overhead, taking in the ebb and flow of waves, the ocean air filling my lungs, became my Zen. Alone in a crowd of sun worshippers, something happened to me. I was transformed into a person who was looking through a tiny crack in my barricaded past, and it was on one particular run that I decided to address it with action. Embarking on a tour boat to view birds might be a humble beginning, but it would also be an opportunity to get out and finally use that camera. Christopher Isherwood wrote *I am a camera.* I, too, be would a camera and record the evidence of my own human experience through new eyes. While I would have preferred Anne Marie's company, I felt a quaint satisfaction with going it alone.

The boat was tied up at the dock outside a stand where a woman issued tickets, and from that point I got behind several people in line waiting to embark. It was smaller than I imagined yet large enough to seat people below the cover as well as on the upper deck. I climbed the stairs to the top where only an elderly couple had already settled themselves. I found a seat near the edge of the deck close to the front to get the best view when a young man in a tee shirt and shorts walked up the stairs. Waves of blonde hair curled around his ears and drooped over his sun tanned forehead, and when he smiled, he flashed his Hollywood set of sparking white teeth. In an instant he was gone again. The dolphins were plentiful that day, my first outing a success, and I managed to fill a roll with birds and shrimp boats and dolphins before leaving the tour boat. As I departed, the towheaded boy offered a hand to the woman stepping off the boat, and turning to face me head-on, offered his toothy smile again as well as a hand to help me down the steps.

"Hope to see you again, Camera Girl!" I smiled and thanked him, surprised that he noticed me but even more taken aback with flirtatious name calling. It was getting late and I needed to run errands before heading home, but the seed of returning for another tour was planted. In fact, my camera and I did this tour three more times before Kevin asked me out.

Harry Wilson owned and operated Harborside Tours. When his son Kevin was not in school—majoring more or less in marine biology at the University of Houston, he helped his father on the boat, checking in guests and taking care of maintenance. His father refused to let him co-pilot the boat, Kevin never having passed his licensing exam, but he clearly enjoyed the company of his son and the extra hand. At the end of my fourth trip up the waterway, he came up to the deck and, in a not so surprising move, slid down beside me.

"Got any good ones today?" I looked at the roll number through the window on the camera and saw I had taken nineteen photos.

"Lots, mainly birds this time." Two shrimp boats had come in with dozens of sea birds trailing them, and warehouse workers on the water's edge occasionally threw fish to the large pelicans hanging around. "Have you been busy helping downstairs?"

"Nah, not much to do today. Dad's got it under control and this week has been pretty boring. But that's not what I came up here for," he said. "Thought maybe we could have dinner one night." Without waiting for my response, he added, "Well, heck, how about tonight?" It seemed last minute to me, but the truth was I was free every night and so I agreed to meet him at The Crab Hut out over the water on the beach side of the island across from Mimi's at eight o'clock. I'd been past it numerous times on my runs, and the familiarity of the weathered boards and shells entangled in old fishing nets draped across the entrance welcomed guests with island charm. Lights from inside the restaurant, which spread out over the water on stilts, softly illuminated the bay. Kevin was waiting for me inside the door, and as I stepped inside, he took my shoulder and pulled me toward him, planting a wisp of a kiss on my cheek.

"Thanks for coming."

"Of course," I said. "This is one of my favorite places."

"Oh, I didn't know you'd been here before."

"Well, not to eat. I run or cycle past it every morning. I just like the way it looks." I was nervous and embarrassed, but he smiled and led me to the hostess who showed us to a table outside over the water, lights twinkling up and down the island. When I look back on that evening, I must have thought it was the most romantic evening I had ever encountered, and I saw myself opening up to the possibility of a relationship with this handsome young beach lover on the path to my newly found enlightenment. I would begin again and leave the past behind. I returned to Kevin's tour boat two more times, unaware they would be the last.

Rain was in the forecast, with light sprinkles already dotting the sidewalk, but I forged ahead, careful not to slip on the damp floorboards of the boat. Kevin was inside the cabin next to his father and the conversation looked serious. I sat inside under shelter from the impending rain, and a few minutes later Kevin joined me. We talked and laughed until the sun peeked through the clouds and he suggested we go up to the deck. Kevin, under the assumption that we had progressed farther than we actually had, reached over to kiss me and, startled, I threw my head back, not so much in retreat as surprise.

"What's the matter? No kiss now?" he laughed, and he grabbed the camera out of my hand, swung it over my head, and teased, "I'll give you your camera back if you'll put one right here," and he pointed to his lips. Challenging me like this over a kiss with my camera held hostage was an act of amorous aggression and the daring fantasy I needed, I reached over for the camera to play along and, in his miscalculation to lift the camera higher, the little black plastic box with the strap attached, Mama's last symbolic gift to me, slipped out of his hand and went flying over my head into the water.

"My camera! Oh, no! All my pictures!"

"Sorry. It was an accident. You shouldn't have tried to grab it."

"What? So it's my fault?"

"You're making too much of this. It's not like you can't get another one. Heck, I'll buy you another one."

"Ugh!" I groaned and sat quietly looking at my hands when Kevin put his arm around my shoulder. I brushed it away. "Don't. Please. Just go. Go back to doing whatever you do on this boat. Please." I turned away and looked out over the water that had swallowed up my camera as the tour boat was heading back to the dock. Kevin sat for another minute and then got up. I presumed he had gone down to help his father, preoccupying himself to avoid saying goodbye as I left the boat. That trip should have been the final one, but in a moment of weakness, I reconsidered what happened. I mean, it was just one little kiss, a game we both played a part in. If my eyes were meant to be the camera that would instruct me on this particular journey, did I learn anything? I decided to try again the next day and repair my image.

This time Anne Marie was practically giddy about going on a dolphin tour. I decided I'd better fill her in on the details of the day before, my outburst at Kevin and my regret. When she had heard the whole story, she said, "Girl, you are definitely not going by yourself. Wait a minute. You're not going back on that boat to take the blame, are you? 'Cause if you are, you can just forget about that. I will not watch you let that guy walk all over you." She didn't know the whole story, but with that stern advice out on the table, we purchased two tickets. I secretly looked around for Kevin. When I didn't see him, and Anne Marie had already boarded, I quietly asked a new deck hand I hadn't seen before where he was. He promptly sniggered and said knowing Kevin he'd be in Houston as long as possible to avoid coming back to work. Without a camera or Kevin to divert my attention, I closed my eyes and let the wind and sea mist sting my face, the plashing of water and the seagulls shrieking overhead a cadency of self absorption. Anne Marie and I were soon talking and laughing and taking pictures of dolphins and fish and seabirds with her imaginary camera. By the time I stepped off the boat, my meager inventory of expertise on men remained as modest as ever, but I consoled myself with the knowledge that Anne Marie was the best girlfriend I had ever had.

It was after four when we knocked on Mary's door. I knew I was taking a chance—it was still her nap time, but I needed her wise ear and I wanted Mary to know my new friend better. Anne Marie was curious about the woman I spoke about so highly and so often. She came to the door as I was about to knock again, and seeing my distraught face, she took my arm and led me in. Anne Marie followed.

"I'll put the kettle on." She looked at my friend. "Come on in, love."

"Thanks, Mary," I said. "I hope we didn't wake you."

"No, no, just having a wee rest."

"I could really use a cup."

"Aye, I can see that. Come in the kitchen and we'll all three of us sit."

"Actually more than tea, if you've got a minute."

"Ah, you'll be wanting a biscuit, too." I smiled for the first time all day. She knew what I meant, but Mary's sense of humor had a way of altering the levity of a situation. "Sit down, pet, and tell me all about it." Mary moved around the kitchen gathering up her supplies. She opened the pantry and pulled out a tin of shortbread. "Lovely biscuits, these are. I'll just put these on a plate."

"Umm, yes. Thank you, Mary."

"Oh, tea and cookies. How very British!" Mary and I both turned and looked at Anne Marie.

"Mary's Irish."

"Oh. Okay. How very Irish," she grinned. Anne Marie wasn't the least bit concerned about cultural formalities, but she took my prompting in stride as usual and had a giggle over it.

I knew I should have waited until the tea was poured, but I couldn't. "Mary, how did you know Carl was the right one for you?" She stopped and looked up and just stared ahead for a moment. Anne Marie didn't say a word but watched Mary intently.

"So that's what would be worrying you, is it?" She pulled out a chair across from me and sat down, forgetting about the tea. "Has the lad on the boat been misbehaving himself?"

"I don't know if that's how I would describe it, but I know he's not the one."

"And how do you know that, love? Wee bit early, eh? You hardly know the lad." The kettle began to whistle and Mary got up to pour water over the fragrant leaves.

"Just a feeling. A strong one, in fact. This thing with Kevin is over, really never got off the ground," I reasoned. "I'm just worried that maybe there won't ever be anyone who is right." Anne Marie opened her mouth to interject but closed it just as quickly.

"Ah, now, you're young, pet. Do you know, I didn't meet Carl until I was singing with the band at the American base in Nottingham, and I was thirty-seven years old. I thought I'd be single the rest of my life, married to my career. For a long time, I was. The times were unsettling. Wartime, you know."

"Thirty-seven?" we both screeched in unison. "I don't think I can wait that long. And I don't have a career. I feel like a nobody wandering around trying to figure out who I am. And so far my luck with men has been dismal." Anne Marie rolled her eyes, crossed her arms, and shook her head. I knew she was dying to chime in.

"Steady on there. What's the rush? Maybe you need this time to sort things out for yourself. What if you were to meet the right one and you weren't ready? Don't you agree, Anne Marie?" Mary got up to pour the tea taking my wide-eyed friend by surprise. She put sugar and milk and a plate of biscuits on a tray and sat down across from me, and my friend just smiled and said, "That's what I keep telling her."

"What was he like, Mary? Your Carl. We've never really talked about him. What attracted you to him? And how did you know he was the one, like the *forever* right one?" She took a sip of tea and thought a minute.

"That was a lifetime ago, Lizzie. I was singing with the band, and one night there he was, right up front at a table with his mates. The Americans were jolly folk back then, having a laugh before flying out. Most of them were pilots, just wanting a bit of fun while they could get it. Not one of them knew if he would be coming back the next day. It wasn't really fun they were after, more of a ceremonial gesture it was, accepting their humanity. When this one, Carl, looked at me with those smiling eyes, I knew there might be something more. My, he was handsome in that uniform. When my set was over, I sat down at a table and he walked up and stood right in front of me. Asked if he could join me, and I couldn't say no. I didn't want to say no. And that was the beginning of a whirlwind courtship. Oh, my, that was such a long time ago."

"But surely you weren't in Nottingham all that time."

"No, by the end of the war I was back in Dublin, but he found me, still singing and playing the piano whenever I could. After all those letters and the war over, he took the ferry to Ireland and stayed in our village for two months courting me, right proper he was, too. My father ran a little fishing boat—catching mackerel and whatever else he could sell, and Carl often went out with him. He was a natural on the water. We were wed in the Catholic Church in a village near Dublin where I had grown up. Carl liked that. He said he'd spent his life in a fishing village. He didn't tell me it was really an island. But I was fair mad about him and we had a good life together, we did." I wanted to ask Mary how Carl died, but she was in the middle of happy reminiscences, and I saved it for another day. My own angst needed the mitigating reprieve of Mary's wisdom about Kevin, in truth, all men in general. On the other hand, what did Mary know about the men of my day? Carl had recognized right away the beauty and talent, the humor and kindness in this woman at a time when he had confronted the savage antithesis, war in Europe. Could a man see goodness only when he was forced to grapple with the ugliness of brutality? Was that what it took to appreciate a life of love and civility? Mary had told me enough to know that their marriage turned out to be more than deference to one another. One look and they had fallen in love, but even as the years passed, Mary could still say he was the best man she ever knew. Perhaps that was the real puzzle for me to solve for myself.

"Enough about me now. I know you didn't come here only to hear my stories. How was your afternoon out on the water?"

Anne Marie answered first, "It was wonderful! I had never seen a dolphin except on television, and the giant seabirds hanging out at the warehouses—such enormous beaks. They swallowed these huge fish that the men on the wharf threw to them," she added. I left that story for another day. I needed to explain what happened on the boat.

"That was today," I jumped in, "but yesterday I went on the boat and saw Kevin. Thanks to him, I lost my camera."

"What do you mean *lost* it? Can you go back and look for it?"

"No. It's gone. Permanently. Lost to the waves of the bay. The truth is, Mary, Kevin was playing around with me, and when he grabbed the camera, it slipped out of his hand and went flying into the water. It was really just an accident. He wanted a kiss and I wouldn't give it to him. I don't know what I was thinking. I was so *stupid*, Mary. And then he wouldn't speak to me. That was yesterday. When we went back to the boat today, he wasn't there, and I don't think he's coming back. Anyway, Anne Marie and I had fun."

"Ah, I see." Mary leaned back and drank her tea without speaking again.

"That's it?" I said, disappointed in this unusual dearth of wisdom.

"No. I really do see what the problem is. You can't fall in love with the lad because you're in love with someone else." My first thought was, she's got it all wrong, and my second thought was *Please, God, don't let Anne Marie ask any questions.* It didn't matter that I hadn't dated anyone seriously since I moved to Galveston. Mary knew there was someone in my past that I couldn't forget. I'd dropped enough hints over the years, but I wasn't ready to have that conversation with Anne Marie yet. One day, maybe, but not today.

"Mary, I have no idea what you're talking about. There is no one else in the picture." I left it at that. "Thanks for the tea. We'd better head out now. I need to drop Anne Marie off and then I could really use a nap." I took our cups to the sink. "Thanks, Mary, for everything."

"Grand, you have a wee rest and you'll be right as rain. Very nice to see you again, Anne Marie," she replied with a smile, but Mary knew more than she was saying and she wisely kept it to herself.

We walked out to the car and Anne Marie didn't waste a second before asking what Mary had implied. "There isn't much to tell—another day. Let's go. I promise I'll tell you the whole boring story later." And being the friend I had hoped for, she accepted my suspension of the anticipated juicy bits. As a satisfactory alternative, she found her favorite station on the car radio, turned up the volume when Queen came on, and sang "We are the champions" with the force of her little voice all the way home.

Gardening, as a sensory experience, allows us to reclaim our
mental and physical health as well as the creative and productive
aspects that encourage us to become the people we were meant to be.
Voltaire wrote, "Life is bristling with thorns, and I know
no other remedy than to cultivate one's garden."

The Art of Gardening by Emily Mayfield

CHAPTER 29

1977 | Shortly before the shop opened, Janie began unpacking a shipment
that had arrived the afternoon before. A box of framed art caught my eye as
she pulled each picture out to inspect.

"This one's nice. I really like the antique gold frame," she said. I moved
closer to see a drawing of a ship with a caption underneath. It read *The USS
Westfield, flagship of Commodore William B. Renshaw, Battle of Galveston,
1862.*

"Battle of Galveston? Who were we fighting in Galveston?" I asked
with more incredulity than I wanted her to see.

Janie looked at the writing under the picture. "It says 1862, so it had
to have been the Civil War, right?"

"The Civil War? No, it can't be. Can it?" I studied the caption again.
Facts were now reconvening in my head, urging a face-off with the presumptions I had held since ninth grade. Reggie had sworn his great-great-great

grandfather had worked to fortify the island for the Confederacy, and I had vociferously shot it down as legend. This *Westfield*—was it proof the war had actually been fought as far west as Galveston? And after course work for a degree in history, why didn't I know this?

"Well, remember that building you passed at 20th and the Strand on your way to the harbor? That was once a Confederate lookout post," she said. Janie was a native of Galveston, an island small enough for every building to be a familiar one.

"What building is that?" I asked.

"The Hendley Building. Back in the mid 1800s it had a wooden observatory on the roof. You could see all the way to the Gulf. In the beginning the Confederates could keep track of Union boats, that is, until the Union got hold of it. You should go there. It's a visitor's center now."

"How do you know all this history? What grade are you in?" I said playfully. Janie laughed.

"Well, when you live on an island and your history teacher plans field trips, you generally stay on the island and visit whatever's available. Actually, my sixth grade reading teacher took us to several places when we read a book that was set during the Civil War."

"Oh, yeah? What book was that?"

"*The Red Badge of Courage*. Do you know it? Can't remember the author though, but it's set during the Civil War. Not Galveston, of course, but that didn't matter to my teacher."

"Yes, I've read it. Stephen Crane," I said but I wasn't thinking of the book. My mind was reeling from unexpected information.

"Well, anyway, we've got some really good pictures for the shop. I guess Mom picked these out. I'll put them in the store room until she decides what she wants to do with them."

I sat behind the counter recalling the robust denial I had thrown in Reggie's face, the fearless clinging to my own interpretation of history, prompted by the state history text, pristine in its exclusive omission of the facts regarding slavery and the Civil War, too, I supposed. He was right after all. He was always right. A trip to the book stall down the sidewalk from Mimi's produced a little book on The Civil War, Chapter Eight explaining how the war was, "fought as far west as Galveston, and after the Battle of Galveston, the Confederacy used hundreds of slaves to fortify the island from the attack of Union soldiers." I bought the book for two dollars as well as a sandwich from the shop next door before returning to work. That night I read the entire book, thinking of Reggie with every turn of the page.

One afternoon when Mimi's was quiet and few customers had stopped by since lunch time, the bells on the door jangled and jarred me from my latest novel. A young man I recognized from high school had just walked into the shop. Bill Nash had been a senior when I entered Carlton High School, the same year as Reggie, and he, too, had had my mother for senior English. He remembered me as Mrs. Rowan's daughter, the one "who was in all the plays." He asked how I came to be on this side of home and then he bought a trinket, a mug with typical beachfront photos on it and *Galveston* written in gold script across the top.

"So what brings you to Galveston?" I said and gave him his change and receipt. He explained how he was in town for a couple of days for a conference at the Galvez Hotel and how he had taken advantage of a break to enjoy the sun. I welcomed his friendly disposition toward me, coming on the heels of Kevin's behavior, and conveyed my hope for a successful stay on the island. He thanked me and as he neared the door, he turned and asked if I would join him for lunch the next day before he drove back to Carlton.

"I'd love to but I can't really leave the shop tomorrow. Sorry. No replacement."

"Problem solved," he said. "I'll bring lunch to you about noon, if that's okay."

"Great! An indoor picnic. Thanks."

Bill was right on time, carrying two large bags into the shop. The moment I saw him I cleared off one of the old tables in the back near the door so I could hear the bells announcing another customer, and together we laid out the trappings of a picnic lunch—fried chicken and potato salad with two slices of apple pie. Nothing I ordinarily ate, but the gesture was thoughtful and I helped myself without hesitation. Before long we were reminiscing about high school days and teachers, which led to my mother, his favorite English teacher, he said. When he brought up *The Scarlet Letter* essay, a particularly difficult assignment, he admitted he hadn't actually read the book, and he laughed and said he was glad he hadn't wasted his time. I disagreed in silence, however. Mama loved Hester Prynne, but Bill never wanted to see that book again. Without warning, it was as if a dark affliction had settled over him. He spoke of her kindness toward Reggie, how she hired him after the incident. He said everyone knew what she had done for him and respected her despite their views on integration. I suppose I shouldn't have been surprised or offended by this information. Everything Mama did I took for granted, appreciated it as much as I could, but still, knowing my mother, I simply expected her to be true to who she was without analyzing it. I had no idea that anyone ever thought about Reggie after he faded from view. In my mind I recalled a cross burning in our yard and the subsequent actions of the community who refused to hear the truth from a colored boy and was ultimately saved by a white girl's alibi, though heavy price she must pay. He told me that not everyone hated blacks. "We were all simply confused by the uncertainty, the unpredictability of the times. We were being asked to change too quickly a paradigm everyone had grown up with." He asked if I ever wondered how the police found Reggie—why he didn't lie there on the ground all night. I remembered hearing the sirens, but Bill didn't ask if I had been there that night. I told him I never thought about it—I naively guessed someone on patrol found him. I left out the part about being utterly heartsick that night. Bill didn't stop at that.

"The police never bothered to go back there," he said. "Nothing had ever happened before, except the couples who parked there late on date nights. Why should they bother?" I was perplexed. Where was he going with all of this? "I'm just saying, not everyone was eaten up with hatred. Somebody called the police and an ambulance as well."

"Like that was supposed to be enough?" I said. "Beat him up to the point of unconsciousness and then call in the medics to save him?" I was allowing my pent up anger to seep out, and I had to catch myself.

"No, but it was something. Not enough, but it saved his life." Then I got it. The truth, imbedded in his words, took away all power to speak. Information contrary to what I had clung to for so long would suddenly shift with little warning and demand that I comply.

"It was you, wasn't it." Bill didn't deny or admit it, but I understood clearly that he had been the one to make the call. "So you were there. You knew who did that to him." Bill quietly answered yes, he knew, and I succumbed to the old feelings again—all the guilt, regret, and emotional attachment to Reggie slapped me in the face. "Why didn't you tell anyone?" I gasped. Bill said he knew he should have but he was afraid of what his friends would have said, and then added that it wouldn't have made a difference anyway. Randy and his boys would have supplied each other with alibis, and they would have sought revenge on anyone who stepped forward. It wasn't a high priority for the police and school officials who just wanted it to be kept quiet and eventually forgotten. After all these years, he said, he wished he had done more.

Bill saw how distraught I was and took his time before speaking again. "I think Reggie knew people cared about him. No one could have treated him with more dignity than your mother. What happened that night was wrong. There's no question. What happened all those years was wrong. We were completely blinded by a way of life that excluded people who were different. And there's more work to be done, for sure. But there were also lots of kids like Randy who tried their best to make sure people who were different would be excluded—especially if they happened to be colored. We were just kids, Lizzie. I'm not proud of it, but the only way to live now is to forgive myself and leave the Randys of the world to the gods, whatever justice may come. At least he's locked up and the world is a little safer. I'm not okay with the part I played in it, but I did what I could at the time."

Listening to Bill's confession was not easy. All the years of guilt, of suppressing the shame of forsaking the one who rose above it all, inflamed my role as the complacent bystander. I pictured myself that night, cowardly leaving the scene and doing what? Feeling sorry for myself and making myself sick while Bill called for help. It finally hit me. It was time to exit this cave of self-loathing and move on. I didn't, or couldn't, do what I should have done that night. Could I forgive myself? One more task, and then I wanted him to leave. I changed the subject with information that I was still having trouble coming to terms with.

"My mother died. I don't know if you knew—it's been almost four years now."

"Yes, I'm sorry. I saw it in the paper when it came out. I knew Reggie worked in your mother's garden every week, and later I saw him at the Green Thumb when my dad and I picked up some plants for our yard."

"That's right. Reggie used to work there sometimes."

"That was just a stepping stone. Apparently he and his cousin set up a landscaping business somewhere in north Louisiana. Last time I was at the Green Thumb, I asked for him and the manager told me he moved away and was starting a business with his uncle and cousin."

"I'm glad to hear it. I sort of lost touch with him." And then with pounding heart I asked him the question I'd been asking myself for years, "Is he married now?"

"That I don't know, but I'm guessing he is. Probably with a house full of kids, too. Isn't that where most of us are now? Well, except for us," he laughed. I laughed along with him and agreed, but not with the same detached ambivalence.

So Reggie was living up to his potential after all. I wasn't really surprised. After all, Reggie was the boy who won writing contests and earned a scholarship to LSU. A brutal beating on graduation night wasn't going to stop him from transforming himself into the man he imagined he would be, insisted that he be. And whether it was out of human tenderness or simple mercy, his compassion had taken care of me, too, even when he must have found me a burden at times. I didn't share this intimate detail with Bill but as I continued my own story, I knew something in me was changing. Were all of these clues for me? My friendship with Mary and the Schwarz family, the camera forever lost in the waves, the discovery of the Westfield and the painful regret of my arrogant dismissal of Reggie's heritage, the irony of Bill's visit—the one person who thought to call an ambulance the night Reggie could have died—were all of these part of the larger plan for me?

"I didn't cope well after she was gone. I sold the house as quickly as possible and left—didn't want anything to do with the memories. I got in the car and ended up here at Mimi's, and I've been here ever since. I haven't kept up with anything or anyone back in Carlton."

"Yeah, I heard about what happened." Bill almost whispered it as if he still felt sorry for me. "I don't blame you for leaving. I'm sorry you had to go through all that." We were both quiet for a moment, and then he got up. "Well, I'm heading back to Carlton this afternoon. Gotta get back to work. It was good seeing you again, Lizzie. Really glad I ran across you." He helped me pick up the empty cartons of food and I guided him to a large trash bin.

"Thanks, Bill. It's good to see you again, too. Have a safe trip home." He was almost out the door.

"Bill?" He turned around. "Thank you for being the one to make the call."

Fig trees, native to Mediterranean climates, prefer to be planted in a warm protected corner of the garden. They produce up to three tasty fruit crops a year as well as quite decorative foliage. Fig trees develop fruit without pollination.

The Art of Gardening by Emily Mayfield

CHAPTER 30

1977 | Anne Marie answered on the first ring.

"You must have been sitting by the phone. Are you expecting a call? Is there a romantic development I don't know about yet?" I laughed.

"Are you kidding. I'm over men, all of them."

"Yeah, right. For today maybe." I asked if I could swing by her place to talk. My conversation with Bill now required the ear of a best friend, and she was happy to see me and even happier to offer advice. I was there in ten minutes.

"I'm going back to school," I blurted out, taking the glass of ice cold tea from her hand. "There comes a time in your life when you realize how ignorant you really are."

"Give me a break, Lizzie. You of all people, ignorant? I don't think so."

"You don't know how ignorant. I've made so many mistakes not just because I've been a wimp but mostly because I always insisted I was right. At least I thought it. Even when I knew I wasn't, Anne Marie. I didn't think it mattered. There's a high level of ignorance in that, but I feel the winds of change acoming. That means I have to go back to school."

"Where? Are you going to leave me stuck here in Galveston?" Anne Marie stood up with her hands on her hips and a smirk on her face. She clearly thought I was joking.

"Sit down. I'm serious. It's just Houston, less than an hour away. Besides, I'm not that kind of person. I make friends for life. Unless you've got other plans."

Anne Marie slumped back onto the couch. "Shut up and hand me that bag of chips, traitor."

"Look, I think I can finish in two years. It'll go by in no time. Besides, you can come to Houston and we can learn the two-step. I hear the cowboy clubs are the rage, and I can come back to Galveston to visit you." When I looked at her, anticipating her usual toothy grin, I saw a scrunched up face with tears threatening to roll down her cheeks. "Hey, did I say the wrong thing? I'm really sorry, Annie. Don't be mad at me. Please." I put my arm around her shoulder and gave a squeeze.

"It's not that," she whimpered, pulling away from me. "I need some permanence in my life, Lizzie. I'm done losing people, just waiting for them to walk out of my life. Maybe you'll come back and maybe you won't."

"Hold on, Anne Marie. You're not the only one who has suffered the loss of people in your life. Everyone has, including me. It's taken me years to get past it. When we met, I was overjoyed that I'd finally found a soul mate, someone I could depend on. I'd hoped you found the same in me. I'm not leaving for good, you know. So what's this really all about?"

By this time Anne Marie was sniffling into a napkin and getting up to refill her glass. She turned around and faced me for a moment without speaking. "There's something I haven't told you. I haven't told anyone actually. No one knows, except the few people who were involved." And then she sat back down and began to tell me the story of why she moved to Galveston all the way from Wisconsin. In her sophomore year of college, she went to a fraternity party with the boy she had been dating, someone she had known for only a few weeks, and, both having had too much to drink, found themselves together in an upstairs bedroom. Unable to remember exactly why, the relationship fizzled out and they ran into each other on campus only once or twice. Two months later, she discovered she was pregnant with one alternative, leave school and live at home. Her parents let her stay long enough to have the baby, insisting the only recourse was to give him up for adoption. Unable to forgive their daughter for the shame and embarrassment they claimed she cast on them, they turned her out. She lived with a friend and waited tables at night while finishing her degree.

"I wanted to move as far away as possible from my mistake and from the people who couldn't find it in their hearts to love an imperfect daughter. So here I am, trying to erase the past and make a new life for myself. Do you know how hard that is?" Her eyes were welling up again, but I took her hands and made her stand up.

"Actually, I do. Listen here, friend, I don't care what mistakes you've made. I've made my share, too. You are one of the best people I know, and I'm not such a bad person either, so this feeling down on ourselves ends here. We're moving on. You got that?"

Anne Marie stared at me as if I'd lost my mind, and then she laughed and said, "Uh, okay...."

"Just *okay*?"

"No! Let's celebrate!" she yelled.

"Ice cream sundaes, definitely ice cream with fudge sauce. And I know just the place. Addie's!"

In light of the new path I was now embarking on, the timing could not have been better. I needed to hear my own advice as much as Anne Marie did. Addie's Café next to Mimi's helped. We parted company there, but not before making plans to see a movie that night. I rushed over to Mary's to tell her the good news.

Mary was sweeping the steps of her house when I pulled up on my bike. Her hair was tied at the back with a yellow scarf and she was humming when she saw me.

"Hello, Missy! Come on up. I've been working long enough out here," and her eyes sparkled.

"Hi, Mary. I'll be right up." After the revelations at Mimi's, I was ready for tea and serious conversation.

Mary's tea table served as a diversionary tactic that provided a balance for the island mentality to which she had long ago acquiesced. From across the wide ocean, she had carried her mother's china tea set that now graced our afternoon tea.

"I'll just take this loaf of bread I'm after bakin' from the oven. We'll put the butter right on the table. You come and take this plate while I fill the kettle." When we both sat down, I broached the subject weighing on my heart.

"Mary, I think I've made an important decision about my life. I need to know what you think."

"Well, go on then."

"Do you remember how I told you about Reggie going on about the Civil War in Galveston, how his great-great-great grandfather was a slave who was forced to work with the Confederacy to fortify the island? And how, like an idiot, I dismissed his heritage?" Mary's face seemed to be searching her mental files. "Well, anyway, I was wrong, so utterly wrong about everything." Mary waited for me to finish. Did she see where I was going with this rant? I had a useless degree in history, and I was becoming more unsettled with it. I started from the beginning. "Someone I knew from high school came into the shop today. He told me that he was the one who called the ambulance when Reggie was beaten up. My surprise was not that he did it, but that I didn't. Reggie was my friend and I let someone else do the right thing. And when I had a chance to make it up to him, I didn't. He tried so often to tell me his side of the story, and I refused to accept the fact that he was right. I've been a terrible friend. Don't you see, Mary, Bill's visit is just one more sign that it's time for me to do something meaningful with my life. Otherwise, why would I keep getting these reminders of how stuck I am?"

"Hang on! That's quite a bit you've just spread out here at my table. Aren't you being a wee bit hard on yourself? What is it you want to do now?

I took a deep breath, intoxicated just thinking of my bonanza of self-discovery. I had so much to say it felt like my brain would explode. "Sometimes I think the past and the future are interconnected with the present, that the line between them is a blur.

Mary frowned and said, "A blur? Go on."

I hadn't really appreciated the value of looking at the past for answers, but the history books hadn't told the whole truth either. I've acted like the past had little to do with the present, or the future for that matter." Mary didn't say a word but I continued. "I don't think my coming to Galveston was an accident or a chance turn off the highway. Everyone's been great, you understand—you especially, but I need to remove myself from a place of shame and sadness and have more time to think clearly. And, Mary, I've done it, here in Galveston. I'm ready now, ready to move forward."

"Aye, pet, it's a blessed day when you can do that." Mary was gazing out the window as if remembering another time.

"It took me long enough," I admitted.

"You're forgetting how much life this old woman has seen, love. I've never once thought time was forever, and remember, I've known firsthand how war makes you think twice about it."

"I know, Mary. I've seen every day how you use your time and how happy it makes you. And you made the most of the past, too, something people my age don't always appreciate, I mean the little time we have, not only to make amends for the mistakes we've made, but to make it count for something."

"Count for what?"

"How about love? Or helping other people? Or just leaving the world a better place than we found it? Isn't that what you did?"

"Aye, but believe me, pet, it's not just the young who struggle with that."

"Well, I've made a decision. I'm going back to school. If I go full time, I can finish another degree in two years. I've finally figured out what I'm supposed to do, and I have to do it now, Mary. I can't wait any longer."

"Done and dusted, eh? And then what?" Mary was cutting straight to the bottom line.

"Yeah, I'm not sure yet what I'll do with it, but something. Teach, write, volunteer—something related to all the lessons history has to teach us. I've managed to get through the hard part just making this decision."

"Well, it's an interesting new development, love. So you'll be leaving."

"I was getting to that. I'll have to live in Houston, at least for the first year. I think I can commute while I write my thesis. I've loved living here, Mary—you and your family have helped me so much, but I think this may be the answer I've been waiting for."

"Then, my clever girl, you must give it a go. Be true to yourself—as long as you come back. I've gotten used to you," she grinned, but in all her practicality got up and walked to the back door. "First, come out here and help me plant my new tree. I've got myself a fig, would you believe, but I'm not so good at using the shovel anymore. I'll do the planting if you can just dig me a proper hole. Come on. I'll show you where I want it." Yes, I could dig a good hole, thanks to Reggie. We left our cups half full on the table and I followed her down the stairs to the garden. Standing near the corner to the left of her house was the slender leafy green fig tree in a large plastic pot. I felt wistful remembering my mother's figs, the day Mama decided she didn't have enough jars. I would never again see figs without thinking of Reginald Washington and the broken pickle jars. "Well, come on. I don't have all day!" she laughed and handed me the shovel.

"Coming, Mary." I dug the hole in what appeared to be fertile soil with little clay in it, which meant the job would be finished with ease. When the tree was planted, Mary attached a support pole to insure the tree's proper growth upward, then stepped back to look at it.

"Grand," she said adjusting the ties on the pole. "Right as rain. In no time at all we'll have lovely brown figs. I'll put the kettle on."

"Yes, in no time at all."

When choosing a tree for your garden, the river birch is highly adaptive.
Able to sustain harsh conditions, it takes root in any kind of soil
and provides light shade, adding color and interest where it is planted.
In Celtic mythology, the birch represents stability and growth
of the human spirit—a powerful garden metaphor for life.

The Art of Gardening by Emily Mayfield

CHAPTER 31

1979 | By the time all the celebrating was over, degrees conferred in ceremonial splendor, I had managed to sail through the job interview that manifested my dream position. I moved back to Mary's to write my thesis the year before, and the timing could not have been more agreeable. Jack's involvement in the community afforded him information vital to my career prospects, which he happily passed on to me. A new division of the library, Galveston's own Civil War Museum, had been in the planning stages for ten years and was now coming to fruition. I promptly applied for the position of assistant director and after a series of interviews, the job was mine. It came with an assistant whose responsibility was to categorize and file the stacks of information and artifacts that had already been delivered and continued to pour in. The lovely new building itself was to receive landscaping from a Houston firm whose winning bid had been accepted with gratitude in light of an already stretched budget. It was a little after four in the afternoon when my assistant Sherry stepped into the office.

"Miss Rowan, the board is ready to meet with the landscaper in the conference room, if you can join them now."

"Right, thanks. I'm on my way." I closed the folder I was in and grabbed a pen and pad, my mind filled with potential locations for designated artifacts. Landscaping would be a welcomed distraction, and the responsibility of keeping the board happy and informed fell in part to me. The conference area was at the front of the building, a long hallway connecting my office to the foyer. When I entered the room, several people were standing around a table chatting casually over cups of coffee. Dr. Will Askew had been selected to head the pride of Galveston's new historical project. His tenure at Rice had produced important research on the Civil War in Texas, and his reputation was known throughout the country. Dr. Askew turned around to speak to me, and the small crowd parted, revealing a tall distinguished looking black man at his side. I couldn't take my eyes off him. I gasped before Dr. Askew could begin the introductions. When he turned toward me, Reggie's surprise became a happy smile of recognition.

"Miss Rowan, I'd like you to meet Reginald Washington, owner of Houston Garden and Landscaping. His company will be taking care of the museum's landscaping needs, the details of which he's prepared to share with us today."

I, too, was smiling as I nervously held out my hand, desperate to manage control over the shock of this unexpected reunion. "A pleasure to see you again, Mr. Washington." Reggie shook my hand and nodded a professional-looking gesture, but our eyes had met, and I knew those eyes well. I tried to read his face but he looked away as we followed the committee to the table around which we would listen to his plans for the next half hour.

"So you two have already met," Dr. Askew said with polite interest. His keen observation detected more than he said.

"Yes, once upon a time long ago," I said, hoping a little humor would deflect any suspicions, and I took a seat across from Reggie.

An hour later Reggie was still fielding questions until the director stood up and thanked him, signaling an end to the meeting. He didn't speak to me until I saw him outside leaning on the door of his jeep. He had clearly been stalling, and I wanted to believe that he had hoped I would find him.

"Reginald Washington, I can't believe it after all this time. How are you? It looks like you've done well these last few years. So, how have you been? How did you—"

"—manage to land this job?" I nodded.

"More importantly, establish a landscaping business in Houston. Congratulations to you."

"English lit wasn't the only thing Louise Rowan taught me, Lizzie. Your mama…." He closed his eyes, remembering. "Your mama taught me everything—about plants, flowers, trees, anything that would grow."

"Yes, she saw great potential in you, but come on, Reggie, you're a self-made man." The ease of our conversation seemed as if six years of silence were a mere trifle in a measure of time.

"When things got difficult, don't you remember, she called the owner of the Green Thumb across town and told them I was a good yard man—would they try me out." Reggie grinned and then his expression changed. "After Randy….,well, anyway, I moved to my uncle's farm outside of Shreveport."

"Yes, Bossier. How well I remember. You weren't even going to say goodbye," I lightly chastised but he ignored me and continued.

"My cousin and I took over his business, growing trees and shrubbery mainly, until I opened a branch in Houston. Been there ever since. So, here I am, still tending a garden. I remember my first book report with Mrs. Rowan. How your mama did love Voltaire. In times of strife…."

"….cultivate your garden. There were some good days, Reggie, despite all the chaos. You've done well. I always thought you should have if….anyway, Mama would be so proud of you." The light was growing dim as gray clouds were moving in.

"I miss her. She saved my life, that lady…."

"I miss her, too. She saved both of us." There was an awkward silence as we both looked away.

"I wouldn't have made a very good lawyer," he said softly, "but I finally got my business degree. I figured if I owned a business, I ought to have the credentials."

"Well done, Reggie, but I'm not so sure about the lawyer part. My mother believed you could do anything, and she was rarely wrong. She thought all you had to do was put your mind to what you wanted and it would turn out right. Now that I think about it, she might have missed the mark with my diving and stamp collecting escapades." We both chuckled remembering, and just as quickly Reggie looked at me this time without hiding the old pain in his eyes.

"Yes, indeed, you have done well," I said as I attempted to lighten the conversation. "What do you mean *when things got difficult*?" I laughed. "One day you were throwing dirt at me and the next you were working for someone else. What was that all about?" I already knew. I never forgot that day, but I wanted to hear it from Reggie finally. And I needed some comic relief.

"As I recall, a white girl was about to get a black boy in a heap of trouble." I did remember, too well, and just standing there in his presence I replayed my embarrassing if not bittersweet scene—me asking Reggie to kiss me. "Lizzie, I'm sorry for how things turned out. We never talked about it, but you were the one who saved my hide in the end, and I never thanked you. You paid for it, too, didn't you." The words had been said more than once as if reliving that nightmare would restore an unremarkable normalcy to the times, but neither of us wanted to persist in the futility of it. "Anyway, looks like you've done all right for yourself, Miss Rowan—I mean, it is still *Miss*, isn't it?" I threw him a frown smile and nodded. He went on, "Assistant director of the museum. My, my. Congratulations. You finally found something you really wanted to do. I'm happy for you, Lizzie."

"Actually, I went back to school, in history again. This is my first job since graduation, and it's the one I really wanted. It took me a while but when I saw a photo of the Westfield Union Civil War battleship in the gift shop where I worked, I realized something about myself. I didn't know as much history as I thought I did, or anything else for that matter." I laughed at my own self-deprecating humor. "And I really wanted to, needed to." Reggie was quiet in the awkward way one feels embarrassed at the truth and unable to speak. I went on with what I knew had to be said. "You were right, you know. I mean, about your great-great-great-grandfather and the war in Texas, in Galveston. Turns out your mother's stories were true. I....I'm sorry I doubted you, Reggie." A tiny drop of water hit the top of my head, startling me, but then another fell and another, yet neither of us budged.

When Reggie didn't speak, I found the courage to say what I had been waiting to tell him. "I owe you another apology, Reggie. A big one."

"Whatever it is, it's in the past and I'd rather not hear it." I detected a move to shut this conversation down.

"It may be a decade before I see you again, so I need to say it now."

"Leave it, Lizzie. Please." Reggie reached for the handle of his car, longing to escape whatever it was that I was about to rekindle, but I pressed on.

"The night of your graduation, Randy put us all in his car and drove us to the back of the school. I honestly didn't know what I was going to witness, Reggie. I was young and stupid and weak. And the thing is, I never told anyone about it. Ever. Not even Mama, especially not Mama. I'm so sorry, Reggie. I wish....I hope you can forgive me. I've carried this around far too long—my albatross all these years. The guilt and sadness every time I've thought about it, about you—such a heavy weight and I don't want to go on like this anymore, especially not now. I tried to tell you when Mama died but I just couldn't. I want to start over. I need a fresh start. Forgive me. Please, Reggie." He turned around and this time he looked right at me.

"I already knew, Lizzie. I couldn't see much that night my eyes were so swollen, but your face—I saw you standing over me."

"Oh, God, Reggie. Why didn't you ever say something?" He shrugged.

"What was the point? It took months to get back on my feet, and if I thought about it at all, after a while I just couldn't see the point." He was still looking at me when he exhaled slowly, paving the way for the unexpected slight he was about to deliver. "Lizzie, there are some things you will never understand about me."

"About you? What do you mean?"

"We live in two different worlds. I'm not saying things aren't better than they were, but we have a long way to go."

"Yes, I know. Believe me. I've just spent the last two years getting caught up with the past. So, what are you trying to say, Reggie? That I'll never understand you because....I'm white? Are we really so different?" Reggie didn't answer. It was the first time he had heard me acknowledge the stark difference between us and he refused to look at me. "You let me carry this burden around all these years." And then a deep sadness fell on my heart, the great weight of disappointment. "I thought we were friends, more than friends really. I thought we had a history together." I kept my voice calm but I was shaking inside at the prospect that Reggie was not going to say the only words that might redeem me. "Well, I guess I'm at your mercy. Can you forgive me?" I was beginning to panic now, afraid he would walk away. "Can you? Please, Reggie. I need to hear you say the words before you leave. Please." Now I was at the point of begging, and I didn't want him to see me cry. It was starting to rain, but we didn't move, he steadfast in his stoicism and I ready to collapse in a puddle of tears. And then he put his hands on my shoulders.

"I do forgive you, Lizzie, but I forgave you a long time ago. Didn't you know? Couldn't you see it?" he whispered. In one graceful move he leaned into me and kissed my cheek, pressing his warm face against mine, his arms wrapped around me and resurrecting those old feelings that were always right under the surface. "I've never forgotten you, Lizzie." And then he was gone. I don't know how long I sat in my car when he left, but I kept touching my cheek, remembering. It was raining hard now. I would be at a conference in College Station for the next three days, but I hoped I would see him again when I returned on Monday.

It was a good conference, the keynote focusing on Civil War slave refugees in Texas, but I was eager to get back to work. I saw Sherry in the hall as I headed to my office.

"Morning, Miss Rowan. Mr. Washington finished and left some paper work on your desk."

"What do you mean *finished*? It's done? I thought they were going to take at least a week for this job."

"Oh, no, the landscapers aren't finished yet. Mr. Washington brought in some people to work the rest of the week, or until they're finished and you're satisfied with the job." Indeed the paper work in a large folder was on my desk as my assistant had said. Apparently Reggie was now in a position to leave the labor to his staff. When I picked up the folder, an envelope addressed to me fell out. The handwritten note was brief.

I planted a tree outside your office window. A birch—you know, herald of new beginnings and all that. Anyway, good luck tonight.

Reggie

Tucking the note in my purse, I turned around to face my window and saw a thin wisp of a tree in its frame. *You'll always find a way back.* Reggie had said those words about me when he planted the birch in Mama's garden, when she called him the Good Gardener. He had planted this tree of hope where she could see it from her window, in remembrance of him and his gratitude to her for giving him a second chance, for the good things to come for all of us. I had found a way back but down a different, unforeseen path.

The official opening of the museum that night turned into a wine and cheese event including several donor speeches, although I was opening the program with a brief back story of the museum from its inception to its current status and the work we would be doing there. To say that public speaking had never been my forte was a critical understatement, but I had grown since meeting Reggie. I wasn't the same person he first knew, that shy little girl afraid of everything and everyone, and I was grateful to acknowledge his role in my growing up. It was a shame he wouldn't be there to see I could actually speak to an audience without falling apart. That evening I'd wear the little black dress I'd been saving. Yes, the black dress and the pearl earrings that said *I am in control of this ship.*

The construction of a small theatre on the second floor of the museum had been a non-negotiable design in the planning of the new building, and the opening ceremonies would begin there, moving later in the evening to the reception hall for appropriate refreshment. Despite my years of experience on the stage, the absence of any transferrable skill from acting to public speaking left me bereft of the aplomb indispensable for the job of speaking before this particular audience of not only well-wishers but patrons with means. When the moment arrived and I was introduced, I got up from my seat, heart pounding and mouth dry, and walked to the podium. Mimi and Jack, Janie and Mary, and Anne Marie were sitting on the third row, smiling as if to cheer me on and I was grateful to see them, the absent miracle baby Mary at home with the sitter. I took a deep breath to calm my jitters and began.

"On January 1st, 1863, the Confederates, under the leadership of Major General John Magruder, retook Galveston with great losses to Union soldiers and ships, and the port remained under Confederate control until the end of the war." *Breathe.* "By late 1863 approximately 150,000 slaves entered Texas from Louisiana, and many in this wave of refugeed slaves, in submission to their owners who had abandoned their plantations in fear of Union occupation, were put to work to fortify the island." As the words that now meant everything to me filled the air of the auditorium, I couldn't have been more certain of being in the right place. At that moment I knew I loved this job, the history of the island and the Civil War that had left its indelible mark there, the island's pock marked buildings that would be forever enshrined as war memorials—the Civil War of which I had been so painfully ignorant. The ardency I felt for the chronicle of events that led me to understand Reggie had also made me love him with an intensity that never diminished across time and space. The thought of him and how words of factual redemption, mine not his, might make him love me back, even when

254

I thought I'd never see him again, assuaged my nerves and I looked up from my notes. A shadowy figure was bustling down the aisle toward a seat near the front. In the darkened crowd of faces I couldn't make out precisely who it was, but the closer he came to the stage, I saw him clearly—a man who seemed to meld into the depth of his dark skin and hair, a lean muscled body that would be his trademark in the way one might recognize the configuration of a familiar word.

EPILOGUE

2003 | His lips brushed my forehead and my eyes fluttered open, fighting back the urge to sleep. Even in the darkness of the room I could see his familiar silhouette against the lighted hallway and strange flashes of light in his hand. A shiny filigreed tree, its branches reaching out to the circle enclosing them, dangled from his fingers, twirling glints of gold and silver.

"Happy Birthday."

"Oh, honey, it's beautiful. Is it a birch?"

"Of course, what else." I reached for the pendant and felt the warmth of his hand.

"I'm going now. The boys will be home this afternoon and I'll be right behind them. Be ready." He put the gold and silver tree back in its box on the table and walked to the door.

"Is that it? It'll be a decade before I see you again," I teased as I reached for the box and pushed my cheek into the pillow.

"Is there something else?"

"Yeah. Get over here." He laughed, put his coat on the chair, and lay on the bed next to me, wrapping his long arms and legs around me. And then he began tenderly unbuttoning my pink satin top.

Our two sons had planned to leave College Station after their last class. Reggie was organizing a surprise for my birthday and they didn't want to miss it. The only surprise was where we would have dinner. He'd been *surprising* me like this for the last twenty years, but I didn't mind. After all this time, I couldn't be happier.

I resigned from my position at the museum and moved to Houston after we married. Reggie's landscaping business kept him there, and I easily

256

got a job teaching history to high school students. When our twin boys came along, I quit teaching and began writing and working in our own garden. As the boys got older and Reggie needed help, I spent a few hours a week at the shop until I became permanent.

Every December Reggie, the boys and I still attend Galveston's Dickens-on-the-Strand celebration, but it's really just an excuse to see Mary, who now lives with Mimi and Jack. Anne Marie and I remain close as ever, and she and her husband Matt visit us often. Mary, as fit as ever for her age, can still coax a tune from the piano. She's not much for technology, though, which is okay with me. She writes long letters every week or so, and I sit down with a cup of tea and read them over and over. Janie married a boy she met at A&M and moved to Austin. Mary Elizabeth goes to UT and sees her sister as often as she can. We try to visit the family several times a year now, but especially on holidays. I never heard from Judy again, and as close as Mama and I were to the Bertrands, that friendship ended the day they moved away from Carlton. I sometimes wonder about Jimmy but I wish him well. As for love and loyalty in friendship, my cup runneth over, more than I ever imagined it would.

When Alfred Washington was released from Angola State Prison, Reggie built his father an apartment on the sprawling grounds in back of our house. He spent the last twelve years of his life helping me in the garden and playing with his grandsons. I like to think they were happy years. One night late in August before school began he went to sleep peacefully and never woke up again. Reggie lost touch with his sister, but he calls his mother every week and she comes to visit us at Christmas when she can.

I still marvel at the way the present absorbs the past and continues its flow into the future. I met Reggie when I was fourteen, yet even now I'm blown away at how, the day I met him backstage, I instantly recognized what I had been missing from a man. It wasn't a father's love I lacked, although that certainly would have made life easier, but rather the kind devotion of a man to my well being, one that sometimes meant a sacrifice but never demanded anything in return. Reggie recognized my stubborn independence long ago and granted me space. To this day he still refuses to argue with me and gives me grace instead of humbling me when I'm wrong. He started that habit a lifetime ago in Mama's garden. For now, I'll just keep time traveling with the love of my life.